Either I'm sleepwalking or this is one hell of a sexy dream...

Lips, warm and moist, covered Maggie's, kissing her in a way she'd always dreamed of being kissed, only better. She should have pushed him away, but suddenly the only place she wanted to be was here in the attic, in this stranger's arms. Rather than run, Maggie tilted her head and parted her lips, kissing him back with a lifetime's worth of pent-up passion.

He slid a hand up to her breast, a groan escaping him. "So beautiful, so damn beautiful." Cupping her, he used his thumb to tease her nipple to life, raising a damp ache between her thighs.

Oh-my-God. Maggie arched against him, reveling in the size and breadth of the hard male body molding to hers. For someone who had never experienced anything approaching casual sex, she was rapidly losing control of the moment—and the handsome, hard-bodied stranger sharing it with her. All that mattered was how much she wanted—*needed*—to make love with him.

As if reading her mind, he wrapped his arms around her waist and laid her down on a nearby desk. "Isabel, thank the good Lord I've found you at last."

Isabel? Who in the world was Isabel?

Blaze™

Dear Reader,

I'm thrilled to introduce you to *The Haunting,* my second book for Harlequin's ultra-sexy EXTREME Blaze line as well as my first paranormal romance. *The Haunting* is very special to me for a number of reasons, including its setting of Fredericksburg, Virginia, where I've made my home for the past five years.

In *The Haunting,* American history professor Maggie Holliday gets not only her dream house, an 1850s Victorian fronting historic Caroline Street, but also her dream man in the form of sexy resident ghost Captain Ethan O'Malley. Logical Maggie doesn't believe in ghosts, or happy endings, for that matter, but an episode of "stranger sex" with Ethan in her attic is about to change all that. To make matters even more complicated, she is the reembodiment of Isabel Earnshaw, the beautiful Southern belle Ethan loved and lost 145 years before and whose diary Maggie discovers behind some loose boards in her attic.

I hope you enjoy their stormy—and very sexy—reunion.

Until next time, here's wishing you a springtime blossoming with second chances....

Hope Tarr
Fredericksburg, Virginia
April 2007
www.hopetarr.com

THE HAUNTING

Hope Tarr

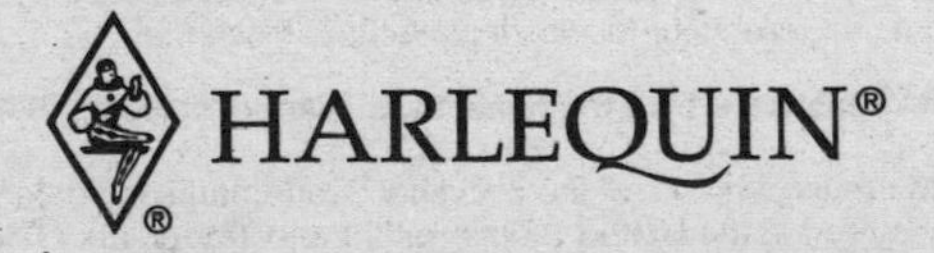

TORONTO • NEW YORK • LONDON
AMSTERDAM • PARIS • SYDNEY • HAMBURG
STOCKHOLM • ATHENS • TOKYO • MILAN • MADRID
PRAGUE • WARSAW • BUDAPEST • AUCKLAND

ISBN-13: 9-780-373-79321-1
ISBN-10: 0-373-79321-9

THE HAUNTING

This edition published by arrangement with Harlequin Books S.A.

www.eHarlequin.com

Printed in U.S.A.

ABOUT THE AUTHOR

Hope Tarr is an award-winning author of multiple romance novels. *The Haunting,* set in Hope's hometown of Fredericksburg, Virginia, is her first paranormal romance and her second book for Harlequin's Extreme Blaze line. When not writing, Hope indulges her passions for feline rescue and historic preservation.

To enter Hope's monthly contest, visit her online at www.hopetarr.com.

Books by Hope Tarr

HARLEQUIN BLAZE

293—IT'S A WONDERFULLY SEXY LIFE

To my former and much-loved historic house at 1310 Caroline Street in Fredericksburg, Virginia, where smiles were shared and memories made.

Never doubt that old houses have souls—and stories waiting to be whispered into a willing ear.

Prologue

A Federal Military Encampment
Stafford Hills, Fredericksburg, Virginia
December 16, 1862

ALL THINGS CONSIDERED, it wasn't a bad day to die. The air was still bitter with cold, but the sky had melted from glacial white to gunmetal gray, with just enough sunshine breaking through the clouds that you could feel the brush of it on your face, soft as a lover's lips. To one accustomed to the relentlessness of New England winters, it was uncommon fair weather for December, a fine day all in all—for those who would be left alive to enjoy it.

Stripped down to his shirtsleeves, Captain Ethan O'Malley sat astride his horse, Thunder, the noose tied to the oak's low-hanging limb and cinched about his throat, his hands bound behind his back. Even with certain death mere minutes away, he wasn't yet ready to give up all hope. He cast his gaze out onto the straggling crowd assembled on the frost-parched grass, searching for some sign—any sign—of her.

Isabel Earnshaw, the Southern belle whose soulful brown eyes, feisty spirit and lithe, long-limbed body had stolen his heart and set his body afire from the very first moment he'd clapped eyes on her. It wasn't as though he'd set out to fall in love with a Confederate. Their first meeting had happened purely by chance a full year before the first shot was fired on Fort Sumter. He'd been passing through Fredericksburg on his way back to Boston when his train had laid over for fuel and fresh supplies. Rather than remain on board in his cramped compartment, he'd strolled the shops on Main Street to pass the time. He'd encountered her in the dry goods store, a bright-eyed brunette with a penchant for crashing into things and a force-of-nature smile that could shake a man down to his very bones. The entire encounter had lasted five minutes, maybe fewer, and yet for the coming twelve months she'd stolen into his thoughts at the oddest times, including at night—especially at night. Lying abed in his lonely barracks bunk, images of her would haunt him, filling his head to bursting with all manner of erotic thoughts—how beautiful her slender form must look freed from her petticoats and frock, how smooth her pale skin would feel beneath his fingertips, how delicious she must taste, not only her mouth but all the rest of her. Like those fantasies, their earthly time together had been bittersweet and all too fleeting.

Futile though it was, he scanned the onlookers again. *Belle, where are you?*

In the main, the dozen or so who'd turned out to watch him die were his comrades-in-arms, Federal soldiers with the 19th Massachusetts Regiment of the Union Army of the Potomac, several of them sporting so-called red badges of courage, scarlet-soaked bandages swaddling fresh wounds. Sprinkled in amongst them were several civilians who'd made camp with the routed troops—a photographer for the *New York Herald,* a mulatto washer woman named Yvette who spoke Cajun-accented English and swore she'd been a notorious

New Orleans voodoo queen in her day and the sutler, Damian Grey. Damian had joined the regiment last spring to supply sundries the commissary didn't stock—horehound candy, gaming cards and dice and whiskey. He had an ear in every tent in the camp—and a tongue as forked as the serpent in the Garden of Eden.

From several paces away, the frock-coated army chaplain cleared his throat. A spare man with thick spectacles and thinning grayish-brown hair, he began droning out a prayer that Ethan's supposedly black soul might find its way to redemption and eternal peace.

Leaving Isabel behind, Ethan would know no peace.

The onlookers cleared throats and stamped cold-numbed feet, apparently eager to see him dispatched so they could break camp and get on with the day's march. Heart hammering, he raked his gaze over the straggling assembly and then beyond it across the river where smoke still rose from the recently razed town.

Belle, where are you? Come to me, sweetheart. Let me look upon your sweet face one last time.

Instead of Isabel, he spotted his nemesis and would-be murderer, Damian, pushing his way to the forefront of the bystanders. Their gazes met, locked, Damian's pale eyes glowing with unmasked triumph. For the first time since they'd led him out of the dependency that served as a makeshift jail, Ethan fought the manacles cuffing his wrists.

Dapper in a derby hat and pressed dark suit, a sprig of lavender pinned to the lapel, Damian sidled up beside him. Chewing on the cheroot wedged into the corner of his mouth, he asked, "How fares our Confederate spy?"

His gaze riveted on the lavender, Ethan saw that the sutler had come forward to strip Ethan of whatever piddling peace he might find in his final moments. “I don’t know, why don’t you tell me? The only spy I see stands before me.”

Craning his knobby neck, Damian took a puff of his cigar and exhaled a perfect smoke ring up into Ethan’s face. “As much as I’d love to stay and watch you dangle, I’m off to call on my future bride. Any tender words of farewell you’d care for me to convey to the fair Isabel?”

As torturers came, Damian had an exquisite sense of timing. Cursing the bonds that held him back from breaking every bone in Damian’s miserable body, Ethan ground out, “Bearing false witness against a man is not a sin the Lord will let go unpunished, particularly when it’s committed by a lily-livered coward like you.”

From what he’d gathered, Damian had spent the Federal assault on Marye’s Heights behind the battle lines drinking coffee and playing cards—and no doubt using the distraction to put into play the final stage of his plot to frame Ethan.

Giving aid and comfort to the enemy, committing acts of treason against the government of the United States of America. The litany of false charges ripped through Ethan’s head like a barrage of canon fire. Even now, with the noose cutting into his flesh and his earthly life reduced to seconds, he couldn’t escape the irony of his situation. Had he really survived the treacherous Rappahannock crossing by pontoon bridge and the bloody battle that had followed only to be court-martialed and condemned to die by a makeshift military tribunal representing the very nation he’d pledged his life to preserve?

“I’ll see you in hell, Damian, and we’ll settle our score there if need be. But settle it we will.”

“Perhaps.” Damian lifted his slender shoulders as though the prospect of eternal damnation was a trifling concern. “I shall think of you from time to time, moldering in your grave while I savor the fleshly pleasures of your bride. Pity you've already broken her in. I would have so enjoyed that, but I venture to say I'll teach her a trick or two." Stepping back, he slapped Thunder's rump. Predictably the stallion started, causing the noose to pull.

Heart drumming, Ethan managed to keep his seat. Crooning sweet nothings to calm the beast, he watched Damian turn and melt into the crowd. "Easy, boy. Easy now."

The chaplain's prayer drew to a close, and a pale-faced Jem Sparks, the company drummer boy, walked up to Ethan.

Pressed into service as the executioner's assistant though he couldn't be much more than thirteen, Jem stood, twisting a white blindfold cloth around and around in his hands. "Sir, they…they sent me to ask if you have any…last requests before…"

"Before they kill me?" Ethan shook his head.

Beyond seeing Isabel, earthly pleasures held no sway over him now. He hadn't touched the beefsteak they'd brought him for his last supper or given a tinker's damn for the quality of the pipe tobacco in his final smoke. But there was one thing he cared about more than life itself.

Dropping his voice, Ethan asked, "Were you able to deliver my message?"

Jem hesitated, gulping as though he were the one wearing a collar of hemp. "I tried, sir, truly I did, but they've got her locked up tight as a drum. I started to climb up the side of the house, but the housemaid caught me and chased me off. I did see the young lady looking down at me from the attic window, though."

Ethan seized on the information like a starving Confederate lunging for a side of salt pork. "How did she fare?"

Jem sucked at his lower lip. "I can't rightly say, sir. It was too far to see clear."

So Isabel was as much a prisoner as he, locked inside her

family's attic, the very attic that had served as their sanctuary from the chaos of the outside world, where they'd met in secret to escape the present and plan the future, where they'd made love that first magical time and every bittersweet time thereafter. Even with death so close he could all but smell it, the vivid memories rushed back to haunt him—Isabel's soft skin trembling beneath his touch as he freed her of her corset and stays; her rich mahogany hair spilling like a silken curtain over the side of his arm as he gently lowered her onto the cloak he'd spread over the dusty floorboards; their urgent, ragged breaths as they approached the pinnacle of their shared pleasure, senses swimming amidst the sweet scent of lavender. She'd used the ribbon from her hair to tie several sprigs of the flowering herb into a neat little nosegay, and hung it from the eave over their heads. Their bridal bower, she'd called it, her mouth trembling and eyes shining with love and unshed tears, for even then they'd known that one or both of them might not live to see a proper church wedding.

There would be no wedding now.

"I'm sorry to have failed you, sir, truly I am." Jem's lament brought Ethan back from the reverie to the present. The boy's sunken cheeks suddenly awash in color, he looked down to the wrung-out cloth in his hands. "I almost forgot to ask, will you be wanting this?"

Ethan shook his head. "I don't think so. I'll be sightless soon enough."

Tears welling, Jem stepped back. "God bless and keep you, sir." Swiping a sleeve over his eyes, he turned to go.

Ethan shifted back to look out onto the crowd, not because there was anyone he particularly wanted to see but because he meant to meet death and his Maker head-on. Instead of focusing on the cold-chapped faces before him, some bleak, others openly hostile, he conjured a mental picture of Isabel that matched the image captured on the tintype he had tucked inside his shirt pocket.

Somehow, my sweet Isabel, I'll find a way for us to be together again even if it means striking a bargain with the devil himself. If not in life, I'll come for you in death, my Isabel. If need be, I'll haunt you as even now your sweet face haunts me.

Below him someone shouted an obscenity and seconds later an egg struck his shoulder. A deserter might draw pity, but a traitor was treated as another animal entirely. With more than twelve thousand of their comrades-in-arms lying dead or wounded as a result of the failed assault, more a massacre than a battle, tolerance was in as short supply as fresh fruit or maggot-free meat. To squander scarce rations, they must hate him indeed. No matter; it was time. He took a deep breath and gave the nod for the hangman.

A pistol's loud report sent Thunder shooting forward. Unseated, Ethan dangled like a fish on the end of a hook. Pain seared through him, scoring his throat, radiating to his trunk and limbs. Succumbing to instinct, he kicked out, flailing feet seeking a foothold on empty air. A bone-deep snapping echoed from within him, the same hard, hollow sound he recalled from the days when he used to help out on his grandfather's farm wringing the necks of chickens. Water streamed his face, his eyes swelling beyond their sockets, and inside his head, the blistering heat soared.

Isabel!

Blessed numbness trickled into his limbs, the pain receding. Darkness wrapped around him like a blanket, warm and womblike, the horizon lit by a pinpoint of star-bright light. Fixing his gaze on the beacon, growing ever larger and blindingly bright, he stopped fighting the rope, stopped kicking the air, his slackening body swinging gently back and forth like the pendulum of the grandfather's clock that stood in the hallway of his family's Beacon Hill house back in Boston. The house to which, after the war was won, he'd meant to take Isabel back as his bride.

Isabel. If only there'd been time to get her away from Fredericksburg, away from Damian, he could be content to simply let go and let the soothing light carry him away. As it was, his love for her was a far more potent force than the pull of any hangman's hemp.

"Ethan Jeremiah O'Malley, release thyself from thy dark, earthbound cares and venture forth into the eternal light."

The booming command resonating from the light was at once a single voice and a cacophony echoing from both around and within him. As much as Ethan wanted to hold back, he suddenly understood that the choice to stay behind or come forward was not his to make.

I shall wait for you on the other side, my Isabel. Until the end of time if need be, I'll wait.

A few more rotations of the rope, a few more feeble contractions of the prisoner's failing heart, and then like a broken pendulum clock, the swinging stilled to a stop. Ethan let go and walked toward the light.

1

Caroline Street—formerly Main Street
Fredericksburg, Virginia
Present Day

"GODDAMNED, FUCKING PIECE of crap..."

Like a cyclone riding the wave of an ill wind, the shouted cursing spiraled from the main floor upward to the attic rafters. Startled, American history professor Maggie Holliday knocked her head against the low-hanging eave, sending dust, cobwebs and dried lavender raining down like confetti on the just-discovered diary in her hands.

Blowing on the tooled leather, she got a whiff of the soothing scent of lavender. For whatever reason, the fragrance held the power to sweep her away to a kinder, gentler frame of mind. All her life, she'd been crazy about anything with lavender in it, from shampoos and perfumes to soaps and sachets. When her Realtor had first brought her up into the attic of the 1850s Victorian, the aroma had wrapped itself about her like welcoming arms. She'd taken it as a sign that the house and she were meant to be.

Finding the diary struck her as similarly symbolic. When she'd come up to nail a loose window shutter in place in preparation for the storm headed their way, she'd never expected to unearth a one-hundred-forty-five-year-old treasure from behind a plank of rotted wallboard. Whether the book had fallen through the proverbial cracks or been placed there purposely was as much a mystery as who had pinned lavender to the eave and why. However it had come to be there, it had survived the past century-plus in amazing shape, the cover barely cracked, the pages yellowed ever so slightly about the curled edges. So far she'd only had the chance to peek at the main page on which Diary of Isabel Marie Earnshaw, Fredericksburg, Virginia was penned in neat, elegant script. Presumably the diarist was an early, perhaps even original occupant of the house she'd just bought, a lovely circa 1850 Victorian in the heart of the Fredericksburg Historic District. Tingling with anticipation, she could hardly wait to take the diary downstairs, find a quiet place and start reading.

Footfalls stomping up the attic stairs confirmed that such guilty pleasures would have to keep until later. Knowing how bad her boyfriend was with books—her treasured first edition of *Uncle Tom's Cabin* had never been the same since he'd touched it—she laid the diary on the built-in shelving, making a mental note to retrieve it later.

The attic door opened, and Richard poked his ash-blond head inside. "There you are."

He crossed the threshold, letting the old door slam behind him. Dressed in a pristine white polo shirt and khaki pants, he looked more ready for a day of golfing than moving, but then he'd done a lot more directing from the sidelines than hands-on helping.

"What are you doing up here, anyway? Didn't you hear me calling you?"

What am I, a doggie dropout from obedience school? Rather than confront him and ruin her first day in her new home with fighting, she summoned her calm, sane voice and answered, "We're supposed to have a storm later, and I wanted to make sure that window was shut properly."

Damn, I did it again. This was her house, not to mention her life. She shouldn't have to explain herself like a guilty teenager caught smoking a reefer in her room. And yet whenever she was with Richard, she found herself doing just that, justifying her every action as if to showcase how normal she was.

Fix one thing at a time, Maggie. With a life as messed up as yours, there are plenty of broken parts to work on before you tackle getting out of your current romantic relationship.

Not that she'd experienced much romancing lately. Richard tended to pout whenever he didn't feel as though he was getting adequate TLC. And over the past two whirlwind weeks he hadn't received much from her. Defending her doctoral dissertation, snagging an assistant professorship in the history department at the University of Mary Washington and purchasing her first house hadn't left her much spare time for stroking Richard's tender ego—or anything else of his.

He crossed the dusty floor toward her, mud and wet grass caking the sides of his deck shoes. Thinking of the beautifully refinished downstairs hardwood floors he'd just traipsed through, she swallowed a sigh. Richard might be a nationally renowned psychiatrist with a thriving Washington, D.C., practice and several federally funded research studies to his credit, but at times like this, he was such a guy—a guy who couldn't be bothered to wipe his feet on the doormat she'd made sure to lay out.

Following her gaze down to his feet, he frowned. "Damn, I just bought these shoes and now, look at them—ruined." He knocked the rubber sole of first one and then the other shoe against the wall, splintering off a hunk of paneling—and a little piece of Maggie's heart.

"Richard, please stop that." Horrified, she stooped to survey the damage. "These boards are more than a hundred years old."

Looking down at her, he shrugged. "From what I can tell, a few rotted boards are the least of your worries. The way those movers were banging around earlier, you're lucky the place is still standing given the condition it's in. Those floors downstairs are riddled with wormholes."

Straightening, Maggie pocketed the broken piece, feeling as beaten up emotionally as her poor wall was physically. "This house was built in 1850 or thereabout. It survived the Civil War and more owner moves than we'll ever know. Those hand-hewn timbers in the basement alone were probably harvested from an even older structure. They're solid as Sheetrock. As for the wormholes, they're part of the period charm."

Richard snorted. "Yeah, right. From what I can tell from walking around that mosquito-infested jungle you call a garden, period charm translates to warped wood and broken slates."

He paused to scratch the insect welts peppering his forearms. Ordinarily she'd offer to go downstairs and dig an antihistamine out of her purse, but she wasn't feeling particularly nice right now.

"Look, Richard, I know the yard is overgrown and I'm going to get to work on that along with managing the mosquito problem. The couple who sold me the house must be in their seventies. The husband is a master gardener, but he hasn't been able to keep the yard up the way he used to. It's going to take me some time, but once I get out there and start weeding and trimming and edging, it's going to be a lovely spot."

A lovely spot she envisioned sharing with a special someone over candlelit dinners on the backyard patio and glasses of mint iced tea on the front porch swing—a special someone, not Richard. Trying to move with his so-called help had been hell on earth, but at least it had cinched her decision. She was going to have to break up with him. It was no longer a matter of if but of when. Before she could find her Mr. Right, she'd have to knuckle down and get rid of Mr. Terribly Wrong.

He shook his head, a condescending mannerism that was getting really old—like the expiration date on their so-called relationship. "Time you won't have once school starts up in the fall. In the meantime, you still have to finish the revisions on your dissertation. Face it, there are only twenty-four hours in a day."

She drew a deep breath, feeling as if she were arming for battle. Even if it was only a battle of wills, these skirmishes always left her feeling drained yet hostile—a combustive emotional mix that was the psychological equivalent of a Molotov cocktail.

"I don't start teaching until the fall, which is months away. Once I do, I'll save a good three hours a day by not commuting."

He rolled his pale blue eyes at her. "You could have had your pick of history departments in any university in the country. You didn't have to settle for an assistant professorship at a Podunk college like Mary Washington or take on a four thousand square foot money pit in a backwater like Fredericksburg."

If he'd deliberately set out to blunt her bliss, he couldn't have done a better job. Hearing the words *Podunk, money pit* and *backwater* in the same sentence was the ultimate put-down, meant to make her doubt herself—again.

Determined not to let him get away with it this time—their

doctor-patient relationship was all in the past—Maggie lifted her chin and ticked off the list of attributes she'd mentally rehearsed since she'd closed on the house the week before. "Fredericksburg isn't a backwater, it's a culturally vibrant city filled with artists and musicians and yes, history, our *nation's* history. Mary Washington offered me a tenure-track professorship. The institution has university status now, one of its English faculty recently won a Pulitzer for her poetry and the American history program has the reputation of being one of the best in the country. As for this house, it passed the termite inspection with flying colors and the home inspection with just a few minor repairs flagged, so I'd hardly call it a money pit. In fact, historic properties typically appreciate more quickly than new ones, so actually this house is a pretty solid investment."

Richard raked a hand through his precision-cut hair. Unlike her unruly waist-length copper-brown locks, his fell back into perfect place the instant he drew his hand away. "There's no need to be defensive. I'm just concerned you haven't thought through the move."

She waved a hand in the air, sick to death of being saddled with a psychological label like *defensive* every time they had a difference of opinion. "Please, Richard, spare me the psychoanalysis. I know it's what you do for a living, but in case you forgot, I'm not your client anymore. You cured me, remember?"

Bull's-eye. She was either cured or she was crazy, but he couldn't have it both ways. For someone who liked to think of himself as Generation X's answer to Sigmund Freud, her barb would have hit smack-dab in the heart of his professional ego.

Tone hurt, he said, "I'm just concerned you're acting on impulse. To make so many major changes only a year out from losing both your parents and only sibling, do you really think it's wise? You can't escape your grief by running away, you know. You're going to have to confront your survivor's guilt sooner or later whether you live in D.C. or Fredericksburg."

Maggie felt tears prick her eyes. Her family's death in a plane crash the year before was her Achilles' heel. As her former therapist, Richard of all people knew how deeply the tragedy had affected her. Just when she told herself she was getting over it, getting strong, he made a point of picking at the scabbed wound.

"I don't have survivor's guilt," she snapped, aware she sounded a little shrill. "Well, at least not anymore. I realize it's not my fault Mom and Dad and Trisha decided to switch flights."

It had been Christmastime, and she'd been in the thick of drafting her dissertation. To make her life easier, they'd decided to spend the holiday with her in D.C. rather than having her come to them as she had in previous years. The direct flight out of Tampa had promised to put them into Reagan National Airport several hours early, in plenty of time to spend Christmas Eve together as a family—only they'd never landed.

He cocked his head to the side and regarded her, all traces of hurt obliterated by his self-satisfied smile. "Are you sure about that?"

Was she sure? One thing she was sure of was that life was unpredictable. There were no guarantees—all the more reason to stop brooding over the past, fretting over the future and start living in the present. Moving to a historic house in the heart of a small town, a real community where she could live and work and get involved in cultural events and civic affairs, had been her dream for a very long time now.

The irony was that it had taken losing what she loved best,

her family, to make it happen. Trisha's death left Maggie as her parents' sole heir. The estate wasn't a fortune by any means, but it was enough to enable her to buy the four-bedroom old house outright, something she couldn't have done on her salary.

"The only things I'm expecting to escape by moving here are gridlock traffic and subdivision housing." Taking off her glasses, she kneaded the headache throbbing behind her eyes. "Richard, please, give me a break. I've just been handed the keys to my first home, which also happens to be my absolute dream house, and I'd like to enjoy the moment, maybe even go for broke and enjoy the whole day. Can't you just be happy for me?" *Can't you just walk out of my life without my having to tell you to get lost?*

"Of course I'm happy for you, baby." Expression softening, he slipped his arms about her waist, and she braced herself not to pull away. Drawing her against him, he dropped his voice and pressed his mouth against her ear. "By the way, have you gotten around to opening my housewarming gift yet?"

At the mention of his *gift,* it was all Maggie could do not to shove both hands against his chest. When earlier he'd presented her with the long, slender box, she'd envisioned a bracelet or maybe a nice fountain pen engraved with her name and new degree. Instead the contents had turned out to be a dildo. The hot-pink, battery-operated, penis-shaped sex toy featured a G-spot locator and clitoral stimulator—the Cadillac of do-it-yourselfers. Along with the vibrator, he'd written her a prescription for Prozac. She'd dropped both in the bottom drawer of her night table as soon as the movers had set it in place.

It was bad enough being thirty years old and frigid—make that *orgasmically challenged*—without getting cheesy sex toys as reminder gifts. As much as she enjoyed the preliminaries of lovemaking, once the main event got rocking and rolling, she just couldn't seem to let go. Sexual dysfunction wasn't what had sent her to seek psychiatric help—Richard's help—but in the course of their intensive weekly sessions, the topic had come up with a host of other stress-related symptoms—nightmares, insomnia, hives and a sudden digestive intolerance to wheat. And yet after only five weekly sessions, he'd declared her cured, dismissed her as his patient and screwed her on his office couch. That was six months ago, and she wasn't any closer to cured than she'd been when she'd first walked into his office, although thankfully the hives had subsided and she could once again pack pasta with the best of them. Looking back with a clearer mind and wide-open eyes, she saw how grossly he'd taken advantage of her vulnerability. That realization packaged with his persistent me-first attitude made it hard for her to feel loving toward him, let alone lustful. Not only couldn't she climax but she couldn't get wet with him, either. You'd think a smart guy like Richard would take the hint.

Pinning her gaze to a point beyond him, she said, "I, uh…appreciate you thinking of me, but the truth is I'm not all that interested in having intercourse with a battery-operated toy."

"Don't knock it until you've tried it." He wiggled his sandy-blond brows and his hips at the same time. Feeling his hard-on pushing against her stomach, she jerked back, repulsed rather than turned on. Frowning, he stared at her for a long moment and then dropped his arms and stepped back. "I know I said I'd take you out to dinner later, but we'll have to celebrate another time. I forgot I have an early morning staff meeting. If I wait until tomorrow morning to drive back, I won't have time to work out before I go in."

A runner herself, Maggie appreciated a hard body as much as the next red-blooded American thirty-year-old woman, but Richard's rigidity in sticking to a strict daily regimen struck her as more fanatical than health conscious. Still, a reprieve was a reprieve no matter the motive.

"Okay, another time then." She followed him down the attic stairs through the main staircase to the front door, making a mental note to come back and retrieve the diary once he'd gone.

He planted a dry peck on her lips and stepped out onto the porch. "Don't work too hard, get a good night's sleep and I'll call you in the morning."

Why was it everything he said to her came out sounding like a prescription? "Okay, great. I'll do that."

Standing in the open doorway, she watched him walk to his car. It wasn't until he pulled the Porsche Boxster out of the parking space onto Caroline Street that she felt her energy returning.

Willie Whiskers, her ultraspoiled, ultraadorable Maine Coon cat mix sashayed up and stroked her ankles. She reached down and scooped him into her arms. Burying her face in his soft, tabby-striped fur, she said, "I don't care what Richard says. This is going to be a good move for us. Fredericksburg feels right somehow. I don't know why, but I fit here."

Feeling right, fitting in—it was time something in her life did.

2

A PLASTIC GLASS OF champagne in one hand and the diary in the other, Maggie stepped out onto her front porch into a picture-perfect spring twilight. She'd always had a strong olfactory sense, and moving to the rail, she breathed in the scents of lilac and daffodil and camellia. The camellia bush was exploding into brilliant pink blooms in the flower bed by her brick steps. No lavender, though, at least not yet. She'd be doing something about that very soon.

There was no sign of the predicted storm yet, so she wasn't overly worried about dampness seeping into the diary's century-and-a-half-old wood-pulp pages. Settling onto the swing seat with a satisfied sigh, she set it to a gentle rocking. Every square inch of her body ached but it was a good ache, an earned ache, an ache that brought about a smile because it came from laboring over something you'd wanted for a very long time but never really expected to have.

Ever since her high school days as a geeky bookworm with a fascination for gothic mystery novels, biographies of American Civil War generals and TV reruns of *The Ghost and Mrs. Muir,* she'd dreamed of owning a historic home with a front porch swing, an English-style garden—and a benevolent resident ghost. Minus the ghost, every other aspect of her personal paradise seemed to be falling into place, a champagne occasion if ever there was one.

Like the diary, the dusty bottle of vintage French champagne set out on her kitchen counter had been a welcome surprise. There hadn't been a note, but she surmised it must be a housewarming gift from her Realtor. She'd planned to share it with Richard later that night, but after their argument she'd told herself that a solo celebration was better than breaking open bubbly with a bully.

Raising her glass, she whispered, "Mom, Dad, Trisha—cheers to you guys," and took a sip.

After absorbing the initial shock of losing her family, the only way she'd known how to cope was to shut down emotionally. She'd existed in a state of functional numbness, performing her job as a high school history teacher by day, working on her dissertation by night, carrying on the bare-bones business of living 24/7 without missing a beat. Nothing and no one could touch her, not really. There was no real pain anymore but there was no real pleasure, either. Overnight, she'd become one of those people—the walking wounded, the living dead.

Her boyfriend before Richard hadn't known what to say, how to help, what the hell to do with her. After a month of trying to fuck her back to life, he'd given up and simply walked away. His leaving had been a relief for them both—he hadn't had to pretend to care anymore and she hadn't had to pretend to be okay.

But a life empty of all feeling was no way to live. It wasn't living at all. After coming across an article in the Health section of the Sunday *Washington Post,* she'd decided to try therapy. According to the mental health experts interviewed, post-traumatic stress disorder wasn't just for war veterans anymore. With terrorist threats, global warming and domestic crime all on the rise, the landscape of daily life was filled with enough danger and uncertainty to drive even the most solid citizen to the therapist's couch.

One name kept appearing among the interviewees—Dr. Richard Crenshaw, a nationally renowned psychotherapist with a private practice in northwest D.C. She'd phoned his office the next day and scheduled an appointment. By the time he'd declared her cured and come down on top of her, sending her sinking into the expensive camel-colored leather of his couch as if it were quicksand, she'd been ready for almost anything if it meant the chance to feel something—anything—again.

Everything had gone more or less okay—not earth-movingly great, not fireworks fantastic, but okay—except for one niggling complication. She hadn't been able to come. Like being one lottery number away from winning the multimillion-dollar jackpot, no matter how close she was brought to the brink, sexual climax eluded her. It had been so long since she'd had an orgasm, she hardly remembered what one felt like.

Her first real sensation of excitement came when she'd climbed out of her Fredericksburg area Realtor's SUV and looked up the stone steps to the house—her house—fronting Caroline Street. One glance at the columned front porch, tall windows with their wavy glass panes and English-style landscaping, and she'd fallen head over heels. The fragrance of lavender greeting her from atop the attic stairs had cinched the deal. Inhaling it, something beautiful and powerful and altogether mysterious had fired off inside her, not just in her brain but in her heart, too. She'd felt as though…as though she'd finally come home.

The argument with Richard, upsetting though it had been, brought one big benefit—he hadn't stuck around to spend the night. With or without the Big O, from what she could tell makeup sex was way overrated. Maybe it worked better after a bring-down-the-roof shouting match but since she and Richard never really got into those, sex afterward felt just as tepid and lacking in resolution as the argument preceding it. More so actually—at least when you argued, you got to keep your clothes on.

Thank God for her girlfriends. Her romance-novelist friend, Becky, had sent her off with a hug and a lifetime subscription to *This Old House* magazine. Her buddy in Baltimore's Little Italy, Lucia, had lined up her brother-in-law's moving company and made sure Maggie got the *family* rate. Her other pal, Sharon, who lived in Fredericksburg and worked in the Human Resources Department at Mary Washington, had called Maggie on her cell the moment the assistant professorship had hit the university's job listing Web page and urged her to apply.

Not once had anyone opened her mouth to voice a negative thought let alone hint that Maggie might be imposing on their time. In contrast, Richard had done nothing but complain since he'd arrived an hour late that morning. As much as he loved to brag about how much weight he could bench press at the gym, during the move he'd barely lifted a finger let alone a hammer. She'd had to nail down that shutter herself while he roamed the perimeters of her property finding problems to point out. Oh, he might talk a good game about his prowess with power tools, but she'd yet to see him do more than change a lightbulb and even then he waited for the last one in the fixture to burn out. The next man she dated was going to be made of sterner stuff. If Richard had lived in the 1860s, he'd never have survived the Civil War—not even as a civilian.

That thought brought her back to the diary. Setting her champagne on the window ledge, she carefully opened the book. As she did, a sprig of dried lavender fell out onto her lap. Even after more than a century spent pressed between the diary pages, it still carried a hint of the herb's distinctive fragrance. What a weird coincidence. Maggie had tucked lavender inside her high school and college yearbooks as well as every photo album and scrapbook she owned. Chills trickling down her spine, she adjusted her glasses and began to read.

February 10, 1861

Dear Diary,

Before today, you were a blank slate or, in my case, a book of blank pages waiting to be written upon, but then that is what my life has been until now—blank, empty, restless with wanting. With all this talk of war—six more Southern states have joined South Carolina in seceding from the Union—come spring there may be no balls or barbecues, cotillions or come-outs to attend, which perhaps is just as well, for when folks do get together, all gay conversation swiftly sours to wondering how soon Virginia will follow suit in the fight to preserve Southern liberty.

But I digress, for the very point of this diary entry wasn't to fret over some silly war that everyone swears the South will win in a matter of months anyhow. No, dearest friend and secret confidant, the entire purpose of my writing is to describe him. Captain Ethan O'Malley, the kindest, handsomest, most dashing man I've encountered in all my born days. And to think, were it not for Mama sending me downtown to fetch flour and brown sugar from Mr. Potter's store, I might have missed him entirely!

I was headed to the counter to pay for my purchases

when men's raised voices from the front of the store had me stalling my steps. "Get on with you, you damned Yank," Mr. Potter yelled. "I don't care how much of Abe Lincoln's gold lines your pockets, I'd see my family starve before I take one red cent from you."

"Now see here, sir, it's a free country and I've just as much right to trade here as the next man," a second man, presumably the Yank, answered. "Whatever money I have was come by as honestly as yours to you—perhaps more so as my interests do not rely on the sweat of slaves."

Being born and raised in a seaport city such as Fredericksburg, I easily detected the shortened *r* and elongated *a* in the stranger's speech marking him as a New Englander. Accent aside, his bold baritone had me lifting my head to peek above the shelving. Even without my spectacles, I could see he was tall and powerfully built. Standing across the counter from him, poor Mr. Potter looked positively puny.

"Get on with you, you abolitionist devil. The only slave on these premises is me, and I still say your money's no good here."

Curiosity has always been one of my more lamentable failings, and I will admit—if only within these pages—that I couldn't bear the thought of the Yank walking out without my so much as glimpsing his face. I bolted out of the aisle—and ran smack into a pyramid of foodstuffs set out for display.

Cans and jars crashed to the floor, scattering pickles and pork and beans over the clean-swept boards, tins rolling to the four corners of the store. I stared about at the chaos I'd created, for once unable to credit the evidence of my weak eyes.

His scowl as black as Abe Lincoln's beard, Mr. Potter rounded the counter and bore down upon me. "Isabel Earnshaw, you'll be the death of me yet. That's the third display you've knocked down this month. When in tarnation are you going to start wearing those spectacles of yours?"

I dropped to my hands and knees to gather up the bits of broken glass, hoping to let the tender topic of eyewear die. "I'm terrible sorry, Mr. Potter, truly I am. Please don't tell my mother. She'll never let me out of the house again if you do." I knew I was a vain girl to carry on so over a silly pair of spectacles and yet the fear I'd die an old maid and go to my grave without ever knowing a man's touch had me shoving them into my pocket every chance I got.

He stood far enough away that his face looked fuzzy, but I could hear the softening in his voice. "Don't fret yourself, Isabel, and for Lord's sake don't go getting cut on account of not being able to see any farther than the end of your nose. I'll fetch the mop from the stockroom. It'll be our little secret this time again but when next you come in, I expect to see spectacles on that pretty face of yours."

I was making good progress on gathering up the broken bits when a burning sensation struck my thumb. I looked down to see blood soaking through my glove. Fiddlesticks. I'd gone and cut myself just as Mr. Potter predicted.

Footfalls crunching on glass came toward me. Thinking it must be Mr. Potter returned, I shoved my bleeding hand behind my back. A pair of big, booted feet that surely couldn't belong to the shopkeeper drew up before me, the tops polished shiny as glass. "The wages of sin, I suppose, or in your case, eavesdropping."

I lifted my gaze and looked up into a grinning and very handsome face. It was the Yank. He must have witnessed my humiliation through the plate glass storefront and come back to gloat.

Mindful that even if I was caught out in a compromising position, I was still a lady—a Southern lady—I forced my chin up and my shoulders back. "I assure you, sir, I was doing no such thing. Why, I've never been so insulted in all my born days."

"That only leaves your unborn ones, then." Before I could answer that glib remark, he reached down a hand to help me up. "Here, let's have a look at that cut."

I hesitated. Though he spoke softly and with a friendly smile, I could see he was a man accustomed to command. Like a guilty child, I slowly brought my bleeding hand 'round from behind my back.

Strong fingers encircled about my wrist, drawing me to my feet. Standing before him, I was keenly aware of how good he smelled, some combination of bay rum and leather and myriad manly scents I couldn't readily identify but wanted to drown myself in all the same.

He gently peeled off my glove, and I felt the tingle of his touch in not just the hand he held but indeed in all of my limbs. He bent his head to examine my injury, a hank of dark hair falling low over his high brow, and I had the urge to reach out with my free hand and smooth its feathery weight back from his face. "I'll be as gentle as I can but best brace yourself," he warned, looking up at me through thickly lashed blue eyes. "This may sting." I felt a twinge and realized he'd plucked out the fragment. A handkerchief materialized in his hand, and he wound it about my thumb to stanch the blood.

He gave me back my hand, and I caught myself staring at his—the dark hairs dusting the broad back, the long, thick fingers that had touched me with such knowing, such gentleness. "Better now?"

I swallowed hard, feeling overheated suddenly though it was a might chilly inside the store. "Y-yes, thank you."

In truth, I scarcely noticed my smarting digit, so caught up was I in studying my savior from under the screen of my lashes. He looked to be a good sight older than I, closer to thirty than my nineteen. Whatever his age, he was quite purely beautiful. His eyes were the bluest I'd ever seen outside of the sky, and I caught myself staring at his mouth, the top lip a bow shape, the bottom lip full and moist, wondering what it would feel like to kiss him. Not the quick, dry peck I'd experienced once so far from a fair-weather beau, but a real kiss, the kind I'd read about in the naughty novels my friend Candice smuggled into my room.

Letting my gaze drop to his powerful torso and slender waist, all at once I understood why Mr. Potter had treated him so sourly. The object of my unabashed admiration wore the dark blue sackcloth coat and kepi cap of an officer in the Federal Army. The broad shoulders I'd been covertly admiring were decked out in the double bars denoting a captain's rank.

As if reading my mind, he shot me a wink and doffed his cap, revealing a crown of thick, wavy hair the blue-black of a crow's wing. "Captain Ethan O'Malley at your service, miss."

I took an unsteady step back. "I'm much obliged for your help, sir."

He shrugged, the movement making me once again aware of the breadth of his shoulders. "I break a lot of things myself…on account of my size," he added with a sideways wink. "My mother says I'm like a bull in a china shop."

"It's my eyes," I found myself confiding, warming to his easy manner. "They've been weak from birth, and I can't abide wearing spectacles."

His gaze met mine and a thrill the likes of which I'd never before known bolted through me. "I don't blame you for not wanting to hide away such beautiful brown eyes."

Habit had me fluttering my lashes, though in truth I was as nervous as a long-tailed cat in a roomful of rocking chairs. He stood so close I could feel his breath falling upon my cheek, all but taste the rich chicory of the coffee he must have drunk earlier and see the eagle motif on the four brass buttons fronting his frock coat.

"May I be so bold as to inquire as to your name?"

Fiddlesticks, where were my manners? "Isabel Earnshaw." I stuck out my hand, careful to keep my hurt thumb at bay.

He took it, cradling it in his big warm one. "Isabel, that's a very pretty name. It suits you, though were you my sweetheart, I'd call you Belle."

Until now the working of my woman's parts had remained more or less a mystery, but when he slid his gaze over me as though we were sweethearts in truth, I couldn't help noticing how my breasts budded to life, the points pressing against the confines of my corset as if begging for his touch.

Face afire, I stepped back, shamefully aware of a sweet, stabbing ache striking low in my belly. "You are forward, sir, to make so free with my given name."

"And you, Miss Earnshaw, are very beautiful with or without spectacles." There it was again, that flash of white-toothed smile that made everything that transpired between us seem perfectly easy and natural as though it was fated to be.

Hoping to return the conversation to a more respectable footing, I found my voice to inquire, "O'Malley is an Irish name, is it not?"

He nodded. "It is. I suppose you could say I'm a son of Erin as I was born in County Cork, but I don't remember much of anything about Ireland. When my parents brought me over, I was just a small child. America is the only country I own as home, the greatest free nation on earth. I'd give my life to preserve it."

This time when he spoke, there wasn't so much as a hint of humor in his bearing or tone, and I was reminded that no matter how blue his eyes or how warm his smile, we were on opposing sides of the current conflict, as far apart as if we hailed from two separate homelands indeed.

Mr. Potter chose that moment to emerge from the stockroom with the bucket and mop. Catching his scowl, I gathered that fraternizing with a Federal soldier must not fall into the category of little secrets he would be willing to keep for me.

He let the mop drop and marched up to the captain, picking his path through the carnage of canned goods and broken glass. "I thought I told you to git."

Stomach dropping to my toes, I turned to Captain O'Malley. His face was flushed, a muscle ticked in his jaw and his blue eyes wore a dark, dangerous glint.

For safety's sake—Mr. Potter's—I stepped between the two men. "It's my fault, Mr. Potter. I cut myself, and

Captain O'Malley was kind enough to come to my aid." Though it hurt my pride something mortal, I held up my swaddled thumb.

Mr. Potter answered with a grudging nod and handed me my market basket. "I'll add these items to your pa's account. You'd best be getting on home."

My cheeks heating, I turned to Captain O'Malley. "Thank you for your kindness, sir, and I am sorry for your handkerchief." The latter was a fib—if not an outright lie—for already I was making plans to preserve it as a memento.

"May I see you home at least?" His chiseled features wore a look that was at once urgent and sad, and for the first time I considered that perhaps he wasn't only flirting, that our encounter, albeit brief, had meant something to him, too.

Aware of Mr. Potter watching us, I shook my head. "I don't live far, just down the street a piece." What I didn't say was that if Pa caught wind of me strolling town on the arm of a Federal, he'd skin me alive. "Good day to you."

Afraid to linger lest I push Mr. Potter beyond his narrow limits, I looped the basket over my wrist and made a beeline for the door. Though I dared not be so bold as to look back, I swear I felt a pair of blue eyes burning a hole through me.

Captain Ethan O'Malley. As I write this, I have your hankie pinned inside my chemise just over my heart. It may soon be as good as treason to admit it, and yet I know I shall carry the fond remembrance of you, my blue-eyed, blue-coated captain for the remainder of my earthly days just as I know that someday, somehow, we shall meet again. In the meantime, I must bring this day's missive to a reluctant close as I hear our maid, Clarice, calling me down to supper.

And yet how can I possibly swallow so much as a single morsel when I am already so very full? Full diary, full heart. Full to bursting…

3

WOW! MAGGIE CLOSED THE diary, eager to read more and yet feeling the need to stop and absorb that first passion-charged passage. For whatever reason, it had affected her in a very personal way, leaving her feeling giddy and hopeful and at the same time more than a little wistful—okay, sad.

Whatever trials and triumphs Isabel had experienced in her life, that life was over and had been for a century, maybe more. And yet looking out onto the very street Burnside's Federal troops had fought their way across during the First Battle of Fredericksburg, Maggie felt as though the past was still very much a part of the present, as though the whispered voices of the long-dead townspeople were tickling the inside of her ear. Smiling at that fanciful notion, she set the diary on the cushion next to her and leaned back, letting her eyes drift shut. With her vision shut off, her other senses came to vivid life. She could smell the gunpowder burning her nostrils, feel the battered street shaking like thunder beneath her feet and hear the shouting of soldiers and the shrieking of neighbors as all around her chaos erupted.

"Isabel. Isabel! Belle!"

Maggie started. Sitting up, she scanned the street below for the source of the shouting. Aside from a motorcycle whizzing past and a black-and-white cat strolling the sidewalk, her neighbors had turned in for the night, the windows of the tidy town houses lining the other side of the street dark other than the occasional flicker of a TV screen. Fredericksburg was an early-to-bed, early-to-rise kind of town, and it was after nine o'clock, late for a Monday. And yet for a moment, or at least a handful of seconds, she'd been sure she'd heard a man shout, "Isabel." It was all easily explained, of course. She'd dozed off. Isabel Earnshaw's diary, an exciting find on so many fronts, had seeded her already fertile subconscious. Though she'd only read the first few pages, already she was hooked. The journal was what academics liked to call a *primary source,* but it also read like a red-hot romance novel.

A red-hot romance novel that for whatever reason seemed to reach across time and speak to her very soul.

THE EPISODE ON THE PORCH had shown Maggie just how tired she must be. Reminded of Scarlett O'Hara's immortal closing line, she told herself that tomorrow was indeed another day. Though the type A side of her personality urged her to push herself and keep going until the last box was emptied, she knew getting some sleep and starting fresh in the morning would accomplish more in the end. Pouring herself a third glass of champagne—she wasn't usually much of a drinker but it had been a big day and the sparkling wine tasted especially crisp and delicious—she headed upstairs to bed.

The movers had set up her metal four-poster in the master bedroom fronting Caroline Street, and she'd carried in the box of bed linens herself to make sure it was within easy reach. Along with retrieving the diary from the attic, she'd made up the bed as soon as Richard had left, needing to do some small, healing task—something that was just for her.

Rounding the bed to her night table, she opened the bottom

drawer to tuck the diary inside and saw the vibrator she'd stowed there earlier. Nestled in its discreetly packaged box, it offered a guaranteed, no-excuses hard-on—at least until the batteries wore down. Still, relying on a fake phallus as a sexual partner struck her as as pathetic as lurking in X-rated Internet chat rooms or dialing a 900 number for phone porn. She just couldn't go there, not just yet.

Hoping that out of sight would equate to being out of mind, she closed the drawer on the sex toy, laid the diary inside the empty top drawer and pushed both compartments closed. Whatever else Isabel Earnshaw had to say about life and love would keep until tomorrow.

Turning away from temptation, she started stripping off her clothes, the Old Navy T-shirt and jeans hitting the floor, followed by her cotton bra and panties. The nightgown she pulled out of her overnight bag was a recent purchase from Victoria's Secret, a small extravagance that, like the earlier champagne celebration, was long overdue. She hadn't worn it yet; indeed, she'd found all sorts of excuses to keep it folded in its pink tissue wrap. Only now did she admit she'd been saving it for her first night in her new house—her first night *alone*.

Reaching up, she unbraided her hair, combing through the waist-length waves with her fingers. Richard was always pushing her to go for a more stylish shoulder-length cut, but like replacing her glasses with contacts, every time she took steps to make the change, she just couldn't go through with it. She might not be the most fashion-forward woman on the planet, but somehow her glasses and long hair had always felt right for her.

Maybe it was the champagne lowering her inhibitions or the heady feeling of home ownership or the cool, floral-scented breeze fluttering through the open window, but whatever the reason she found herself stepping up to the antique dressing mirror, a gift from her girlfriends on her last birthday. Sharon and Becky and Lucia were always telling her how lucky she was to be born tall and naturally thin, *model genes* Sharon called it. Until her sexual shutdown, Maggie had never given her body all that much thought but now she found herself mentally cataloging her assets, starting with a flat stomach and long legs. Okay, her thighs were a little on the thick side, but she liked to believe that owed to muscle built over years of running, not fat. Her breasts were nicely shaped though smallish, but most of her previous boyfriends, including Richard, were self-proclaimed ass men. When they'd first started sleeping together, Richard had gushed over her tight little tush until she'd wanted to smack him silly. Turning to look back over her shoulder, she didn't see what all the fuss was about. It was just an ass, after all, though she was pleased to see there was no sign of sagging

She slipped the nightgown over her head, the cream-colored linen-cotton blend sliding over her skin like a lover's lips, the hem brushing her ankle bone—a minor miracle when you were almost five foot nine. Just as well Richard hadn't stayed because he would hate the old fashioned style, but then his taste in lingerie ran more to Frederick's of Hollywood. Maybe it was just her repression at work, but somehow strutting around in a baby-pink sequined teddy trimmed in faux feathers seemed more silly than seductive. In contrast, the gown's delicate seed pearl smocking and wrist-length tulle sleeves suited her taste exactly. Wearing it, she felt soft and feminine, desirable and yes, sexy. Definitely sexy.

If I'm going to fly solo, then I'm going to fly solo the old-fashioned way, sans flavored gels or body sprays, edible underwear or battery-driven props.

Facing her reflection, she cupped her breasts, circling the nipples through the thin nightgown and then tenderly tugging on the hardened points.

Hmm, so good.

She slid her hands downward to her belly and lower, fingertips skimming the crisp curls crowning her pubis, the cool breeze from the open window brushing over her bare skin like a lover's lips, her heart's desire emerging as a silent prayer.

I want to come. I need to come. Please let me come.

She reached down and caught the hem of the nightgown, lifting it to her waist. Widening her stance, she dropped her gaze to her genitals. According to Richard's instructions, this was the point at which she was supposed to look into the mirror and repeat I love you, Maggie again and again. Supposedly the exercise helped to rebuild the self-acceptance and self-love needed to orgasm, but Maggie had her doubts. Chanting endearments while she stimulated herself seemed even sadder than fucking a toy, a new low to which she wasn't ready to sink, at least not yet.

Instead, she slid one hand between her thighs and concentrated on clearing her mind. Trying for an attitude that struck a middle ground between hopeful and relaxed, she ran a single finger back and forth over the slit parting her inner lips. Pleased to find she was moister than she'd expected, she moved upward to her clit. Circling, she mentally switched out her hand with a man's bigger, stronger one—broad-backed and blunt-fingered, the top dusted with dark hair, the nails clipped short and kept very clean.

He gave me back my hand, and I caught myself staring at his—the dark hairs dusting the broad back, the long, thick fingers that had touched me with such knowing, such gentleness.

Maggie stilled her hand. It was the passage from Isabel's

diary, only the voice repeating it inside her head was her own and yet not quite, the cadence of Southern-accented syllables and elongated vowels feeling both foreign and oddly familiar. A chill swept over her, raising gooseflesh. The argument with Richard had upset her, but she wasn't buying that it alone was to blame. The culprit was the diary. Finding it had flipped the lid on her very own Pandora's box, messing with her already messed-up head. For whatever reason, she was identifying with a nineteen-year-old Civil War era woman and not necessarily in a healthy way.

She tried bringing herself back to the present, but it was no use. The spell was broken, the mood wrecked. She wasn't getting off, she was getting sore, and she had no one to blame but herself. Her boyfriend's wet-blanket attitude might have dampened her first day in her new house, but her first night she'd ruined all by herself. *Way to go, Maggie.*

Tears in her eyes, she let the nightgown drop, yanked back the bedcovers and fell into bed—and almost immediately to sleep.

MAGGIE HEARD THE BATTLE AS if the violence were taking place just outside her open window. "Fall in. Fall in!" "Hold the line. Hold, I say!" "Jesus, I'm hit. I'm hit!" *Crack! Boom!*

As if peering through a rabbit hole, she saw herself not in her bedroom but hunkered down in a small, squat room—a cellar. Nor was she alone. Her parents and Trisha were there, too. They looked much as they had the last time she'd seen them alive except for their midnineteenth-century hairstyles and clothing. Somehow she knew their family name wasn't Holliday. It was Earnshaw.

Sitting cross-legged in a corner of the earth-packed floor with Trisha—Lettie—lying across her lap and her Maine coon cat, Jefferson Davis, cowering beneath her full skirts, Maggie felt the thunder of exploding shells and striking artillery shake the house from rafters to foundation, resonating in her breast along with her fast-beating heart. Only her name in this life wasn't Maggie. It was Isabel.

Lettie lifted her swollen cheek from Isabel's breast and looked up at her with terror-stricken eyes. "I'm scared. I don't want to die."

Earlier, the twelve-year-old had been hit by flying debris when a musket ball blasted through the brickwork of their kitchen. Fortunately she'd suffered no worse than bruising and broken skin, though Isabel worried the true damage might run deeper than any harm inflicted to flesh or bone.

She hugged the trembling child tightly against her, wishing she might block the sounds of death and destruction from her tender ears. "Don't worry, puss," she said, brushing plaster dust from Lettie's crown of copper curls. "Everything's going to come out all right, isn't that so, Clarice?"

Looking over Lettie's head, she exchanged glances with their housemaid, Clarice. Huddled into the opposite corner, her cast-off cloak wrapped about her big, soft body, the African woman's eyes were round with fear, but for the child's sake she summoned a smile.

"'Course it is. Miss Lettie, you listen to your big sister, you hear. The Lord never did make a Yank who could shoot straight."

The shooting began at five o' clock though it had commenced with friendly fire. On General Lee's orders, signal guns from the hilltop behind Braehead had released two successive shots to warn the townspeople that a battle would soon commence.

Clarice had roused them all from their beds. "Miss Isabel, Miss Lettie, wake up. The Yankees are coming. They got two pontoons nearly across the river."

The Federals, including Ethan's own Irish Brigade, had been holed up at Chatham Manor in the Stafford Hills for the past two days, their engineers braving Confederate fire to build pontoon bridges to ford the river. Isabel had dressed herself and had gotten Lettie halfway so when the bombardment began. Snatching up blankets, cloaks and a terrified Jefferson Davis, the five of them had raced down to the cellar. Throughout the long, hellish day, intelligence of the carnage came to them by way of fleeing neighbors and Confederate soldiers. The town was afire in many places and an entire row of buildings on Main Street was burnt to ash. The Hall and Sons Drugstore had been looted not once but twice, and the rumors were flying fast and furious that the Yanks meant to torch not just the warehouses and stores but the houses, as well. Any civilian male found possessing a firearm was to be shot on the spot. Isabel cast a look to her gray-bearded father, sitting cross-legged with his rusted hunting rifle loaded and cocked, and a tremor ran through her.

"Damned Yankees," Pa muttered for the umpteenth time, training his weapon on the cellar stairs.

Sitting on a milk stool beside him, her mother intoned the words to the Twenty-seventh Psalm again and again, tongue stumbling over "Though an host should encamp against me, my heart shall not fear."

But Isabel's heart did fear, not for herself or even her family so much as for Ethan. They at least could hole up below ground whereas he was in the thick of the fray. Had he survived the river crossing or was he even now lying dead or wounded, felled by a Confederate sniper's bullet? Assuming he lived, he must be close by, part of the Federal advance. Would his big, gentle hand be the one to toss the torch through their already shattered kitchen window, to pull the trigger on the gun that would release the bullet into her father's skull?

Boom!

The ball slammed into them, the thunder of it sending the single candle crashing onto its side. The flame smothered on the earthen floor, leaving them in darkness dense as pitch. Even wearing her spectacles, Isabel couldn't see the hand she stretched in front of her.

Pounding, the sort that came from the butting of musket muzzles, sounded from the main door above. "Come out, you damned rebels, else we'll smoke you out."

Isabel squeezed her eyes shut and pulled Lettie closer. *Ethan, I trusted you. You promised to see us spared. You promised to come for me. You promised not to die.*

Oh, God in heaven, Ethan, please don't be dead. I couldn't bear that. I couldn't bear to go on without you.

4

"ETHAN, PLEASE DON'T BE DEAD. Please don't be..."

Maggie came awake to damp sheets wrapped around her legs and the sounds of banging battering her ears. She bolted upright, cracking the base of her skull against the metal headboard. Rubbing the sore spot, she looked out into the darkness trying to place where she was—her old apartment in D.C., the guest bedroom at Sharon's or Fredericksburg circa 1862? Somehow none of those felt exactly right, though the last felt closest to the truth. Before full-blown panic could set in, a small, bushy-tailed creature leaped onto her lap, bringing her back to the familiar. Kitty motor running at full throttle, Willie kneaded the blanket in her lap, an anchor to the present—to normalcy. All at once, she remembered—Caroline Street, historic house, first night. The fragments of memory fused like puzzle pieces, forming a complete picture of the present—present as in 2007.

Wow, that was one hell of a dream.

Shaky still, she reached across to the nightstand to switch on the lamp. Putting on her glasses, she looked over in time to see the numbers on her digital alarm clock turn over from 11:59 to 12:00—midnight on the dot. She'd been in bed just about two hours and yet she felt like Rip Van Winkle—only instead of sleeping away twenty years and waking up in the far future it was as though she'd slept, or rather traveled, more than a century back in time.

But what really bothered her about the dream wasn't the mismatching of eras so much as the exchanging of identities. Why had she transposed herself onto Isabel Earnshaw? What could she, a thirty-year-old American history professor brought up in the postfeminist age, possibly have in common with a Southern belle from a previous century?

Outside her open window, the predicted storm raged full throttle, thunder boomers striking fast and furious, sheets of rain spraying through the screen. Hair standing on end, Willie sprang off the bed and scrambled beneath. Wishing she might do the same, Maggie got up, grabbed a fistful of tissues and bent to wipe up the rainwater before it could soak into the hardwood finish. She turned to toss the sopping tissue in the trash when a heavy clapping caught her attention.

It was the same noise she'd heard that morning, the one that—along with the thunder—she must have incorporated into the battle backdrop of her dream. Fully awake, she realized the sound came from inside the house, specifically, the attic. With all the wind and rain, the shutter she'd nailed in place must have worked loose again. She hesitated, weighing whether she should go back to bed and try to block out the noise or bite the proverbial bullet and stay up to deal with it. At times such as this, a part of her wished she wasn't quite so alone, that she shared her bed with a man who wouldn't think twice about going up into the dark attic and taking care of the problem for her. Not Richard, who, as far as she could tell, didn't even own a hammer, but a real man, an old-fashioned man with big, capable hands equally suited to fixing loose shutters and making tender love to his sweetheart.

But it was 2007, not 1862, and the sad fact was she was all alone, she was all she had. If she wanted to log in any z's over what was left of the night, she was going to have suck it up, go upstairs and nail the friggin' shutter down herself.

Humming an old feminist song lyric about being a woman who roars, she grabbed her flashlight and hammer from the top of the dresser and ventured out into the hallway. The clapping grew more pronounced as she approached the attic door. Opening it, she reached for the light switch just as another thunderclap rocked the house. It passed and she flicked the light switch only no light came on. That last boomer must have taken out the electricity. *Damn, this night keeps getting better and better.*

Hoping her flashlight battery had sufficient juice to carry her through the night, she climbed the creaking stairs, the old boards splinter rough beneath her bare feet, her left hand holding the flashlight, her right hand wrapped about the hammer's handle. At the top of the stairs, she pushed through the attic door. A draft of rain soaked air hit her even before she'd stuck one foot over the threshold. Feeling like the too-stupid-to-live heroine from a bad gothic novel, she stepped inside and shone the light on the window. The shutter flapped like a ship's sail, not because it was broken but because the window was pushed up, wind and rain rushing inside. She must really be losing it because she clearly remembered closing and bolting it before coming downstairs yesterday morning to meet the movers. Oh well, it was a good thing the noise had woken her, otherwise the boxes of books she'd stacked there would have been soaked through, her library of first-edition volumes ruined or at least badly damaged.

A heavy hand descended on her shoulder.

Maggie screamed and spun around, the flashlight falling

to the floor and her head butting against the intruder's rock-hard chest. Her fight-or-flight response kicked in, and she brought the hammer back and then forward, sinking it into her attacker's broad shoulder.

Only instead of the anticipated painful howl and backward stagger, he didn't make a sound or budge. The hammer met with no resistance beyond air though she didn't see how she could have missed him.

He reached a big hand between them, lifting the tool from her suddenly slackening fingers. "Hush, Belle, I've not come to harm you." The hammer disappeared, and he planted a big-palmed hand on each of her shoulders.

Heart pounding, she fought to free herself. "I don't know who Belle is, you pervert, but I'm not her, so let me go. Let me go!" She kicked out, going for his groin with her raised knee, but once again she missed her target. So much for those self-defense classes at the Y.

To her surprise, he dropped his arms to his sides and stepped back. Breathing hard, she stared up at him, a tall tower of a man, broad shouldered and wearing the Civil War regalia of the Federal Army.

He shook his head, eyes reflecting a strange, piercing light. "Isabel, my Isabel, I heard you calling to me, and I've come for you. I've found you at last."

His face was in shadow but the light from the full moon filtering through the window illuminated sculpted features, a somewhat hawkish nose and a sensuous pair of full lips. And his eyes, though it was too dark to see their color, raked over her with such wonder, such…yearning.

"You must be crazy, I didn't call you. I don't even know you."

Heart racing as though she'd made one too many trips to Starbucks, she scanned his solid frame for signs of a weapon.

None seemed to be in immediate evidence, and though she had no doubt he could easily strangle her with his hands alone, she relaxed fractionally. Even in her present predicament, the researcher inside her kicked in, cataloging every detail of his costume, authentic down to the four brass eagle buttons fronting his single-breasted dark blue sackcloth coat and the captain's double bars sewn onto the epaulets topping each broad shoulder. He must be a Civil War reenactor who for whatever reason felt entitled to camp out in an apparently unoccupied house, a homeless person with a penchant for American history or a psycho with one of the personality disorders Richard was always running on about.

Unnerved by his unblinking, mute stare, she backed up. "Look, I don't know who you are or what you're doing in my attic, but if you go now, I won't call the police." That was a lie, of course. Assuming he agreed to leave—and talk about a long shot—she fully intended on dialing the 9-1-1 emergency number the second he cleared her door.

Instead of coming after her, he stood in place. "So you'd call the constable and make a jailbird of me, would you now?" He shot her a wink.

Constable? Jailbird? Really, some of these reenactors took the hobby entirely too far.

"Ah, Belle, the Lord alone knows how I've missed you." He swooped in, enfolding her in a full-body embrace and lifting her off her feet.

She raised her cheek from the scratchy wool of his coat to scream but before she could get out a sound, he captured her mouth in a kiss. Lips—warm, moist and mobile—covered hers, kissing her as she'd always dreamed of being kissed, only better. *Either I'm sleepwalking or this is one hell of a sexy dream.* As large as he was, his hold on her was light, exquisitely gentle. He ran his big hands up and down her arms, smoothed his palms over the small of her back and framed her waist as though she were some rare, cherished object he feared to break. At that point, she could have pushed away and perhaps even made it to the door, but suddenly the single space she cared to occupy in the whole of the universe was right there in her attic—in a stranger's arms. Rather than run, she tilted her head and parted her lips and slid her tongue into his mouth, kissing him back with a lifetime's worth of pent-up passion—passion that seemed to be thoroughly, gloriously returned.

He slid a hand upward from her waist to her breast, a groan escaping him. "So beautiful, so damned beautiful." Cupping her, he used his thumb to tease her nipple to life, raising a damp ache between her thighs.

Oh, my God. Maggie arched against him, reveling in the size and breadth and power of the hard male body molding to hers. For someone who had never experienced anything approaching a casual sexual encounter, she was rapidly losing control to the moment—and the handsome, hard-bodied stranger sharing it with her. Whether a reenactor hopped up on too much history or a certifiable nutcase, whoever and whatever he was, for the time being it didn't matter. All that mattered was how very much she wanted—needed—to make love with him.

As if reading her mind, he wrapped his arms about her waist and lifted her off the floor, setting her down on some smooth, solid surface it was too dark to see.

"Isabel, my sweet love, thank the good Lord I've found you at last."

Had she heard him correctly? Had he really just called her Isabel? Either that was one hell of a coincidence or she really was hallucinating. She started to break in with, "But I'm not—" when he ran his hands, so warm, so strong, so knowing, along her legs from ankle to thigh, carrying the hem of her nightgown up to her waist. Cool air brushed her bare skin, raising gooseflesh, and she suddenly remembered she wasn't wearing panties, that a complete stranger was seeing straight down to her most private place. She started to tug the garment down.

"Don't." Strong fingers banded her wrist, drawing her hand away. "I've waited so long, an eternity. I need to see you, touch you, suckle the sweet fruit of your womanhood once again. Give me leave, Belle. Dear Lord, give me leave lest I die a second death."

The sweet fruit of her womanhood? Die a second death? On second thought, maybe the intruder was a wannabe actor. He certainly showed a flair for the dramatic as well as an amazing command of period vernacular, nor did it hurt that he was blessed with a handsome face and killer body. He might have been a hero from the pages of one of Becky's historical romance novels. Maggie doubted her comparatively staid subconscious could have thought up such fantastical packaging, but before she could ask him why he kept calling her Isabel— Belle—he angled his face to hers and covered her mouth once more, his kiss more hungry than gentle this time, the heat of his big body radiating toward her like rays from a tanning bed, burning away all conscious thoughts except one.

I have to have this man.

Crazy as it was, she felt like a virgin again, not because she was nervous but because she was very eager to touch and taste and explore the unknown that was him. Whatever bedroom gymnastics she'd performed to please past lovers faded into insignificance. Everything she did or was about to do with this man—this stranger—felt like a first. It was as if with the brush of his mouth and the touch of his hands he were washing her clean body and soul, rendering their lovemaking rainwater fresh and breathtakingly new.

He broke contact with her lips and lowered his head, laying a trail of damp kisses starting with the sensitive spot behind her ear, the line of her throat leading into the curve of her shoulder, the tips of her breasts—laving her through the thin fabric, then pushing one sleeve off her shoulder and down. Taking her nipple into his mouth, he pulled hard but not too hard, the perfect pressure. Blessed wetness jetted between her legs, and she no longer cared that she wasn't wearing panties. In fact, she was really glad she wasn't.

Touch me, oh please, touch me.

As if she'd spoken aloud, he slipped his hand between her spread thighs and found her with his finger. He slid the thick digit inside, crooking it ever so slightly, gently stroking the ultrasensitive spot of her vagina that, until now, no one had ever found.

Maggie threw back her head and moaned as pleasure so keen it danced on a knife-edge of pain poured over her, bringing her almost to the breaking point—almost but not quite. Limbs trembling and nerves pulsing, she shifted on her bottom. "How did you know? How *could* you know?" Anchoring her hands to the shelf of his beautiful shoulders, she thrust upward, seeking to drive him deeper still, harder still.

His breath was a hot, husky whisper in her ear. "I know because I know you, Belle. I can read your body as though it were the back of my own hand. I know just where and how you like to be kissed and touched and tasted. I know when to gentle my touch and when to firm it. I know the little moans you make when you want me to enter you soft and slow and the throaty cries you give to let me know you crave it harder, faster. And yes, Belle, have no fear, I know exactly what to do to bring you to the pinnacle of your pleasure."

Her glasses had disappeared at some point though she couldn't say where. Resting his forehead against hers, he watched her face while he fingered her, intoning endearments obviously meant for another woman and yet feeling so very right for her. Under any other circumstance having a man call you by another woman's name would be the king of turnoffs but in this case the false identity combined with the darkened room and the scents of lavender and rain and a century's worth of mustiness lent a surreal quality to the situation, making it seem all right, or at least marginally better, because she could trick her mind into believing she was dreaming still or sleepwalking or outright hallucinating, that this wasn't really happening. But it was happening. She was about to go all the way with a total stranger, an intruder, in her attic, and she couldn't find the will to care—let alone stop.

And there would be no stopping, no pulling away. She'd reached the point of no return, the outpost beyond reason. He hadn't done more than remove his hat and yet there she sat, perched atop what she gathered must be an old secretary desk, her nightgown pushed up to her waist, her legs spread wide apart, her sex pulsing around that thick, probing finger. Stranger though he definitely was, hallucination perhaps, she'd never before felt so utterly at home with a man. She was so open to him, so incredibly wet she could feel the liquid warmth blanketing her inner thighs and trickling down her leg. She badly wanted him to replace his finger with the big, stiff cock she'd earlier felt pressed against her, but before they shared that ultimate pleasure, there was something else she wanted from him, something for which she didn't have the courage to ask, at least not in words.

Threading her fingers through his hair—so silky, so soft—she slid her hand to the back of his head, drawing him closer, drawing him down. He followed willingly, kissing a path from her breasts to her belly and lower still, not stopping until he was kneeling before her, his head level with her splayed thighs. Disappearing between them, he found her with his mouth.

Oh, my. Talk about feeling like you'd come home—or stumbled upon the long-searched-for prize. Never in her life had a man pleased her so thoroughly or so well. Unlike Richard or her previous boyfriends, her mystery lover seemed in no rush to reach the main event. He teased her clitoris with the point of his tongue, lapped at her labia as though it were some juicy, exotic fruit of which he couldn't possibly get enough. In between, he took breaks to press soft, sweet kisses to the insides of her thighs, to look up into her eyes and affirm how delicious she was, how much he wanted her in every way. His obvious pleasure in her had a potent effect on Maggie. Instead of worrying she might be taking too long to come, or that once again she might not come at all, instead of worrying about those and myriad other matters beyond her control like the circumference of her thighs—too wide—or the size of her bust—too small—for the first time in her adult life, she gave herself permission to step outside of her overworked, overburdened brain and live totally and completely in her body. She leaned back and let the cleansing pleasure wash over her, *through* her, refusing to think beyond how amazing it felt to be with him, how fundamentally good and right. She no longer cared if he was homeless, a robber or an escapee from the nearest nuthouse. She was oblivious to everything beyond her absolute need to be with him. If she had one unfulfilled wish it was to know his name, not for filling out a police report later but for the joy of shouting it when her time came. Instead she settled for repeating a series of anonymous endearments that had never before been so very heartfelt. "Oh, baby," and "Yes, sweetheart, there. There!" and "Oh my, what are you doing to me?"

The orgasm hit—fast, hard, furious. Had she been standing, the force of it would have knocked her to her knees. Like a thunderbolt ripping through a placid summer sky, there was no real warning. Suddenly it was upon her, she was in it and there was no recourse but to ride out its rage.

Coming down from the clouds, Maggie opened her eyes and looked into her lover's shadowed face. "That was so good," she whispered. "I never knew it could be so good."

"It can be even better, sweetheart. Let me show you again just how much better." He slid a warm hand between her thighs, parting them even wider, and a moment later she felt his member, so very big and so very hard and so very thick pressing into her.

"Not so fast." Tempted as she was to take him inside her in one rock-hard thrust, doing so would be tantamount to chugging a glass of fine wine in one sloppy swallow. Determined to savor every glorious inch of him, to draw out their pleasure for as long as she might, she pressed both palms to his chest. "Fair is fair. I don't care if you're my hallucination or just the hands-down best dream I've ever had, I get to see you, too."

A frantic urgency tore through Maggie. Now that she'd dined on ambrosia, a single serving was nowhere near enough. Somehow in the darkness and without her glasses she unbuttoned his uniform coat, sliding the sleeves over his bulging biceps and then off, and then went to work on the linen shirt beneath. Buttons popping, she yanked it open, revealing a magnificently planed chest dusted with dark hair. She raked her fingernails through the coarse matting and then, needing to taste as well as touch, dipped her head and sucked his flat nipple into her mouth.

He rewarded her with a throaty groan and slid a heavy hand into the back of her hair, crushing her against him. "So warm, so beautiful, so alive. You make me feel so very alive, my Isabel."

Even in the midst of her passion, she noticed how he kept saying *alive* as though it was some extraordinary state. But this wasn't the time for bogging herself down with thought when there was still so much to see and do and explore with him. Lifting her head from his chest, she realized he still wore his neckwear. A muscular neck had always been a particular turn-on for her, and she could tell from the power and breadth of the rest of him that his wouldn't disappoint. She wanted to bare his throat, nibble and lick and suck his Adam's apple and then slide her tongue along the line of muscle at the juncture of his powerful shoulder, marking him in a way that would last at least into tomorrow. Giving herself up to the moment, she reached up to the white scarf wound cravat-style about his throat.

"No!" Face fierce, he grabbed hold of her wrists, forcing her arms down to her sides.

Confused by his reaction, Maggie felt her libido drop a notch. "What is it? What did I do?"

He let go of her and took a step back, shaking his head as though she'd betrayed him somehow.

"Hey, where are you going? Look, I'm sorry, I didn't mean… If you don't want your neck touched, I'm cool with that."

Maggie blinked. That champagne must have caught up with her along with her bad eyes because though he still stood before her, the outline of his body looked fuzzy now, the lower half flickering in and out of view like the picture on a shorted-out television screen. Whether he was a dream or a hallucination, either way she wasn't ready for this, for them, to be over. She stretched out a hand to beckon him back, but instead of meeting with firm, blood-warmed flesh, it passed through him as though…as though he wasn't really there.

"Weary, so weary." Expression bleak, he backed away until he came up against the closed door. "Must…rest now, but I'll be back for you, my Isabel. I'll be baaaack…" Like a dissipating fireworks constellation, brilliant but brief, he vanished from view, pixels of light fading to ash and finally nothingness.

Maggie squeezed her eyes closed and then opened them again to dust motes floating like fairy dust in the cool, still air. Her sexy stranger was nowhere in sight. Feeling very cold and very alone, she felt around the darkness for her glasses.

She found them folded beside her. Putting them on, she called out, "Hey you, where'd you go?" She pulled down her nightgown and slid off the desktop, landing on wobbly legs. "Look, calling the cops is totally off the table at this point. I just want to talk to you."

Talk—that was a fib if not exactly a lie. Talking would come later, maybe when she was tracing slow circles over the broad canvas of his sweaty, muscled back. For now what she really wanted was to finish what they'd started, to give back some of the pleasure she'd so greedily taken. The tabletop sex had made for one hell of a thrilling fantasy ride but, rubbing her sore behind, she decided she wouldn't mind finishing out the night on her bed's ergonomically correct mattress.

But first she had to play out the current round of hide-and-go-seek. "I guess I'm it, huh?" She found the flashlight on the floor and used it to scour the four corners of the room, but he was nowhere to be seen. Given the sloped roof, there weren't all that many places a tall man might hide, especially one built like a professional football player. Her gaze came back to the still-open window. Outside, the storm's violence had tamed to a soft, steady downpour. She supposed he could have climbed out onto the slates and scaled the roof, but unless he was a comic book hero, part mountain goat or someone with a serious death wish, he wouldn't have attempted it, certainly not in the middle of a storm.

The alternative that came to mind was scarier still—she'd finally gone over the edge. No wonder the bag lady who fed the pigeons at the Dupont Circle fountain while keeping up a steady dialogue with invisible friends was always so smiley. Given what Maggie had just experienced, the old girl might be having one hell of a party inside her high-topped elastic-waist pants. If Maggie had guessed going nuts could be this much of a kick, she'd have gotten comfy with being crazy a long time ago.

A less dramatic possibility was she'd been sleepwalking. It had been years since her last episode, but she still remembered the scary sensation of waking up and finding herself nowhere near her bed. One time her dad had found her as far as the backseat of the family car, pajamas on and packed book bag beside her as though ready to get a head start on the ride to school.

In this case, she'd gotten a head start on a very different, very adult kind of ride. Regardless of whether her sexy stranger was housebreaker or hallucination, out-of-work actor or a sleepwalker's wet dream, the episode had achieved one major milestone—she'd come. After more than a year of straining to reach climax—and then giving a performance worthy of Meg Ryan in the diner scene of *When Harry Met Sally* when she didn't—she'd finally made it. Her mind might be en route to derailment but her body was back on track and working just fine. The stickiness between her thighs didn't lie nor did the raw, metallic taste coating the inside of her mouth where she'd bitten the inside of her lip. She'd come. Whatever else about her still needed fixing, at least she could cross *orgasmically challenged* off the list.

She walked over to the wall switch and this time when she flipped it, the light came on. Better. The returning electricity shone light not only on the dark paneling but on the significance of what she'd just done. Even if her sexy stranger was a hallucination, on some level she'd cheated on her boyfriend. That she didn't feel worse about that was a telltale sign that she and Richard were as good as broken up. The next and final step would be to make it official. Now that she'd had amazing sex—okay, the prelude to amazing sex—in whatever form, there was no second-guessing herself, no going back.

That her mystery lover hadn't called out any random woman's name but *Isabel* specifically struck her as strong support for the hallucination hypothesis—that and his dissolving before her eyes. On the other hand, it was dark, she hadn't been wearing her glasses and the climax had been so potent she might as well have knocked back a pint of Jack Daniels along with the champagne. If her sexy stranger was a reenactor camping out in her attic, who was to say he hadn't discovered Isabel's diary before Maggie had, perhaps even been the one to put it there in the wall? If so, then his dressing up as a Union soldier and calling her Isabel might have simply been his acting out a fantasy. Afterward, he'd taken advantage of her blissed-out state to slip out of the house. For all she knew, he might have walked right out her front door.

And yet when she went downstairs to check, all the doors and windows were still locked—from the inside.

5

ONCE SHE SETTLED BACK IN bed, Maggie slept like the dead. It was past ten when she woke the next morning with a hammering headache, a vague feeling of fatigue and a slight tenderness settling into certain places. With daylight streaming through her window, it was easy to believe the episode in the attic was simply an elaborate and very sexy dream. That worked until she got up to go to the bathroom for some Motrin and spotted the dirt smudges on the back of her nightgown—and the love bite blooming on the side of her neck. Sitting on the edge of the bathtub picking a splinter from her big toe, it was clear she really had been up in the attic. Equally clear was that she hadn't been up there alone.

Hallucinations didn't leave hickeys. She'd been up in that attic with someone. And yet the doors and windows had all been still locked and her bedroom window showed no signs of tampering. The attic window was the only conceivable way out, and she still couldn't wrap her mind around anyone being crazy enough to climb out onto a steep pinnacle of slippery slate in the middle of a storm. Then again her sexy stranger had been wearing a Civil War uniform and living in the attic of a vacant house—hardly hallmarks of normalcy.

Could there be some other way in and out of the house she'd yet to discover? Padding back to bed, she thought of the diary stowed in her night table. If the house had any secret passageways or hidden trapdoors, surely Isabel Earnshaw would have known about them. Whether or not she would have seen fit to record them on paper was another matter, but it was worth checking out.

She took the diary out of its drawer, opened to the next entry dated almost a year later and sat down on the side of the bed to read. Talk about anticlimactic. The passages following the description of Isabel and Ethan's sexually charged first meeting were mostly sparse laundry lists detailing the minutiae of daily life once the war began—a rather understated account of the Northern troops taking possession of Stafford Hills across the Rappahannock River; the staggering cost of household staples like beeswax, cotton goods and metal items such as sewing pins; and the scarlet fever that had swept through the town the previous winter, but nothing about the house per se and nothing about seeing Ethan O'Malley again. Skimming the entries, Maggie felt her hopes for a fairy-tale ending sinking like the *Titanic*. Until now she hadn't realized just how much she was counting on living vicariously through Isabel's innocent and oh-so-romantic eyes. Halfway through, she'd almost given up hope of the young diarist ever reconnecting with her dashing Union Army captain when an uncharacteristically wordy entry caught her eye.

Friday, May 2, 1862

Today a large cavalcade of Federal officers and accompanying horsemen rode through the town, their occupation made complete by the construction of pontoon bridges across the Rappahannock, enabling them to ford the river from their encampment at Stafford Hills. Women and children, boys too young to fight and old men lined either side of Main Street to watch the procession pass in sullen silence. Standing among them, I looked up into the faces of our oppressors. Though my family and neighbors never lost an opportunity to vilify the Yankees, beyond their blue uniforms, I can't say they looked or bore themselves any differently than our much revered Grays.

I was about to turn away and head for home when my gaze alighted on the visage I'd all but given up on ever seeing again. It was Captain Ethan O'Malley of the sky-blue eyes and broad smile. He wasn't smiling now but somber-faced as a judge as well as thinner than I remembered him. Even so, a thrill the likes of an Independence Day fireworks display shot clear through me. I wanted nothing more than to run to him and yet I dared not so much as lift my hand to wave. Instead I stood stock-still, willing him to look my way, my heart flipping over with gladness when he did. I fancied I saw a flash of awareness in his eyes, a telltale lifting of the brow that bespoke of recognition, but before I could be sure, he passed me by.

Excitement mounting, Maggie raced ahead to read the next entry dated two days later, a Sunday. Writing, even in one's journal, on a Sunday would have been forbidden back in Civil War times. To break the Sabbath, Isabel must have been bursting with news.

Sunday, May 4, 1862

Anyone reading this diary entry must conclude I have either gone mad or become the most wanton, wicked girl in the whole world, for this afternoon I cast aside all my scruples and threw myself at Captain O'Malley.

Many of the Federals attended Sunday worship along with the townspeople. Indeed, the Baptist Church was so crowded with blue uniforms we counted ourselves fortunate to find a pew. My searching gaze alighted on Captain O'Malley seated across the aisle with his fellow Federals. All through the sermon, I tried to catch his eye, but he refused to so much as glance my way. The one eye I did catch I would have gladly done without. Several times I looked over to where the soldiers sat only to find the opaque gaze of the sutler, Damian Grey, fixed upon me.

After church let out, I made an excuse to my parents that I had to see my friend Candice about a Bible study lesson we were contriving for the little ones. Instead I followed Captain O'Malley down the street and into the lending stable where the Federals were quartering their horses. He was bending to cinch his mount's saddle strap when I took a deep breath and pulled the heavy door closed behind me.

Despite the pains I took to be quiet, his soldier's senses must have detected my presence almost at once. He whirled about, one hand flying to his sidearm. Seeing it was only me, he relaxed his stance, though his handsome face wore a scowl. "Miss Earnshaw, what the devil are you doing here?"

I was both surprised and pleased he remembered my name, too pleased to mind the rebuke. "I saw you in the cavalcade earlier this week and then in church this morning. I didn't think you remembered me."

He stepped away from his horse and came toward me, his handsome face registering an urgent sort of gladness. "You're not the sort of woman a man forgets easily—or at all." His beautiful lips curved upward in a hesitant half smile that had my heart skipping beats. "But you should go now. It wouldn't do for you to be found here alone with me."

He was thinking of my reputation which, if not ruined, would be much tarnished upon our discovery. And yet since the war, such matters seemed trifling. Determined to hold fast to my courage now that I'd come thus far, I looked up into his face and said, "I've no intention of going anywhere, Captain O' Malley, at least not until you've set my mind at ease on one point—whatever have I done to offend you?"

A look of puzzlement crossed his handsome face. Even hollow-eyed and lean-cheeked, he really is the most beautiful man. "Offend me? Isabel, Miss Earnshaw, I assure you, you are quite mistaken."

I took heart in the fevered light in his eye and the way he kept running his gaze over me as though seeking to record every detail of my presence. "Then pray explain why you've taken such pains to avoid me these past days. Why, in church this morning, I might as well have been made of glass or air for all you noticed me."

"Sweet little fool," he said with a shake of his head, and if it wasn't for the melting look accompanying those words, I would have picked up my skirts and fled before I abased myself further. "If I keep myself from you, it is because you are so very lovely and innocent, so very perfect in every way save one—your allegiance to the South in this war. If I stay away from you, Miss Earnshaw, it is because I can't trust myself to do otherwise, for to come within arm's length of your dear self is to risk losing all reason, all honor."

"And what if…what if I don't want you to stay away?" At this point, I was trembling in every part of my person, not from fear but from the thrill that being close to him always seemed to bring.

He took a step toward me and laid his big, warm hands atop either of my shoulders. Dropping his voice to a husky whisper, he looked deeply into my eyes. "If you don't take yourself out of here right now, I may find myself obliged to kiss you."

A strange, frenzied excitement seized me then. I turned my face up to his, my tingling bosom rising and falling with each ragged, rushed breath. "Is that a threat or a promise, Captain?"

He swallowed hard, bringing his Adam's apple into prominence, and sinful girl that I am, I couldn't wait to have the taste of his flesh on my tongue. As if reading my thoughts, he lifted his hand to my face and traced my lower lip with a single, roughened finger, then slid the thick digit ever so slowly between my parted lips to touch my tongue.

"A bit of both, I reckon."

Maggie closed the diary feeling as though the temperature in the room had gone up several notches. Though Isabel Earnshaw was too much of a Southern lady to say so, reading between the proverbial lines, she surmised the reunion in the stable had ended with Isabel and Ethan sharing their first kiss, perhaps more. And yet somehow she knew, just knew, it wasn't the stable in which they'd made love the first time but the attic—Maggie's attic. How could she be so sure?

Eerier still, Isabel's description of Ethan O'Malley matched to a T the sexy stranger she'd had her brief but memorable encounter with the night before, even down to the captain's bars he carried on his oh-so-broad shoulders. She could almost believe the good captain and her intruder were the same man. But that was crazy. Even if he'd survived the war and lived to see old age, Ethan O'Malley would have been dead for more than a century. The intruder in her attic had been very much alive and around her age, thirty or thereabouts. Could he be an O'Malley descendant, perhaps? Fredericksburg might have become a bedroom community to Washington, D.C., prompting certain die-hard old-timers to rail against the Yankee locusts taking over the town, but the city still had its cadre of old-money Southern families, many of whom could trace their residency back to the days of George Washington. And yet hadn't Isabel mentioned in her diary that Ethan O'Malley was from Boston?

The sound of Maggie's cell phone ringing pulled her sharply back to the present. She crossed the floor to where she'd plugged it into the wall charger. Glancing down at the display, she saw it was Richard, the very last person on the planet she wanted to talk to, especially after last night. She hesitated and then clicked the cell on.

Richard's clipped tones blared out from the receiver. "I don't know about you, but I didn't sleep worth a damn." He didn't bother with saying good morning or asking how her first night in the house had gone—typical.

Holding the cell to her ear, she sat on the edge of the bed. "I can't say it was the best night's sleep I've ever gotten." The best orgasm definitely, but not the best night's sleep.

"There was a bad storm here," he said, forging ahead as though he hadn't heard her. "The power's been out since midnight."

"Midnight, really?" That got her attention. It was just around midnight that she'd gone up to investigate the flapping shutter—and ended up going down with a certain sexy stranger.

"When I drove to the gym this morning, several trees were down and power lines out with them. Look, I know I said I'd help you get set up, but I think I'd better stick around here until the road crews have a crack at cleanup."

Hoping she didn't sound too eager, she said, "No, no, of course you should stay safe. There's no point in taking unnecessary risks. I'll be fine. I have power and tools and, well, power tools, too. If I need to, I can ask Sharon to lend me a hand after she gets off work."

"You're sure?" He sounded almost as relieved as she felt.

"Positive."

There was a prolonged pause and then he asked, "Aren't you going to ask me how my meeting went? Really, Maggie, you live in your own head entirely too much."

That might be true but last night living in her head had amounted to living large—make that *extra* large. "Sorry, I'm not awake yet. I had kind of a rough night myself."

Instead of asking what had gone wrong, he said, "Do you want me to write you a prescription for some Ambien?"

First the unasked-for prescription for Prozac and now the push for her to start taking sleeping pills—Richard must be a pharmacist's dream come true. "Not that kind of rough. We had a bad storm here, too." Talk about living inside your own head. "With all the wind, that shutter in the attic came lose again and the banging woke me up. I...I had a hard time getting back to sleep."

A *hard* time, indeed. Remembering the feel of her intruder pressing against her, she felt herself getting wet all over again. Along with sexual desire, the memory sparked a surge of guilt. This wasn't right. She had to break up with Richard. It wasn't fair to either of them to keep their relationship in limbo any longer.

She scoured her brain for a delicate way to broach the topic when it occurred to her that admitting her infidelity might more than fill the bill. Who knew, but maybe Richard might welcome the excuse to end things between them.

Bracing herself, she began, "Listen, Richard, there's something I need to tell you. Last night, I had this really weird experience, and I think it must mean that—"

"Sorry, Mags, gotta run. I've got a new patient out in my waiting room, and I haven't looked at her chart yet."

He was the one who'd called her and yet the moment the conversation shifted from him, he decided he didn't have time to talk—typical, but maybe for the best given the busy day she had ahead of her. Topping her to do list was getting to the bottom of what had happened last night.

"Um, okay. I guess I'll catch you later, then."

"Yeah, I'll give you a buzz. Ciao."

"Okay, bye." Stunned by his curtness, she clicked off the cell.

Sinking back against the banked pillows, it occurred to her that her sexy stranger was in so many respects Richard's polar opposite, dark where Richard was fair, broadly built where Richard was narrow—and sexually generous where Richard was selfish. If she'd been with her soon-to-be ex-boyfriend in that attic, she would have spent most of the time on her knees.

Maggie put the diary away and got up to dress, glad to feel the headache wearing off. Her unresolved relationship with Richard was a barrier holding her back from a lot of things, namely the ability to fully enjoy her life. But before she dealt with him, she needed to deal with getting her house in order, or in this case, her attic. Whatever had happened up there last night, she was determined to get to the bottom of it before the day was over.

6

ONCE SHE MADE THE COFFEE and fed the cat, Maggie kicked into gear, conducting a thorough room-to-room search. So far Isabel's diary hadn't yielded any clues about the house, and Maggie was beginning to suspect it wasn't going to. In the absence of insider information, a practical, hands-on approach was called for. Almost all old houses had secrets and maybe in addition to the diary, this one harbored if not a hidden passageway, perhaps a trapdoor leading to the outside. It didn't hurt to hope. In that vein, she spent several hours knocking her knuckles on walls and tapping her heels on flooring only to affirm everything was exactly as it appeared to be—solid plaster, solid wood. When lunchtime rolled around and she'd turned up empty, she gave in and accepted the obvious if unromantic explanation—there wasn't anything to find. Her sexy stranger had entered and exited through the attic window, end of story.

On the positive side, that meant he must be a flesh and blood man, not a hallucination and certainly not a ghost—of Ethan O'Malley or anyone else. Neither hallucinations nor ghosts left hickeys—at least she didn't think so. Standing at the kitchen counter slathering mustard on her Swiss cheese and rye, she told herself she'd been with someone up in that attic, and if that someone had gotten in once without her knowing it, who was to say he couldn't do so again?

Rather than wasting time worrying about the state of her sanity, she should be worrying about the state of her security—her *home* security. Seeing the situation in the bright light of day, she told herself she was lucky she hadn't been beaten or killed or, at minimum, robbed of her few valuables. Sandwich in hand, she got out the phone book, scanned the ad listings until she came to a home security company she recognized as reputable and told the young woman answering her call she wanted the most foolproof, state-of-the-art system on the market.

Two hours later, she had a deluxe security system in place complete with door and window sensors, interior motion detectors, siren and a master control panel with so many buttons it looked as if it had been lifted from the console of the starship *Enterprise.* Before leaving, the technician gave her a brief walk-through and then handed her an instruction manual thicker than the Bible. Watching his van pull away, she released a relieved sigh. Her checkbook balance might be substantially lighter, but you couldn't put a price on safety. Provided she kept the system activated at all times, the space was sealed as tight as Fort Knox, which meant there would be no further nocturnal run-ins with sexy strangers. That should have been reassuring, and it was, but it also struck her as more than a little sad. The episode in the attic had been the hands-down sexiest, most thrilling thing to ever happen to her and yet at the same time she'd also felt inexplicably safe and cherished, lusted after and yet…loved.

A sexy intruder in her attic was about as close to a resident ghost as she was likely to ever come. In a crazy way, she'd gotten to live out her fantasy. From here on, she'd have to do a better job of watching what she wished for.

LOOKING DOWN ON ISABEL'S machinations to secure the house from his attic perch, Ethan could only shake his head. The intervening century and a half hadn't changed her, not a jot. In her current life, she might be known as Maggie Holliday and communicate in a queer dialect the likes of which he'd never before heard, but there was no doubt the tall, lovely brunette he'd held all too briefly the night before was Isabel, his Isabel, down to the beauty mark gracing the corner of one eye, the crescent-shaped birthmark topping her left shoulder and the stubbornness streaking through her as strong and hot as white lightning. Haloed by moonlight, she'd looked even lovelier in the lacey, loose-fitting nightgown than she had in the heavy petticoats and corseting of their time, her burnished mahogany hair falling freely to her waist like a silk skein, not pinned and hidden beneath a bell-shaped bonnet as it had been when they'd first met.

Ethan raked his hand through his collar-length hair, though in truth he couldn't feel a thing, not the grazing of his fingertips against his scalp nor the weight of his legs swinging over the side of the rail. After one hundred forty-five years of separation, the powers that be had finally granted him permission to borrow back his body for this, his first visit to earth since his physical death. Unfortunately, taking human form after so long away was a good deal more involved than slipping in and out of an old, familiar suit of clothes. Embodiment brought the burden of responsibility and also the unfamiliar feeling of physical weight. It also consumed a goodly portion of his finite reserve of earth energy, the fuel that had enabled him to cross back over to rejoin the living. Taking human form, even temporarily, was akin to dipping up buckets of water from a shallow well. Sooner or later the well would run dry, and he would be called to cross back over to the other side whether or not he'd tracked down Damian and settled matters between them as he'd sworn to do on that brisk December day back in 1862. With his soul's eternal rest at stake, and that of Isabel's, too, he didn't want to squander so much as one drop of his precious energy.

The soft, reedy strains of a harmonica pulled him from his thoughts, signaling he was no longer alone. Ethan looked up to see his spectral sidekick and former camp cook, Harold—Hap—Longacre float down onto the beam beside him.

The horizontal slash of a Confederate cavalryman's saber had lopped off Hap's head at the Battle of Marye's Heights. Until he found his killer's spirit and the two made their peace, he was obliged to haul the dismembered head about with him wherever he went, a scary sight even for the spectral world.

"Why so down in the mouth? Sky's blue, grass's green and girl's still pretty as a picture." Hap lifted the head off his shoulders like a box lid, set it atop his knees and gave the grizzled crown a good, long scratch—not that ghosts suffered from itches or other bodily sensations, for that matter, but Hap was a notorious showman.

"I've betrayed Isabel's trust in me."

Hap raised a bushy gray brow. "How's that?"

Ethan propped his jaw on one fisted hand and admitted, "I seduced her—again."

Hap's weathered face cracked into a grin. "Well, good on you, Cap. How'd you manage it, the seducin' part I mean? No, don't tell me, lemme guess. You bamboozled her out of her knickers with the old sleight o' hand."

Ethan lifted his head from his hand. "I didn't even think of that."

"Then you put a spell on her so she would think she was a flower opening up to the sun?"

Ethan shook his head. "Of course not." Hap might not be able to grow another head but over the past one hundred forty-five years he'd obviously grown quite an imagination.

"Oh, no, I know, even better, you got your mitts on some of that Yvette gal's love potion and slipped some into her food when she weren't lookin', right?"

"I didn't even think of that."

"Then what?"

Ethan let out a long sigh. "I used the oldest, dirtiest and most tried-and-true trick in the book."

"Sir?"

"I got her drunk."

The French champagne he'd left for her on the counter had been a fine vintage indeed, from Napoleon the Third's own cellar. Even so, he hadn't expected Isabel—Maggie—to quaff three glasses of the stuff. The earlier argument with Richard must have created an even greater disturbance in her energy field than he'd credited.

Hee-hawing, Hap slapped a weathered hand against the outside of his thigh, setting the head in his lap rocking like a hobbyhorse. "Well, that'll work, too, I reckon. So what's the problem?"

Ethan hesitated to vent his maudlin thoughts in the presence of such eternal optimism. "I was thinking maybe I should leave her be and go back before she's any the wiser."

Hap frowned. Reaching down, he adjusted the head in his lap. "Why in blazes would you go and do a fool thing like that when you've been living, so to speak, for this chance for one hundred fifty years give or take?"

It was no more than the truth. For one hundred forty-five

years now he'd been shoring up astral energy like a miser hoarding gold, preparing for the time when he would cross back over to earth and reunite with Isabel, or rather her soul's reembodiment. It wasn't until Isabel—Maggie—had moved back into the house she'd inhabited one hundred forty-five years ago, the very house where they'd dared to meet in secret and plan and love, that the elements were sufficiently aligned to make his long-awaited reentry possible.

In the interim, he'd watched and waited much like a boy might wait for a chicken egg to hatch at a state fair. He'd seen her born—or rather reborn—as Maggie Holliday, watched her take her first step, her first bicycle ride *sans* training wheels and, yes, experience her first kiss. Looking on as she'd locked lips with a pimply faced boy in an ill-fitting tuxedo and metal-covered teeth, he'd had to hold back from throwing down thunderbolts worthy of Thor. When she'd received the phone call relaying the tragic news that her family had perished, he'd stood by while she grieved, his soul absorbing as much of the ache as he could. Though invisible to her mortal eyes, he'd been very much with her all the time. When she'd walked into her water closet with the intention of swallowing a deadly dose of pills, he'd seen history about to repeat itself. Refusing to simply stand by and let it, he'd stepped between her and the medicine cabinet, wrapping his energy field around her like physical arms. Instead of dooming her chance of eternity yet again by taking her own life, she'd folded to her knees on the tile floor and wept and wept, never once suspecting her tears were soaking into his very breast, his very soul.

To save them both, he had to make Isabel—Maggie—remember, he had to make her believe. To jog her soul's memory, he'd appeared to her dressed in full uniform though he'd left off wearing weapons of any sort so as not to frighten her. But instead of remembering, she held on to the fool notion he was either a housebreaker or a hallucination. But then modern people seemed to rely a great deal on so-called expert advice in the form of self-help books, television and a mysterious entity known as the Internet. The common sense so prized in his day seemed to be sorely lacking—entirely missing was the faith.

The previous night in the attic had been nothing short of transporting and not only because he'd gotten to slip back into his physical body. He'd forgotten all the pleasures physicality brought, and when you were not only in your body but using it to make love to the woman who was the love of your life, sentience was pure, unadulterated magic. Just touching her, he'd felt his fingertips singing—and his manhood thrumming.

Maggie might not yet remember their past together, but he would have thought their present-day lovemaking must mean something special to her, too, and yet mere hours later she was spending the better part of her day working on ways to bar him from not only her house but also her life.

Was this what modern people called a one-night stand?

Turning back to Hap, he gestured to the ethereal window at their feet. Like watching a diorama, he could peer down through the parted mist and see in microcosm Isabel's every movement. "She doesn't want me. Look at the trouble she's taking to keep me out."

Hap lifted his headless shoulders in a shrug. "So the gal's playing hard to get, so what? Some things never change regardless of the year, but it'll take more than any newfangled locks to keep the likes of you and me out."

Dragging his gaze away from Isabel—Maggie—standing at the kitchen counter poring over her new security system manual, he turned back to his friend. "I know that and so do you, but she doesn't." If she was this afraid of him, thinking he was a housebreaker, how much more terrified would she be once—*if*—he revealed the truth?

It hadn't helped matters that he'd lost his earthly foothold last night and faded out at the very worst of times—just when he'd been about to enter her. After one hundred forty-five years of floating in the ether world, such an earthy experience would be a jolt to even the stoutest of astral bodies, and a century and a half of abstinence had lowered his passion threshold considerably. He'd felt the riptide force of her climax run through him like an electrical current, the charge of it wreaking havoc on his energy field, his carefully crafted purpose and, yes, his self-control. Her reaching up to untie his neck cloth had been an added shock. Back in his day, it was the man who took control of the undressing, not that he'd have minded sharing that pleasure with Isabel's decidedly modern incarnation. The catch was that taking back his physical body had meant taking it back in as-is condition complete with burns and scars from the hanging rope. Considering how hideous his wounds would look to her, vanishing had seemed the better part of valor.

Hap's finger snapping drew him back to the present—and the problem at hand. "Don't be too hard on the gal, Cap. It's not her fault she don't remember." Apparently Ethan's wasn't the only soul that had perfected the art of reading minds.

"Maybe she doesn't want to remember."

The Civil War had seen friends and family members killed, dreams lost and an entire way of life wiped out forever. Even his and Isabel's most private, beautiful moments had been overshadowed by a sense of poignancy and impending doom. How could he blame her for wanting to block out the memory of a past so fraught with peril and pain?

Hap raised his head in his hands and gave it a vigorous

shake. "All of us before we're birthed have a veil put over our third eye, so we focus on the life we're coming into and not the past ones. I reckon it's up to you to make her remember, to make her believe."

Hap was right. Humans were born, or rather reborn, in a state of amnesia. As a general rule, the powers that be didn't want souls focusing on the triumphs and tragedies of past lives at the expense of the lessons to be learned in the present one. Occasionally a memory from preexistence slipped into consciousness, hence déjà vu, but for the most part, humans came into their new lives as blank slates.

"I'm doing what I can. I appear to her in my uniform, the same one I wore the day we met. I loosened that shutter to bring her up to the attic and then guided her over to the wall where she'd find the diary. And still she's hell-bent on believing I'm some sort of..." He hesitated, searching for the word. "Reenactor."

Like the carnies of his day, reenactors seemed to travel in troupes, staging battle scenes and balls and generally playing at the past rather than pursuing honest employment. Her other assumptions about him—madman, felon or figment of her imagination—were even less flattering. The last troubled him most of all because it meant she didn't trust in her own heart's wisdom, let alone the soundness of her mind. Tapping into her swirling thoughts, he saw they were a tangle of dark and conflicting emotions: frustration and sadness, intense sexual longing but also fear—fear that she might be losing her mind. He laid the blame for the fear squarely on the slender shoulders of the miserable quack she'd taken as her beau. The churlish way the cur had spoken to her earlier had made Ethan's blood boil—metaphorically speaking.

But dishing out his just desserts to Isabel's beau was secondary to his mission of finding Damian and settling the score between them once and for all. To accomplish that, he would require the help of the other member of their tragic romantic triangle—Isabel. After all they'd been through together, after all they'd shared, he'd thought getting his beloved to remember again would be the easy part. But he could see he was going to have to woo and win her all over again—and after one hundred forty-five years, his Romeo skills were more than a little rusty.

BEYOND BREAKING FOR A RUN around town, Maggie spent the day unpacking and setting up the house until evening. She was just thinking about dinner when Sharon showed up at her door. For the past five years Sharon had lived in Fredericksburg in the loft apartment of a subdivided 1880s house on lower Charles Street, one of the few downtown rentals that allowed pets—in her case, the demon dog, a sweetheart of a rottweiler mix named Minnie, after the mouse.

"Hey, girlfriend, I hope you don't mind my stopping by without calling, but I wanted to drop off your housewarming gift." She handed her a small box, the gift wrap imprinted with her signature gold stars.

Tearing away one corner of the paper, Maggie opened the lid. Inside was an antique-style soap dish holding three decoratively molded scented guest soaps—lavender, of course. Remembering how the scent of lavender had seemed to swirl about her last night, growing stronger and sweeter just before she'd come, she felt embarrassment heat her cheeks—and a telltale tingle warm the place inside her thighs.

"Thank you, sweetie, this is perfect. You know me too well. You have time to come in for the tour?"

"That depends." Sharon hesitated, violet-blue gaze peeking past Maggie to the inside of the house. "Is Darth Vader lurking about?"

The *Star Wars* villain was Sharon's code name for Richard. Maggie had introduced the two over drinks at Clyde's in Georgetown a couple of months ago, and it had been a case of mutual dislike at first sight.

"Nope, the coast is clear. Richard went back to D.C. yesterday afternoon." She backed up and waved Sharon in.

Looking relieved, Sharon followed her inside the house. "I thought he had some big celebration dinner planned."

"I thought so, too, but apparently it was a choice between wining and dining me or working out at the gym. The gym won."

"Bastard." Sharon shook her head. "That settles it. You and I are going out—my treat."

An administrative assistant in the university's HR Department, Sharon couldn't make all that much money. Maggie shook her head. "No way are you paying for me. Besides, I can't go out like this. I'm a mess." She spread her hands to indicate her dusty T-shirt and jeans. As for her hair, she hadn't touched it since pulling it into a messy ponytail before her run.

Sharon was one of those women who always looked a hundred percent put together. Casually but smartly dressed in a chocolate-colored cotton wrap dress, high-heeled wedges and chunky silver and amber jewelry, she shrugged. "So go change. I'll hang out and wait. It'll give me a chance to catch up with my bud, Willie, here." She stooped to pet the cat. Hearing the voice of a prominent member of his fan club, Willie had trotted into the foyer as soon as Sharon stepped inside.

Maggie hesitated. She needed to do more than change. Before going out, she really needed to shower, too. "It's going to take me at least a half hour to pull it together, and it's almost eight o'clock now. Are you sure anything will still be open by the time we get out of here? I'm guessing Tuesday night is probably pretty dead in a small town like this."

Smiling, Sharon scooped a purring Willie into her arms. "Stick with me, Mags. I know just the place."

7

LOCATED ON WILLIAM STREET in the heart of the Fredericksburg Historic District, Bistro Bethem was a local restaurant that served seasonal modern American cuisine with a distinctive Southern flair. In recent years, the establishment had added weekly live music to its menu of events. Two hours and two margaritas into the evening, Maggie was pleasantly tipsy if not exactly drunk, toes tapping to a local musician crooning the lyrics to Bob Dylan's "Knockin' on Heaven's Door," one of several acts billed as part of Bob Smith and Friends. Unlike other open mike nights Maggie had attended, all the musicians in Bob's lineup were really good, including Bob himself, who performed the first solo set of mostly blues tunes. Apparently the secret was out because when they'd walked in around nine o'clock the place was packed, both the inside seating and café tables occupied and the bar area with standing room only.

Seated across from Sharon at one of the indoor tables, Maggie leaned across and admitted, "You were right. I really needed this."

A grin wreathed Sharon's face from one triple-pierced ear to the other. "I hate people who go around saying 'I told you so' but well, I told you so."

Casting her gaze about the crowd, Maggie said, "I can't believe this is a Tuesday night. It's so crowded you'd think it was the weekend. I wish Richard were here to see it. He'll never believe me otherwise. He acts like I've moved to Green Acres."

As soon as she spoke the words, she realized she was lying—to herself. She didn't wish Richard was there. In fact, she was really glad he wasn't.

Sharon lifted her glass of pinot and took a sip. "That's because Richard's an ass."

A few months earlier, Maggie would have rushed to defend him but now she turned to check out some of the other guys at the bar, a clear sign she had one foot—and several additional toes—out the proverbial door.

Sharon's voice had her turning back. "Mags, what are you doing, huh?" Setting down her wine, Sharon sent her a serious look.

"Uh, having a margarita—actually a second margarita—with one of my best gal pals, why?"

"Don't be a smart-ass. You know what I mean. What are you still doing with Richard? I know, I know, you were going through a rough time and he was…well, for good or for bad, he was there for you. Look, I'd be the last woman on earth to knock taking advantage of a warm body and a willing ear to get through the tough times, but in this case, I just don't get it. From where I sit, you've got it all going on. You're brilliant with the Ph.D. to prove it, you're funny and kind and in case you somehow missed all the male ogling coming your way tonight, you look like a friggin' supermodel. Frankly, it's a damned good thing you're so nice because otherwise it would be really easy to hate you. So why are you wasting yourself on a jerk like Richard?"

Ordinarily this would be the point at which Maggie would counter with a laundry list of all Richard's finer qualities—the M.D., the stellar reputation in the medical research community, the good looks and hard body—only she found none of those things impressed her all that much anymore. Missing from the mix was compassion, empathy and just maybe a soul.

Maggie blew out a breath. She wasn't really in the mood for a deep discussion, let alone a relationship intervention, but it seemed there was no escape. "I'm going to break up with him." Catching Sharon rolling her eyes, she added, "No, really, I mean it, I am. I just feel like I need to get my house in order first, not the house I just bought but my life. As soon as I get these revisions in on my dissertation and get into a groove teaching my fall classes, I'll be able to breathe again, start making plans—changes."

Sharon blew out a breath. "You're waiting until the fall to break it off? But it's only spring. Time's wasting, girlfriend, and there are plenty of other hunks in the sea. Speaking of which…" She glanced over to the bar where a thirtysomething hottie in a sports coat and comfortably worn jeans leaned over to get his check.

Maggie nodded. "That's Mac McMillan, a fellow come-here like us. He's involved with the police department somehow, as a detective, I think."

Sharon turned back to their table, eyes bright as headlight high beams. "If you don't want him, I just might take him."

Maggie spared Mac a brief glance. He was a good-looking man, no doubt about it, but her thoughts kept circling back to the tall, dark and handsome reenactor who apparently had felt entitled to camp out in her attic. For any number of reasons, he was going to be a tough act to follow, let alone top. Just thinking about him, she could taste the tang of his kiss; feel the heat of his big, hard body wrapping around hers and smell the musky scent of him, some heady combination of wool and leather and…well, man.

Maggie smiled. "He's yours. I'm spoken for, remember?" In her mind, she wasn't talking about Richard but instead her sexy stranger. Even though she knew last night had been a one-shot deal, every now and then she caught herself glancing around the room in the hope of seeing dark hair, blue eyes and broad shoulders.

Grinning, Sharon reached for her drink. "Thanks but this is a strictly girls' night out. No stinkin' boys allowed. As for you, promise me one thing. When you do get around to breaking it off with Darth, no more dating shrinks, okay?"

Chuckling, Maggie raised her glass and touched it to Sharon's. "You've got yourself a deal."

MAGGIE STEPPED INSIDE her front door a few minutes short of midnight, humming the bars to an old Stray Cats tune. She'd lived in D.C. for several years and rarely had stayed out past nine on a weeknight. Compared to her northwest D.C. neighborhood, downtown Fredericksburg was party central. Go figure.

The margaritas and time with her friend had both been medicinal. At several points during the night, she'd been on the cusp of confiding the attic episode to Sharon but had lost her nerve every time. For starters, Sharon was a longtime volunteer with the local rape crisis hotline. Maggie's admission that her hunky hookup was also guilty of breaking and entering would have invited a safety lecture with at least one really scary story tossed in. Some things were better left unsaid.

And yet remembering how her sexy stranger had kissed and fingered and licked her until she'd wanted to scream out her pleasure, she couldn't believe he'd done anything all that bad. The more she thought about it, the more convinced she was that he must be some eccentric local—she was already discovering that Fredericksburg had more than its share—

who'd known the house was sitting empty and taken advantage of the situation to camp out rent free. If that were the case, then the alarm system sign in her front yard flower bed and the decals on her doors and windows should discourage any future visits.

That ought to comfort her, and it did, but it also made her more than a little sad. The orgasm had been A-list and not only because it had been a year in coming, so to speak. Even without the physicality of sexual climax, the short but sweet encounter was the hands-down most scintillating thing to happen to her in the whole of her rule-driven, task-oriented life. She couldn't imagine anything ever matching it. There had been several attractive men at the bistro tonight, but no one who had remotely measured up. Logically she knew the sexy setup must have played a part in the amazing chemistry she'd felt. A deserted attic chock-full of historic artifacts; a tall, dark, uniformed stranger waiting in the shadows; a storm raging outside—the scenario might have been lifted from one of Becky's romance novels. Perfect—it had all been so very perfect, down to the lavender scenting the rain-soaked air.

Last night had amounted to throwing up the lid on her personal Pandora's box. Sure, she'd had decent sex in the past, but now she realized that before the encounter with her sexy stranger, she'd never known passion, not really. Now that she'd had a glimpse into what she'd been missing, she couldn't imagine going back. Maybe it was greedy of her, selfish even, but she wanted to feel that rush of excitement again, that incredible thrill that came from being in the arms of someone who was as crazy hot for you as you were for him.

It was the stranger part that just wasn't working for her. As much as she wanted passion in her life, she also wanted to share it with someone who would stick around the next morning to eat scrambled eggs and toast, drink coffee, read the newspaper and maybe later even take a walk or rub her feet. Maggie wanted someone she could believe in, someone with whom she could dream.

What she wanted was a soul mate. But when you were thirty and living in a small town where single women outnumbered single men ten to one, what were the odds of finding one of those?

AS SLEEPY AS MAGGIE WAS, once she undressed and slipped into bed, her wired mind kicked into overdrive. She felt like Alice in Wonderland only instead of being induced to drink from a bottle or to eat a small cake, it was as if the diary was calling out to her from the inside of her night table drawer—take me out and read me! After fifteen minutes of counting sheep and trying to block out her alarm clock's rhythmic ticking, she gave in, switched on the lamp and took out the diary. Head propped on pillows, she laid the diary on her tented knees and opened to where she'd left off.

The next entry was dated at the end of August, a gap of several months. Isabel must have been too busy or too distracted by a certain Union Army captain to take the time to record her thoughts.

August 26, 1862

The rumor circulating about town is that the Federals have received orders to decamp and march on Richmond. While Ethan will neither confirm nor deny it—for him to do so would be treason—I fear he will be leaving with his regiment any day now. With so little time left to us, and so many curious eyes upon us—the pale blue ones of a certain sutler in particular—we've begun meeting in the attic of my parents' house, sweltering though it is.

This evening I waited for dusk to fall and then stole upstairs. Tying a handkerchief to the attic window, I sat down to wait, hands clasped and heart thundering. True to his word, Ethan materialized at the window mere moments later. I was on my feet in an instant, helping to pull him through. The moment he landed inside, I was in his arms, his cool lips catching mine in a kiss that was at once thrilling and firm. Kissing him back, I felt my fears melting away like snowcaps struck by January sunlight.

Drawing away, he looked deeply into my eyes. "God, Belle, how I've missed you. How good it feels to have you in my arms again."

He reached into my bodice and brought my breasts together in his hands, circling the tips with his thumbs and raising the tingle between my thighs to a full-blown ache. I knew I ought not to let him touch me so, that our being together like this without benefit of marriage was terribly wrong, sinful even, and yet with the war making every day so very uncertain and our every stolen moment together such a gift, I couldn't find it in my heart to deny either of us.

As if reading my guilty thoughts, Ethan drew his hands away and settled them on my waist instead. Resting his forehead against mine, he breathed in gulps of air as though he'd just run a great distance. "I should stop now before…before things go too far." I could tell from the urgency in his voice and the fevered look in his eyes he didn't want to stop any more than did I. He started to turn away, but by then my decision was made.

I took hold of his wrist, drawing it back up over my belly and settling it on my breast. "Belle?"

I shook my head, warming in a way that had little to do with the heat. "Don't stop, Ethan. I don't care what comes after. I want this, I want you, only wait one moment."

I turned away and pulled out a sprig of lavender from the little jelly jar I'd set out on the old secretary desk. Reaching into my hair, I took my ribbon and tied it about the herb, making a tidy bouquet of the bunch. "This will make it perfect." Smiling back at him over my shoulder, I hung the lavender on a long nail protruding from the beam. "Now it's our bridal bower, sure as if we were man and wife in truth." Turning back, I sent him a wobbly smile and opened my arms.

Ethan stepped into them. "God in heaven knows how I do love you, Belle. Once the war is won, I'll make you my bride in earnest, I swear it."

Once the war was won. I no longer cared which side won or lost, I only wanted it to be over. No matter whether it was the North or the South that went down in history as the victor, we were all losers for having allowed our homeland to be so torn asunder.

I wrapped my arms about his neck, wishing I might never have to let go. "I love you, too, Ethan, with all my heart forever more."

Forever more. For the next sweet, stolen hour, he made gentle love to me and for that brief time at least, the madness of the world beyond the four walls of our little attic seemed far away indeed.

Maggie closed the diary with a sigh. Setting her folded glasses on the night table, it occurred to her that the journal was much more of a window into Isabel's most private world than a historical resource. A part of her felt like a voyeur for intruding. And yet another part of her felt as though doing so was her right, as though the diary belonged to her and not only because she'd discovered it in her attic. More than once she'd paused in reading, struck by an eerie sense of familiarity, as though the faded words in their neat, elegant script had been put there by her own hand. Realistically she knew there was a scientific explanation for déjà vu, that the sense of having been there and done that was the *illusion* of remembrance rather than remembrance itself, and yet she couldn't help feeling as though she was reliving an episode from her past, a past that was every bit as real to her as the events of her current life. In her mind's eye, she saw Ethan O'Malley stepping behind Isabel—her—felt the thrill of him sprinkling sweet, soft kisses over her nape and shoulders, felt his calloused fingers working to free her from the confines of her gown and petticoats and corset, heard his whispered endearments as he lowered her onto the cloak-covered floor and then came down atop her. Remembered—yes, not imagined but *remembered*—how she'd turned to him and wound her arms about his neck and arched toward the lovely blunt pressure of his exploring fingers, felt her body's answering call in the way nature guided her to lift her hips to his questing hand.

Her mind circled back yet again to the previous night's encounter. Just what had that been about? Was it possible that prolonged sexual frustration could drive you mad, sort of like the old, archaic Freudian notion of hysteria only in reverse? Had the inability to climax made a bottleneck of her brain, blurring the line between what was real and what was fantasy? Or was it that she was lonelier than she wanted to admit, so lonely that her overburdened subconscious had resorted to inventing a sexy intruder to keep her company? If that was the case, maybe she should swallow her pride and take that vibrator for a test run after all. A sex toy was no substitute for a man, let alone a relationship, but she hoped that climaxing would quiet not only her sexually tense body but her troubled mind as well.

Even though it was foolish of her—she was alone in the house, after all—when she got up to put away the diary, she made it a point to cross the room and close her bedroom door. Coming back to the nightstand, she took a deep breath and pulled open the bottom drawer.

The dildo was heavier than she remembered but then she'd only handled it for the few seconds it had taken to shove it inside the drawer. Wielding it like a wand, a very adult wand, she had to admit that other than its Pepto-Bismol pink color, it was remarkably lifelike, not to mention impressively well-endowed—certainly a hell of a lot larger than Richard was. Given his defensiveness over his modest-size member, she was surprised he hadn't viewed the toy as a rival.

Willing herself to relax, she slid beneath the sheets and opened her legs. It was moment of truth time. "Can I really do this" warred with "can I really afford not to"? The latter argument won out, and she edged her thumb toward the toy's switch, sliding it into the On position. The faux phallus jumped to life—a slow, salacious swirl against her palm. Even though she'd established she was all alone, embarrassment stung her cheeks.

"I did make love to you that evening, most passionately, not once but several times."

"Ahhh!"

Her scream echoing in her ears, Maggie looked down to the sexy Civil War reenactor standing at the foot of her bed and shoved the vibrator behind her back. Even with her glasses off, he stood out crystal clear from the blurred backdrop of her bedroom. Caught in the act of getting it on with a bubble-gum-pink battery-operated toy—how much more humiliating could life get?

Hoping he hadn't seen, she demanded, "How did you get past the security system and back inside?"

His gaze slid over her, making her very much aware that while he was fully and formally clothed, she wore only a cotton sheet. "I didn't get back in. I never left."

He'd been hiding in the house the whole time! Freaked out, she snapped the covers up to her chin. "Well, I want you to leave now."

Clutching the sheet, she mentally calculated the distance between the bed and the cell phone plugged into the wall charger. To reach it, she'd have to give up the sheet and take the plunge—or rather lunge—in the nude. Realistically she knew he'd already seen, or at least felt up, everything she owned and yet the prospect of streaking in front of him was daunting all the same.

He shook his head, his smile gentle. "I'm afraid I can't leave, not until my mission is completed or my reserve of earth energy runs out, whichever comes first."

Mission? Earth energy? Not in her wildest dreams—or hallucinations—could she have come up with something as crazy as that. Reenactor or not, the guy must be certifiable. Spotting her terry cloth bathrobe lying across the foot of the bed, she reached out and grabbed it. She ducked beneath the sheet, dragging the robe with her like an alligator going underwater with its prey.

Struggling to get her arms into the sleeves, she surfaced for air. "Look, you," she said, spitting stray hairs from her mouth.

"I don't know what kind of arrangement you had with the previous owners, but when we were negotiating what came with the house, you weren't included in any itemized list I ever saw. I bought this house. It's mine. I own it, which means you're either trespassing on my property or breaking and entering—your pick."

Fixing solemn blue eyes on hers—there was enough lamplight to make out their deep cobalt color—he asked, "Why are you always pushing away people who care about you?"

She cinched the tie on the robe and shot out of the bed. "I'm not bluffing, I will call the police." Grabbing for the cell, she looked down and, squinting, pushed the three-digit 9-1-1 emergency number.

She'd expected him to tackle her, but instead he didn't budge. "And just what shall you tell them?"

More irritated than frightened, she lowered the phone without pressing the Send button. What was this, the Spanish Inquisition? It was bad enough being caught in bed on the brink of having sex with a hot-pink dildo without having to play twenty questions.

Fisting her free hand on her hip, she met his gaze head-on. "Well, I suppose I'll start by saying there's an intruder in my house who refuses to leave—how's that?"

"And yet when the authorities come to search, they will discover the doors and windows locked, the alarm enabled and no earthly presence beyond you and your cat. They will think you mad as a march hare." His gaze dropped to the cell phone in her hand. "Isabel, please put down that device and listen to me."

Mad—how could he possibly know that prospect haunted her more than any fear for her physical safety? Determined to stay focused, to stay strong, she hiked up her chin and pulled back her shoulders. "My name is Maggie, Maggie Holliday, and this *device,* as if you didn't know, is called a cell phone."

He stood staring at her, and she couldn't shake the sense that those kind eyes of his were looking straight through her, reading not only her mind but her heart, too. "You're not mad, sweetheart. Your mind is as sound as Jefferson Davis's lockbox."

Suddenly he was beside her though he'd been standing several feet away, and she hadn't seen him cross the room, not even a blur of movement. Before she could fathom how he'd managed to move so quickly without seeming to move at all, his big, warm hand found hers.

"Isabel, stop fighting the truth and listen to me, won't you?" He gently disengaged her death grip on the phone and set it aside.

She was shaking, but she had too much pride to let him see—and too much pride to continue answering to another woman's name. "Stop calling me Isabel. My name is Maggie."

He shook his head, his gaze intent on her face. "Like it or not, you are the embodiment, or rather reembodiment, of Isabel Earnshaw. You lived one hundred forty-five years ago in this very house. Our Federal forces captured the town for the first time in the spring of 1862 and though we'd met the winter before, it was then I began courting you in earnest, albeit in secret. We became lovers for the first time in the attic of this very house as you've just read in the diary—*your* diary. That sprig of lavender hanging from the nail in the attic was placed there by your own hand. It has defied nature and remained intact all these many years, nourished by our love, watered by your tears."

Wow. Either he was putting on one hell of an act or he actually believed what he was saying. "Okay, okay, assuming I am the reincarnation of Isabel Earnshaw, then that must make you—"

"Captain Ethan O'Malley at your service, Miss Earnshaw." He stepped back and executed a formal bow.

It was nowhere near Halloween, but Maggie opted to play along. "How come you get to be reembodied as yourself?" If there was a flaw in his story, and there had to be a ton of them, she wanted it put out there on the proverbial table.

He held his arms out from his sides and stared down at his legs and feet as though he'd only just discovered them. "Actually my human body is only a loan."

"A loan?" This was getting weirder by the minute.

He nodded, sending a hank of dark hair falling over his forehead. "You see, sweetheart, I'm what you might call a ghost."

8

"ACTUALLY I PREFER THE TERM specter or apparition—it just seems more respectful—but if ghost suits you better, I won't complain." He had the audacity to wink.

Oh, my God, I really am going crazy. Going, going…gone! Maggie sank down on the side of the bed and covered her hands over her ears. "Stop it. I won't listen to you anymore. Tomorrow I'm calling Richard, and I'm getting him to write me a prescription for an antipsychotic. If that doesn't work, I'll admit myself to an inpatient program. Whatever it takes, I am not going to let you drive me crazy. You are not here. I'm not really seeing you—or hearing you, either."

"Richard." He spat out the name. "Don't tell me you'd take the word of that lily-livered quack over the truth of your own heart?" He shook his head, not condescendingly as Richard did, but in a way that conveyed not so much disappointment as…sadness. "Why, Isabel, you used to be so fearless. It was one of the qualities I loved best about you. Whatever happened to the brave, stouthearted lass you used to be?"

Despite the craziness of her situation, his question got her thinking. What had happened to that hopeful, happy little girl who'd spent summer nights making wishes on every star she could find on the off chance one might fall to earth, who'd scoured her backyard lawn searching for four-leaf clovers, who'd believed in Santa Claus, the Easter bunny and the tooth fairy long past the time when most of her peers had graduated to MTV and training bras they didn't yet need? Wherever that girl was, Maggie suddenly, desperately wanted to bring her back.

Fighting tears, she turned her head away. "I honestly don't know what's happened to her—to me."

The mattress dipped as he sat down beside her, the warmth of his thigh brushing against hers. "Then let me help you find her again."

He wrapped his arm about her shoulders and drew her against him. She knew she ought to pull away and run for the hills, or at least to the next-door neighbor's, but suddenly leaning into all that male strength, even if the source was a crackpot or a figment of her imagination, was too tempting to resist.

"You see, Belle," he said at length, "Though in this life you're known as Maggie Holliday, Isabel Earnshaw was your first embodiment as an earth entity, the origin of your soul's birthing. Some souls complete their work in a single lifetime but most require additional embodiments. In your case, you were meant to return to Fredericksburg, to live in this house again and to discover, or rather rediscover, your diary."

If he knew about the diary, he must have been watching her. "You've been spying on me." She pulled away.

He lifted his squared chin and turned to face her. "I'm no spy," he declared in the same sharp tone he'd used when referring to Richard. "But I can tell you this, that device you have beneath your pillow, you shan't have need of it."

"Device?" It took a moment for her to realize he wasn't talking about the cell phone but the vibrator. Shit! In all the commotion, she'd as good as forgotten her guilty little secret. Wondering what else he may have seen, she dropped her head in her hands. "Just go away, wherever ghosts go, and leave me alone."

"Alone. Is that really what you want?" He sounded hurt.

Pulling her head out of her hands, she looked over at him and nodded. "Yes."

"At the risk of being indelicate, permit me to point out that prior to my arrival you were on the verge of fornicating with a faux phallus—a faux *pink* phallus. I'd say you spend far too much time alone in bed as it is."

Oh, God, he has seen. Kill me now—please! "Who are you—*really?*"

"Your lover, your soul's mate as you are mine. Had our past lives turned out differently, I would have taken you as my wife to love and cherish for all time."

She looked up. "You wanted to marry me?" Even if he was crazy and insisting she was someone else, this was as close to a marriage proposal as she'd come so far.

He nodded. "Had things gone differently, I would have taken you back to Boston as my bride, to my family's house on Beacon Hill. We would have made love each night in the big four-poster bed my parents brought over from Ireland and rocked our babes to sleep in the cradle my grandfather carved with his own hands. And when our time came and death took us, we would have been laid to rest side by side in my family's burial plot."

"It sounds lovely, like paradise."

"It was and would have been, but all may not be lost. Last night when you stood before your mirror, it wasn't only your body begging for release but your soul calling out to mine."

Heat hit Maggie in the face. Despite the things they'd done together the night before, knowing he'd watched her masturbate, or at least trying to, was almost too much humiliation to take. She shot up from the bed. "I don't know who you are or what your con is, where you've drilled the peephole, but I want you out of here—now!"

He rose up beside her, but instead of leaving, he cupped her chin in his hand and slowly, gently, turned her back to face him. "Belle, my sweet Belle, let me ease that ache between your thighs. Let me love you as I once did."

Being propositioned by a figment of your imagination—or a horny ghost—could this night possibly get any weirder? "How can you when you're…you're not really here?"

In answer, he slid his hands to the tops of her shoulders, bringing them both down onto the mattress. Head meeting the pillow, Maggie reminded herself she'd been about to have intercourse with an inanimate object, a battery-dependent toy. Who was she to hop on—make that *hump*—her high horse? Was having sex with a fantasy really any worse?

Safe sex couldn't get any safer than this.

And yet to consciously copulate with someone who presented himself as a ghost was just flat-out crazy, wasn't it? Talk about some weird fetish. What next, picnicking in graveyards, screwing in funeral homes?

She lifted her head to look at him. "Maybe I haven't always made the best choices in boyfriends, but so far every guy I've slept with has been solidly alive. This is a first for me."

Straddling her hips, he angled his face to hers, the corners of his sexy mouth lifting in the barest hint of a smile. "Hush, sweetheart. Doubting only spoils the magic."

Palms braced on either side of her head, he feathered soft kisses over her forehead, eyelids and the corners of her mouth. She could feel the stubble on his jaw, the delicious weight of him pressing her into the mattress and the thrill of his hard-on brushing against her lower belly. In every way that mattered, in every way that counted, he was real, he was with her and more than that, he was the embodiment of every fantasy she'd ever had.

Looking up into her sexy stranger's steady gaze, Ethan's gaze, she felt his warmth melting away her doubts and fears as though they—and she—were made of candle wax. To have a lover look at her as he was doing had been Maggie's heart's desire for a very long time now. Much like her historic house, it was something she'd yearned for yet never really expected to have. Whoever and whatever Ethan was, this time they shared was a gift—and suddenly Maggie wanted nothing more than to cast aside her doubts and fears and open herself to receive.

And not just receive but also give back as she hadn't had the time—or nerve—to do the previous night in the attic. To let go of her inhibitions, her shyness, her self-doubts and be the no-holds-barred lover she'd always wanted to be, known she could be, if only she'd had the right partner to share the sexy ride with her.

As if reading her X-rated thoughts, his smile broadened and his eyes blazed. "I'm here with you, Belle. Here to bring your every fantasy, your every unspoken desire out of the darkness and into the light. Here to love you as you've dreamed of being loved, as you deserve to be loved without shame, without apology and without regret. Here to help you see the truth locked inside your own beautiful soul. I'm here, dearest Isabel, to help you believe again."

ETHAN HADN'T SET OUT TO GET Isabel into bed, at least not at first. Like earth, the astral realm had its share of cads and ne'er-do-wells, but he wasn't one of them. Until the previous night's episode in the attic, he'd kept himself solidly on the straight and narrow. But then Isabel—Maggie—wasn't just some astral body with whom he wanted to go bump in the night. She was the love of his life—and afterlife. Even with one hundred forty-five years' worth of pent-up desire pulsing through his energy field, he wanted more from her than a casual coupling.

Although he still felt a twinge of guilt about the champagne incident, staging their attic reunion hadn't been a purely self-centered act. Maggie might not yet know it, but hers was a soul torn between two worlds. Until she cast aside her earthbound doubts and fears and owned the truth of who she was and what she'd done to be condemned to successive embodiments—the astral version of body hopping—the past would never be put right. Just as he would be fated to wander the earth in search of his nemesis, Damian, Maggie would be reborn or, rather, reembodied again and again, always single and subconsciously seeking her soul's mate. To successfully complete their respective journeys, they must come together once more. Until then, eternal rest would remain beyond their reach.

Pretty weighty stuff for a second date.

Success hinged on Maggie opening up her mind and relaxing her will to believe again. So far, she was showing herself to be every bit as stubborn and headstrong as she'd been back in 1862, perhaps more so. She was the reembodiment of Isabel Earnshaw, all right, but it was clear she wasn't going to take his word for it. Before she could be brought around to accept the admittedly extraordinary truth, she would have to *feel* it for herself.

He slid her robe down and brushed his mouth over the small red mark staining her otherwise porcelain-perfect skin—so warm, so silken smooth and so very alive. Alive—dear Lord, how he'd missed that feeling.

She hooked a hand to his shoulder, and he saw that she was staring at his neck. "The other night when I started to unwind your neck cloth, I sensed you didn't like it. You didn't, did you? Why?"

Her unwitting reference to his ignoble death had him feeling vulnerable, spiritually stripped bare. The very last thing he wanted was to spoil their lovemaking with dark thoughts from the past. "Some things are better left unsaid—and unseen."

He felt a sudden tug on his energy field, and then a prick at the back of his neck. Like a balloon on the receiving end of a hat pin, he felt his energy draining. Damn, Damian must be close, closer than he'd credited.

Not wanting to show himself as weak before her, he hastened up. Even the act of swinging his heavy human legs over the side of the bed suddenly seemed to take an enormous amount of energy. "I should leave you to your rest. Sleep well, my love."

"You're going?" She pushed up on one elbow, looking both puzzled and sad. The robe dipped open to reveal the tops of her beautifully shaped breasts, the silken skein of her hair framing the curve of her lovely, long neck and alabaster shoulder.

Standing at the foot of the bed, he looked back at her, so beautiful, so desirable and so clearly desiring him in return. "I thought you wanted to be alone."

"And if I don't anymore?" She arched a dark brow, a sensual invitation as old as Eve.

He hesitated, his cursed pride warring with his desperate need to be with her. "Then you'll have to ask me to stay with you. You have to want it, too, enough to invest your energy in the asking. Otherwise, I won't have the strength to stay in my body and be with you."

Whereas even thinking about Damian resulted in a depletion of his energy, being with Maggie, or even near her, had the opposite effect. She filled him up, completed him as only one's soul mate could.

It was her turn to hesitate. Biting her lip, she admitted, "I've never once asked a man for sex in my whole life."

He couldn't help smiling at that. It might be 2007 and she might be a typical modern woman in many ways, but she still carried about with her the prim and proper vestiges of her nineteenth-century self. "I'm not any man. I'm your soul mate, your other half. Ask, Belle, please ask."

She cleared her throat, two hot, pink spots appearing on either cheek. "Very well, Ethan, I want you to spend the night with me. I want to make love with you."

Ethan didn't have to be asked a second time. In the span of a single human heartbeat, he was in bed beside her, opening her robe, licking the rosebud tips of her breasts into hard little points, reaching down between them to comb his fingers through the crown of coarse curls between her thighs, finger seeking the pretty pink clit he couldn't wait to play with, to taste and tantalize a second night.

She lifted herself without him asking, and he slid the robe down and then off. The other night, he hadn't gotten the chance to properly appreciate her. Even though he could have laid her lovely, long-limbed body bare in the blink of an eye, he took pleasure in undressing her the old fashioned way, with his hands—and his eyes. Now that there was time—and he reckoned with their combined energy, he could likely last until dawn—he slid his hand down the length of her, taking his time to marvel over the satin smoothness of her belly, using his hands and fingers in different ways to touch her, all the while thanking the powers that be for the gift of having his body back, not only so that he could receive pleasure again but so that he could give it also.

He gently raked the fingers of one hand through the coarse curls covering her pubis, remembering how delicious she tasted, thinking how mouthwatering she looked and smelled. The mound of Venus they'd called it in his day. He dipped his head and pressed a kiss to the soft skin of her lower belly, pleased when she shivered.

She looked up at him with wide, knowing eyes. "I want to see you, too. Whatever you're willing to give between now and dawn, give me that at least."

"All right, then." He blinked, willing his heavy wool jacket and trousers to fall off along with his belt and high-topped boots. All he was left wearing were his small pants—and the neck cloth.

"Better?" he asked, hoping it was enough and yet not too much.

"Much." She reached between them, her slender hand massaging the erection weighing between his legs. "You're so beautiful here and everywhere else." *So beautiful I want to take you inside my mouth and lick and suck and taste you, and then feel you come against the back of my throat.*

Startled, he stared down at her, wondering if this once he might not have misread her unspoken thought. "I beg your pardon?"

A wicked gleam lit her eyes. "If you want me to believe you're real, that I'm not dreaming or hallucinating, then you're going to have to let me make love to you, too. It's the twenty-first century. Women don't lie back like cold slabs of bacon anymore. If we're going to be lovers, then be my lover—in every way."

Ethan smiled to himself. Apparently some things had changed, even improved, in the ensuing century and a half. "Then tell me what you want from me. Tell me in exact detail."

This time Maggie didn't hesitate but took up the challenge.

"I want to take you in my mouth and give you the kind of pleasure you gave me the other night." Her voice, though soft, was very firm.

Even without benefit of astral energy, she had the three buttons on the flap of his small pants undone and his penis between her kneading hands before he could so much as form a word in answer.

Somehow, and he wasn't entirely certain how, Ethan had lost control of the situation. The seducer had become the seduced. He was on his knees as Maggie was on hers. Facing him, she bent her head and laid a trail of warm, wet kisses starting at his nipples to pectorals to belly and beyond.

She sucked him all the way into her mouth, and he exhaled a very heavy, very human breath. Feeling weightless and slightly weak though he was very much in his body, he slid a hand into her hair. "Woman, what are you doing to me?"

Rather than answer in words, she slid her tongue up and down his shaft, then moved to tease the sensitive seam at the head of his penis, all the while stroking his balls and backside with sure, deft fingers.

She pulled back to look up at him, mouth moist and eyes sparkling. "Hmm, you do taste good—heavenly, actually." Holding her gaze on his, she ran her tongue along the contour of her lower lip and then sucked it into her mouth, a sigh escaping her.

He didn't have to trouble himself to read her thoughts to know what she was thinking, feeling. He could tell by her rapt expression that she was tasting him, savoring his essence and finding him as delicious, as addictively enticing as he'd found her to be the other night.

"You said you saw me standing in front of the mirror the other night. You must have seen me touching myself. Would you like to watch me now?" Apparently it was her turn to read his mind.

Though it wasn't really a question, Ethan answered anyway. "Yes."

Resting on her heels, she slid her palms over her breasts. Riveted, he watched her capture her nipples, rolling them between her thumb and forefinger, bringing the tight little buds to life.

"Do you like watching me?" She slid her hands from her breasts to her flat belly, fingers pointing downward.

Ethan's mouth went dry. Sucking in a breath, he admitted, "Yes, yes."

She slid her hands lower and spread herself with her fingers. Watching her slender digit slide inside her glistening pink flesh, Ethan felt very much a man—a human man—poised to explode.

When she started circling her clit with a single, shiny wet finger, Ethan knew he'd come to the limit of his earthly self-control. He reached out and captured both her hands in his. "I need to be inside you." If she denied him, he couldn't say what he would do.

Fixing her passion-drugged gaze on his, she nodded. "I need that, too." *I need to feel you inside me, I want to feel you inside me and at the same time part of me needs to feel like I'm your prisoner or at least your slave, that you want me so much you'll do anything to have me even if it means deciding for us both.*

Reading her dark, sexy thoughts, inhaling her musk and her heat, Ethan felt as though steam must be coming out his very pores. "I have done everything I could to have you. I will do anything I have to, in order to keep you. If there's a slave among us, sweet Belle, it's me. And like any slave worth his salt, I cannot deny my mistress."

Wrapping his hands about her slender wrists, he bore her

down on the lavender-scented sheets, carrying her arms high over her head and guiding her hands to the metal headboard. Locking her gaze on his face, she grabbed hold of the posts and spread her legs wide.

Ethan looked down at the beautiful woman splayed beneath him, her dusky pink nipples standing out as hard points and her pretty pink labia drenched with desire and acknowledged that indeed, it was good to be alive—again.

"Hold on, Belle, hold on for dear life." Straddling her, he positioned himself over her moist pink slit.

Looking up at him with shining eyes, she clenched the bedposts tighter. "For dear life," she repeated and cinched her long legs tight about his waist.

He entered her slowly, giving himself to her inch by inch rather than all at once, not because he expected her to be a virgin—it was 2007, as she'd pointed out—but because their first time together in this life was simply too special to rush.

"Oh, Ethan." He glanced up to her white-knuckled hold on the posts, knowing it meant he wasn't hurting her but pleasing her greatly.

He pulled out of her just as slowly and just as thoroughly as he'd entered. She shivered and begged for more, her lithe body straining for a release he swore to himself he would die a second death rather than deny her.

Entering her again, he bent his head and sipped at one succulent nipple, milking her with his mouth. "You feel so good around me, Belle, so tight and so wet."

In answer she bucked beneath him, her moon-pale skin pearled with sweat, the musk between them rising up like steam. She was so close to her release, he could feel the power of her harnessed orgasm pulsing through not only her energy field but also his.

"Please, Ethan, please—now."

He pulled out of her, ignoring her cry of protest. Sliding down the length of her body, he drew her legs wider apart and took her with his mouth. He found the fruit of her womanhood, the sheltered pearl of her clitoris, and stroked his tongue over her once, twice, thrice…

"Oh, Ethan!" Maggie's hands fell away from the posts, her body quaking beneath him as he entered her again.

The clenching and unclenching of her inner muscles around him after one hundred forty-five years was more than Ethan could bear. He reared back and drove into her yet again, hard and fast, full and deep, taking as much as she would give and then giving her more still.

"Belle!" The spasm overtook him, the contraction so strong it shook him to the core of his being and beyond. He released himself inside her, giving her the essence of his physical body, his life force, along with all the love stored inside his soul.

Afterward, he lay beside her and gathered her up in his arms. Settling her damp head in the curve of his shoulder, Ethan had never felt more complete in all his life—or afterlife.

WEARING A RALPH LAUREN monogrammed bathrobe, his hair shower damp, Richard sat in the leather desk chair in his condo, stubbing out his fifth cigarette in a row. It was after midnight and he saw his first patient at 8:00 a.m., but he could already tell he wouldn't be sleeping tonight. Maggie. Ever since their argument the other day, he'd been obsessing over her. He'd jerked off a little while ago in the shower but thinking of her tall, slender, tight body, how incredible she'd looked in that Frederick's of Hollywood thong she'd worn the last time he'd fucked her, he felt himself hardening all over again.

She hadn't enjoyed it, not the fucking and not the lying in

bed afterward. He'd known that even then. It had been months since she'd gotten wet for him, never once had she gotten off, though in the beginning she'd put on one hell of an act.

He'd figured once she moved into that precious money pit of hers, and saw firsthand why Fredericksburg went by the nickname of Dead Fred, she'd be more than happy to move back north. The crazy thing was she actually seemed to *like* it there.

What he didn't like was the change in her attitude. The other day, she'd defended her precious house like a mother lion defending her cub. The fact that she'd gone ahead and bought the damned thing in spite of his objections was a sure sign his hold was slipping.

But what was really killing him was the sudden suspicion that the money pit might not be his only rival, that she might be seeing someone on the side. When he'd announced his intention to drive back to D.C. rather than stay in Fredericksburg as planned, she hadn't been able to rush him out the door fast enough.

He tapped the two theater tickets against the chrome side of his desk. He fucking hated musicals, but Maggie loved them, and until he figured out what was going on with her and reestablished his control, he might have to make a concession or two. Women with tight asses, long legs and doctoral degrees didn't grow on trees. That she also happened to be amazing in bed, always so much more eager to give than to receive, made her just about the perfect girlfriend.

Maggie was a keeper. If it took burning her precious historic house to the ground to hold on to her, then that's just what he'd have to do.

9

HER CELL PHONE'S RINGING pulled Maggie into wakefulness. She stretched out a hand next to her, her palm meeting with cold, empty space. Whether he was a ghost on leave from the netherworld, a mental patient on the lam from white-suited attendants or her very own sexy hallucination, Ethan was gone. Gone but not forgotten. He'd left his mark in the musky scent of him on her body and her bed sheets, the lovely tenderness between her thighs and the incredible tangy taste of him inside of her mouth.

Vaguely aware of a dull headache drumming her temples, she cracked open an eye and glanced over at the alarm clock. Six o' clock! Senses spiking into adrenaline overdrive, she leaped out of bed. The last time she'd gotten an unexpected early morning wake-up call, it had been the airline informing her of the plane crash.

Heart pumping, she remembered that last night Ethan had taken the phone out of her hand. Where the hell was it?

Trailing the sound to the dresser top, she picked it up and flipped up the casing. "Hello."

"Hey, babe, I came into the office early to get some paperwork out of the way before my first appointment and thought I'd give you a buzz." It was Richard. He sounded wired, like someone who'd had way too much coffee but otherwise he seemed fine, chipper even. "Three guesses why I'm calling."

She sank down on the edge of the bed. Six o' clock in the morning was too early for guessing games or uninvited phone calls. "I can't imagine."

"Well, how's this for a hint? Guess who just snagged two tickets to Debbie Allen's *Alex in Wonderland* at the Kennedy Center?"

She dragged a hand through her tangled hair. "Uh, I don't know."

Nor, at the moment, did she greatly care. She braced a hand on the mattress, thinking how big and empty her bed seemed without Ethan in it. He'd left her just before dawn, supposedly to do the cosmic equivalent of recharging his batteries. She hoped that meant she'd see him later that evening but of course there was no way to know for sure.

"I did."

"Oh, that's great." Still not totally awake, she wondered at Richard's sudden interest in seeing a musical, a form of theater he'd always professed to hate.

"The performance starts at seven-thirty sharp in the Terrace Theater. I'll be coming from the office so you'll need to meet me in the theater lobby. If we get there a little early, we can catch a drink before the show."

"You mean tonight?"

"Yeah, pretty exciting, huh?"

"It sounds really nice, but I can't."

"What do you mean you can't?" His raised voice had her holding the cell away from her ear. "Jesus, Maggie, I went to a lot of trouble to get these tickets. Can't you take a break from the money pit for one evening?"

The money pit—so much for his wooing her. A part of her felt like setting him straight then and there. She could picture the scenario now. *Richard, I'm sorry but there's someone else. He's a ghost and we've been having hot astral sex in my attic and now my bed.* She knew she could never do it—but it sure was fun to think about.

Richard's ranting snapped her back to the present. "You said you wanted to go, and I went out of my way to wrangle two seats for tonight. It's a limited engagement, so it goes without saying tickets weren't cheap and they're nonrefundable."

Did he want her to write him a check or what? Despite the lack of notice, a few weeks ago she would have dropped everything to accommodate him but being with Ethan, whoever and whatever he was, was already changing a lot of things in her life, including her perspective on relationships. She wasn't willing to walk away from her own life's unfolding drama to suit Richard's schedule. Instead of feeling guilty for letting him down, she felt annoyed. Every nice thing he did for her no matter how large or small—and usually small won out—seemed to have some invisible string attached.

"Look, I'm sorry, really I am. I'm just not feeling like myself."

That was nothing if not the truth. She pressed a hand to the side of her head, willing the pounding to settle. The headache was a symptom of stress, it had to be. At this point, she couldn't decide if she was Maggie, Isabel or some combination of the two. Whoever she was, she still needed to break up with her boyfriend, though sitting on her bed buck naked and still half-asleep didn't strike her as the best circumstances for making her big stand.

Backpedaling, she said, "I've come down with a spring cold or allergies or…something. If I go, I'll end up coughing through the performance." *If I go, I may just miss my chance at eternal love, this time forever.* "If it's a cold, I don't want to get you sick."

Predictably that had him backing off. Richard was a fanatic

about germs. He washed his hands at least thirty times a day. She'd always found that a little, okay a lot, obsessive, but of course she'd never said so.

"Are you sure a cold is all it is?" he asked. Maybe it was only her own guilty conscience, but she would have sworn she detected suspicion underscoring the question.

"Of course that's all. What else could possibly be going on in a sleepy little backwater town like this?" God that sounded bitchy. Softening her voice, she added, "I'm sorry. It's just this cold getting me down. I'd better go."

Clicking off the cell, she braced her elbows on her tented knees and leaned forward, massaging her temples. Isabel Earnshaw. Maggie Holliday. Was it really possible that two women separated by more than a century could be one and the same soul?

Can they really both be me?

THANKS TO RICHARD'S WAKE-UP call, Maggie got an early start on the day. After popping an Extra Strength Motrin, she pulled on a scoop-neck T-shirt and jeans and then went downstairs to pour food into Willie's bowl. Wired as she was, there was no need for coffee. Instead of stopping to make it, she headed straight for the Central Rappahannock Regional Library where she hoped to find some answers.

The library was a short one-block walk down Caroline Street, and Maggie found herself wishing it was farther so she'd have more time to mull over what was happening. Admittedly she'd been a little tipsy when she'd come in last night, but the two margaritas had worn off before she'd gone to bed. She distinctly remembered setting the alarm and locking the front door, mainly because she'd double-checked and then triple-checked herself. She didn't see how she could have been dreaming. Another hallucination was the only plausible explanation. Hallucinating two nights in a row—there was no way that could be good. And if her lover, if Ethan, really were a ghost, what then? Looking on the bright side, dating a dead man would mean not having to worry about birth control, sexually transmitted diseases or dirty socks on the floor. The situation was win-win—at least until she wanted to leave the house.

It was shaping up to look like she either needed a shrink or a ghost buster and by the end of the day she was determined to know which. She was a Ph.D., by God, an educated and rational being. She ought to be able to get to the bottom of whatever she had going on inside her head—and her house.

Located on the library's basement level, the Virginiana Room housed records related to Virginia history. When Maggie walked up to the reference desk and explained she was doing some research on her house, the librarian on duty greeted her with a friendly smile, introduced herself as Carol and then spent the next few minutes walking her through the collection's holdings of birth and death certificates, cemetery and burial registers, census information, marriage licenses, military records and wills and deeds.

Maggie spent her first hour unfurling copies of the Sanborn insurance maps on file. The plot on which her house sat was originally part of a larger parcel that included the modest frame structure built by George Washington's brother Charles as a private home later to become the public tavern known as the Rising Sun. Since the Revolutionary War, the land had been parceled off a number of times. By the 1850s, what was left of the original plot more or less aligned with the current survey markers, and the property had passed into the hands of the Earnshaw family. Jerome Earnshaw owned a lumber mill just outside of town and in the spring of 1852 he built two mirror image side-by-side Victorian-style structures. The one next to the tavern he rented to his foreman. The other, Maggie's house, he took as his family home.

The Earnshaw house survived the 1862 battle, one of a handful of homes on that portion of Caroline, then Main Street, left standing after the rampant torching and looting by Federal troops. Isabel's words from the dream rushed back to her. *Ethan, I trusted you. You promised to see us spared. You promised to come for me. You promised not to die.* Had the gallant captain made good on his word and seen his sweetheart's home spared?

Returning to skimming the records, Maggie came across an 1863 obituary. In what had to be the irony of all ironies, the Earnshaw family survived the 1862 battle only to die a few months later when their carriage hit a rut in the road and overturned. According to the newspaper account, Jerome, his wife, Patricia, and their daughter Lettuce were killed instantly. Maggie recalled that in her dream, Isabel—Maggie—had held her little sister, Lettie, in her arms during the bombardment. For sure, Lettie was the nickname for Lettuce, but what about Isabel? She read the article again but there was no mention of the oldest Earnshaw daughter. No mention of Isabel.

What had happened to Isabel? Though Maggie was only halfway through the diary, she'd glanced ahead to see the date of the last entry, December 16, 1862, the day after the battle had ended in victory for the Confederates. Isabel had obviously survived the siege to write about it in her diary but after that, what had become of her? There was her birth record from the parish registry but none of any subsequent marriage—or death. Likewise, the cemetery and burial registers turned up empty. It was as if she'd simply vanished.

The romantic in Maggie desperately wanted to believe Isabel and Ethan had eloped after the war and gone north to live happily ever after, but that explanation simply didn't feel right. If that were the case, surely they would be together in the spirit world or reembodied together, not separated by an energetic wall of time and space. No, something must have happened to Isabel, something sufficiently scandalous that the social historians of the day had chosen to sweep it under the rug rather than record it for posterity. A cold, queasy feeling of foreboding settled into the pit of Maggie's stomach, making her glad she'd skipped breakfast. For whatever reason, she couldn't shake the feeling that whatever ill had befallen Isabel was no accident but had involved the purposive taking of the young woman's life.

Giving herself a brisk, mental shake, she told herself to focus on facts, not feelings. Tracing the title on the house, she saw that it was sold at auction to Damian Grey of Massachusetts, a sutler by trade. To afford the five-thousand-dollar purchase price, a small fortune back then, he must have done quite well for himself during the war. Maggie recalled Isabel mentioning him briefly in her diary as a civilian who'd camped with Ethan's regiment. Why would a former Federal sympathizer settle in a Southern city like Fredericksburg? Thinking about the chilly reception so-called Yankee locusts received from certain old guard townies even today, she doubted the uneasy climate of the Reconstruction South would have made Fredericksburg much of a home sweet home for him.

Perhaps the reception Damian Grey received had driven him away after all? Subsequent searching revealed that though he held the deed for thirty more years, he moved out after less than a month, closed up the house and left Fredericksburg for Richmond. Upon his death in 1892, the property passed to a distant cousin. There were a series of subsequent owners over the years, most recently Doris and David Smithfield, the elderly couple from whom Maggie had purchased it.

Feeling as though she'd taken a whirlwind tour in a time machine, Maggie exited the software search program and switched off the computer. Eyes crossing from four hours poring over microfilm, microfiche and maps with minuscule print, she stopped by the reference desk on her way out.

From behind the counter, Carol looked up from the index cards she'd been collating. "Did you find the answers you were looking for?"

Maggie hesitated. Talk about an existential question. "Well, I found out some, a lot actually, but there are still some gaps."

Carol nodded, looking sage. "There always are when you first start delving into the records, but hang in there. Practice makes perfect. In the meantime, if there's something you're looking to have answered particularly, some burning question, why not write down your query and one of the duty librarians will get to it as soon as she has the time."

"Really? That would be great. I'd really like to know more about one owner in particular, a Northerner named Damian Grey. He bought the house at auction but lived in it less than a month. Only instead of reselling or renting it, he apparently just closed it up and left town."

"That is curious." Carol passed her the pink request slip and a number two pencil. "Well, write it down, and we'll see what we can find out."

Maggie wrote down her request along with her cell phone number. Handing the slip over, she said, "Thanks, Carol, you've been great. If something turns up, would you mind giving me a buzz?"

Carol beamed. Pursuing a quest such as this would be a librarian's raison d'être. "Be happy to."

Maggie stepped out into the library's sunlit front courtyard, an accordion folder bulging with photocopied documents tucked beneath her arm. Feeling weak as though she really might be coming down with some sort of bug, she took a seat on one of the benches by the fountain to gather her jumbled notes and equally jumbled thoughts. She'd just opened her notepad when her cell phone went off. Digging it out of her bag, she saw it was Richard again. In all likelihood, he was calling to bully her about the tickets.

Steeling herself, she clicked on the phone. "Hi, Richard, what's up?"

"I just called to see how you were feeling." Two teenagers with skateboards chose that moment to let out a hoot as one boy completed a near perfect front-side flip. Damn! "What was that noise? It sounds like you're in a park or something."

"Oh, that's just the television. So, um, did you find any takers for those tickets?"

"I ended up selling them to my secretary. It turns out her husband is a big Debbie Allen fan. Apparently he was crazy about her in *Fame*."

Maggie didn't have the heart to point out that Debbie Allen was the producer and choreographer of the program, not a performer in the production. "That's good." Leave it to Richard to sell rather than just give expensive theater tickets to a clerical employee he probably paid barely above minimum wage. Generous guy—not.

"Listen, I hope you'll be better by this weekend because I was thinking I'd come down on Saturday and we'd spend the day together. I'll pack a bag to spend the night and then head back to D.C. after brunch on Sunday."

At his mention of spending the night, panic rose. After

being with Ethan, there was no way she was letting Richard anywhere near her bed.

"You want to spend the weekend in Fredericksburg?" Second only to finding out Ethan was a ghost, news like this counted as the granddaddy of shocks. Ordinarily Richard acted as though Interstate 95 ran exclusively northbound. To volunteer to drive south, he must sense he was in big-time trouble.

"I was thinking maybe it was time I give you the chance to show me just what you think is so special about it."

"Are you sure I can't meet you somewhere in D.C.?"

As much as she disliked the capital city, it would be much easier to break up with him there and then make her getaway. If he met her in Fredericksburg, she'd be stuck with him for possibly the whole day, not to mention have the drama of their breakup unfold on her home turf. Another Battle of Fredericksburg—that she could do without.

"You're the one who's always going on about the historic charm and small-town ambience. Think of this weekend as your chance to prove it."

Ordinarily she overlooked his more minor faults but now that she'd made the decision to ditch him, his peevish tone and grandiose attitude really got under her skin. "I'm not the tourism director, Richard," she answered, not caring that she sounded snappish. "It's not my job to sell the city to you or anyone else. I just happen to be one of the approximately twenty-one thousand people who like living here. What can I say, we're an odd breed." She didn't add that at least one of those twenty-one thousand residents was, technically speaking, a specter.

To her surprise, he backed down. "Look, Mags, I didn't mean it that way. I know things haven't been so great between us lately, and I'd like the chance to change that. We can even have that romantic dinner I promised—a sort of all-in-one celebration of you getting your Ph.D. and the new house."

A month ago she would have given her eyeteeth to hear him make such an offer, but now she simply couldn't find it in her heart to care—a heart Ethan had touched deeply along with every square inch of the rest of her. After making love with him, the thought of sitting across the table from Richard and having to hold up a conversation made her feel even more tired—and slightly nauseous. Still, she was a grown-up, and she and Richard had been seeing each other exclusively for six months. Ending their relationship involved more than just giving back his high school ring or varsity letter sweater. He deserved to be broken up with face-to-face.

"Um…okay." She had it on the tip of her tongue to tell him not to worry about packing that bag, since he wouldn't be staying over, but she held back. He'd only press to know why and before she knew it, she'd be breaking up with him over the phone—a tempting but cowardly act.

"Great. Why don't you call and make reservations for us at that train station restaurant you liked so much? Just make sure you request a table in the smoking section, okay?"

Richard would never dream of applying the word addicted to himself, but when it came to nicotine, he was as hooked as any heroine street junkie. With her sensitive nose, she couldn't stand the way the smell clung to her hair and clothes, not that Richard cared about any of that. He was one of those self-absorbed smokers who blew smoke in your face, and when your eyes watered, asked if you were coming down with a cold.

Being with someone as giving as Ethan, however briefly, cast Richard's selfishness into even sharper relief. They might not be able to leave her house together, at least not in daylight, but then again, every relationship came with its challenges.

Even if he returned to the astral realm without so much as a goodbye, he'd changed her life irrevocably, forever.

"I'm pretty sure Claiborne's is nonsmoking. Just about all of the restaurants in town have gone smoke free." She'd given him an out, and she realized she was holding her breath in the hope he would take it.

"I guess I can always go outside if I need—*want*—to smoke."

Go figure! She'd spent months wishing Richard would be more romantic, more considerate, more…interested in not only her but in other people beyond himself and his paying clients. Now that he was making some effort in that regard, she didn't want him—not in her house, not in her town and, frankly, not in her life.

She had to tell him. But even Richard with all his faults deserved better than being broken up with over the phone. "Uh, okay, I guess I'll see you on Saturday."

"Not before noon, though." He yawned into the receiver. "I'm beat from getting up this morning. I've really got to catch up on my sleep this weekend, otherwise I won't have a ghost of a chance of making it through that National Institute of Health symposium next week."

Maggie smothered a yawn—and a smile. "Richard, I know just what you mean."

10

ETHAN SAT IN THE ATTIC, twirling a sprig of lavender in his hand and trying to get a grip on the rush of human emotions he was feeling. The previous night in Maggie's bed had surpassed even their attic reunion in terms of physical passion and soul-deep connection. He'd left her sleeping like an angel and returned to the attic enveloped in an aura of sensual satisfaction.

Richard's phone call had blunted not only Maggie's bliss but his, as well. Richard had begun siphoning the life from her, literally, almost from the moment she'd clicked the call on. Attuned to her as he was, Ethan immediately felt the fluctuation in her energy field, which had gone from golden glowing and gloriously open to a stagnant muddy gray.

Ethan knew it wasn't very noble of him to eavesdrop but he hadn't been able to resist, not because he was overly curious—he wasn't—but because, when it came to Maggie, he felt powerfully protective, the emotion underscored by a dark and deep-seated fear. In his lifetime, Damian Grey had stolen her away after leaving Ethan powerless to protect her. Though Isabel's tragic action had rendered Damian's victory a hollow one, it was Ethan and Isabel who had paid the price of Damian's treachery—with their lives.

I'll see you in hell, Damian, and we'll settle our score there if need be. But settle it we will.

When Ethan had made that vow one hundred forty-five years ago, he'd hadn't known there wasn't any such place as hell, at least not in terms of the fire and brimstone picture painted by clergy from their pulpits. The truth was hell wasn't a physical place but rather a state of being. Every man and woman carried the seeds of their own torment within their souls. Earthly life presented an opportunity to work through one's failings but the learning didn't stop when your heart ceased beating—if anything, it began in earnest. Contrary to popular myth, heaven wasn't a pearly gate–bordered playground for harp-strumming angels and frolicking cherubs. Once a soul passed on, the powers that be put you through your paces, challenging you to overcome whatever internal obstacles blocked your ascendance to the next highest level of being. It was usually at that crucial point that another embodiment was scheduled, only in Ethan's case a special exception had been made. Instead of getting a new body, he'd been allowed to borrow his former body back—but only for as long as the energy he'd earned would support it. Like a horseless carriage that had run out of fuel, once his energy was used up, he would have to go back whether or not he'd found Damian.

So far he hadn't had any luck tracking the devil down in the afterlife, the astral plane or present-day earth. And yet in whatever state of being Damian existed, Ethan was convinced he existed still. There were times such as last night when he felt his enemy's presence as a physical stabbing; at others, it was a subtler sort of haunting—a sudden whiff of the cheroots Damian had favored in life, the clicking of his boot heels as he stole up from behind.

A demon soul such as Damian's wouldn't elect to stay in the astral realm or the great beyond where he'd have to work at ascension. Hard work, like truth telling, had never been the sutler's strong suit. For an entity such as Damian, paradise would be right here in the dog-eat-dog world of modern-day earth.

THAT EVENING MAGGIE LEANED over the bathtub and lit the votives one by one, the haunting strains of Loreena McKennitt's *Book of Secrets* CD playing on her boom box parked on the washstand counter. Interspersed with the candles lining the surrounding tile work shelf were a few of the treasured seashells she'd collected over years of family vacations spent on the quiet beaches of North Carolina's Outer Banks. The antique-style slipper tub with its rolled edges, high back and oil-rubbed bronze lion's feet was her pride and joy, a decadence she couldn't really afford but had simply had to have. As soon as she'd closed on the house, she'd called her contractor and insisted he find a way to sandwich it inside the small hallway bathroom that served as her master bath. He'd hemmed and hawed but in the end he'd gotten the job done though he'd charged her an ungodly amount. It didn't matter; it was worth every penny.

She stripped off her robe, savoring the feel of the silk sliding over her skin before laying it aside nearby. Turning back to the tub, she lifted her leg over the side and stepped into the warm water. *Ah.* Easing herself beneath the bubbles, she had to admit that sometimes being a type A personality had its advantages. She'd been officially moved in just a few days, but barring the ubiquitous home projects, the house was in full working order. Even in the midst of debating her sanity, she'd gotten the curtains hung, the boxes unpacked and all the drawers and closets organized complete with see-through, stackable plastic storage bins courtesy of The Container Store.

It felt good to be home.

Along with her glass of wine, a lovely pinot purchased

from Kybecca, a locally owned wine and gourmet shop, her lavender-scented soap and bath oils lay within the lacquered brass caddy, a cool little accessory that fitted across the tub's top. She reached for the bath beads, taking a moment to appreciate the pretty packaging before dropping a few into the steaming water—such lovely, lovely decadence.

She took a sip of the wine and leaned back, regarding her tented legs, the tops of her knees peaking out from the suds, savoring the sensation of the water lapping against her sensitized flesh, the tips of her breasts and the lips of her labia. Whether real or imagined, Ethan had given her the most amazing gift—he'd put her back in touch with her body. Even before she'd climbed into the bath, she'd been aware of the rhythmic throbbing taking place low in her loins, the slippery wetness between her thighs. She hadn't needed a battery-powered dildo or a prescription for Prozac to get her groove back. The seeds of her sexuality had been there all along, dormant and waiting for her to unchain her heart and open her mind.

It was all so very lovely, so perfect, or at least it might have been, only something, or rather someone, was missing. Ethan. Whether a ghost or a figment of her fractured mind, for the present moment she didn't really care. She just wanted him there with her to share the wine and the warm water and the music, a flesh and blood man whose clothes she could peel off, whose warm, bath-scented skin she could lick and taste and suck.

Oh, Ethan. As lovely as this is, it would be so much lovelier, so absolutely perfect, with you.

"I'm always with you, Belle, whether or not you see me."

She started, knocking her head against the porcelain. Even though she'd been thinking of him, wishing he were with her, having him check in and out without so much as a door opening or a discreet cough took some getting used to.

Embarrassed, she could barely meet his gaze. "Don't you ever knock?"

Casually outfitted in a white shirt with the sleeves rolled up to reveal muscular forearms and buff-colored riding breeches, he smiled down at her and shook his head. "Out of practice I'm afraid."

She angled her face to look at him and, she hoped, to be kissed. "It's after midnight. I didn't think you were coming."

"I wasn't going to but then I heard you calling for me, and I couldn't stay away."

Maggie thought for a second. "I didn't call you."

Dropping down on his knees beside her, he leaned over the tub's edge and brushed her mouth with his, a soft, gentle caress that still set her pulse pounding along with other distinctly southern portions of her anatomy. "Not in so many words, perhaps, but never doubt that thoughts are things. Earlier you weren't certain whether you wanted me to come to you or not, but just then I heard your soul calling out to mine as loudly and as clearly as that church bell."

"What church bell?"

As if on cue, the bell of the Baptist Church sounded, striking out the single hour.

His gaze slid over her, from the haphazard twist of hair she'd pinned high on her head to her bare shoulders and the slopes of her breasts to the knees and toes poking out from the frothy water. Grateful for the cover of bubbles, Maggie slid farther down in the tub. Stupid to be modest when he'd already seen, touched—and tasted—every inch of her. But this was different somehow. She'd only had a few sips of wine. She was fully awake. Whatever happened between them, she couldn't pretend it was a dream.

She picked up her wine and knocked back a healthy

swallow. Dutch courage her grandmother had called it, but whatever form courage took, she'd never needed it more. Remembering her manners, she held out the glass to him. "Care to join me or is being dead enough of a natural high?"

Waving the glass away, he shook his head. "No, you're not dreaming or hallucinating, either. I'm really here. And there's no point in trying to hide yourself from me because I can see you clear as day beneath the froth." His gaze settled on the tops of her breasts above the waterline, and she felt her nipples swelling into taut, achy peaks. "By the by, your friends are right—you have a beautiful body. I was admiring it earlier."

Thinking of how slow and deliberate she'd been in taking off the robe, Maggie felt her face heat. "You don't mean…I mean, you don't watch me while I shower…do you?"

His brows drew upward, his sensuous mouth snapped into a serious line, his lips looking as deliciously moist and impossibly soft as she remembered his kiss to be. Dead or alive, he really was the most beautiful man. Recalling the feel and taste of him, she felt the now familiar tingling between her thighs.

"A gentleman doesn't resort to chicanery to glimpse a lady in dishabille. To do so would be unnecessary at any rate." A mischievous glint lit his eyes and turned up the corners of his mouth—his kissable, sexy mouth.

She stared over at him aghast. "Are you saying you can see through not only bath bubbles but also…um…clothes?"

He reached across to touch her cheek, the edge of his sleeve dipping into the water and yet managing to somehow stay dry. "Isabel, my love, I can see through to your very soul."

MAGGIE SAT AT HER KITCHEN table the next morning sifting through the documents she'd photocopied from the library and replaying the previous night with Ethan in her tired but very happy mind. The bath hadn't been the only element that had made their third encounter so deliciously steamy. Once she'd gotten over her initial embarrassment, the idea that her lover had the ghostly equivalent of X-ray vision had amounted to one hell of a turn-on. By the time they'd finished making love on her bathroom counter, Maggie had been thoroughly sated—and her mirror thoroughly fogged.

Smiling to herself, she'd just jotted down a note to remind herself to check back in with Carol at the library when Sharon's call came through. "Guess who has the rest of the day off?"

Maggie flipped the folder closed. "You?"

"Yep, the powers that be decided to have the administrative offices painted before school starts, and HR was this afternoon's lucky winner. And it's a Friday—can life get any better?"

At Sharon's reference to *the powers that be,* Maggie couldn't help thinking of Ethan—and smiling. Over the past few days, she'd easily smiled more than she had in the past year at least. If only she could find more energy to enjoy her newfound happiness. She was on her second cup of coffee, and she was still having trouble staying awake. Between fatigue and the headache she'd woken up with, it wasn't shaping up to be a superproductive day.

"Any chance you can meet me at Hyperion?" Sharon asked.

Maggie hesitated. She had a home owner to do list longer than her arm, the edits on a doctoral dissertation to complete and Isabel's diary to finish along with the fruits of her research quest. And yet wasn't life altogether too short not to take out time to be with the people you loved?

"So, Mags, what do you say?"

"Give me ten minutes to walk up, and I'll see you there."

LOCATED ON THE CORNER OF William and Princess Anne Streets, Hyperion Espresso was a hub for downtown activity patronized by politicians, painters and musicians, students from the college and busy moms with babies in tow. Open from early morning until late in the evening, the locally owned coffee shop was almost constantly crowded. Carrying two café mochas and a sticky bun to share, Maggie and Sharon found an open streetside table and settled in. Thinking about her previous night with Ethan, the amazing ways he'd touched and tasted and pleasured her both during and after her bath, Maggie found herself battling a smile. Afterward he'd wrapped her in a bath towel and carried her back to her bed. She'd never before felt so excited to be with someone, to simply be alive.

Stirring a second packet of artificial sweetener into her porcelain cup, Sharon looked over and asked, "Do we need to trade seats and get you out of the sun?"

"Nope. I put on my sunblock before I left the house. Why?"

Sharon studied her for a moment before answering. "I dunno, your face... You look kind of flushed. No, flushed isn't the right word. It's more like you have this...glow about you." All of a sudden, her eyes widened and her brows shot up. She dropped the sweetener, packaging and all, into her cup. "Oh, my God, you've had sex, haven't you? *Good* sex."

No longer bothering to fight it, Maggie felt herself breaking into a broad Cheshire cat grin. "*Great* sex, as a matter of fact."

Sharon held up her palm for a high five. "Praise the Lord and pass the sticky buns." Taking a bite from their shared pastry, she added, "Give it up, Mags. Who is he, because I know he can't be Richard?"

Maggie felt her smile slip. "I can't tell you."

Sharon made a face. "Oh, c'mon, you can't toss out a

teaser like that and then leave me hanging. You met him in Fredericksburg didn't you?"

"Well, er…yes."

Sharon was beaming. "I knew it. There are only six available and remotely datable men in the whole friggin' town, and you've just taken one of them out of play." She hesitated, smile dimming. "It's not the cute cop, is it?"

"No."

Sharon picked the paper out of her coffee and took a sip. "In that case, which of the remaining *five* available guys is he?"

"I wouldn't exactly say he was available."

Sharon frowned. Leaning closer, she whispered, "He's not married…is he? Look, girlfriend, take it from someone who's been there and done that and, well, just don't go there. Believe me, you'll only get hurt."

Maggie shook her head, beginning to regret spilling the beans. Talk about opening Pandora's box—along with her big mouth. "No, he's not married. It's just…complicated."

"Complicated as in he's gay, bisexual, in prison, fixated on his mother, likes to dress up in women's lingerie, is cruel to cats—what?"

In spite of the seriousness of the situation, Maggie burst out laughing. Their buddy Becky, known as Rebecca St. Claire in the romance fiction world, might be the bestselling writer among them, but when it came to real life, Sharon had the hands-down most wicked imagination of their group. "None of the above."

"Well, that's good, isn't it? That eliminates just about every bad thing I can come up with other than… Wait, he's not a serial killer, is he?"

Blowing on her steaming latte, Maggie shook her head. "Negative on that one, too."

"So what's the problem?"

Maggie shrugged. "I suppose you could say he's someone from my past."

"Shit, you're not seeing that jerk who dumped you after the crash, I hope?"

"No, nothing like that. My *distant* past." Talk about an understatement. According to Ethan, they'd been lovers since 1862. On the positive side, it meant at least he didn't have a commitment problem. "You've never heard about him before but he's…well, he's wonderful."

"Well, in that case, I'd have to say go for it, girlfriend."

"Really?"

Sharon nodded, suddenly looking far away and more than a little sad. "Second chances at love are like falling stars or four-leaf clovers. When one comes your way, it's always for a reason—and you'd better not blow it second-guessing yourself."

11

SINCE IT WAS SUCH A NICE day, warm but not yet hot, they decided to do some shopping after they finished their coffees. There were a few things Maggie wouldn't mind picking up for the house but mainly it was just fun to look. Fredericksburg might still be a little rough around the edges, but the city had made enormous strides in revitalizing its commercial district since she'd discovered it driving back from the Outer Banks a decade before. Antique malls and Civil War memorabilia shops stood side by side with newer stores like Walker Home and e.e. Smith that carried an array of hip home furnishings, eclectic artwork and funky household items.

Located in the same block as the Visitors' Center, Beck's Antiques sold high-end American and British antiques from a restored Federal-style brickwork building. As much as Maggie appreciated antique furniture, it was the extensive collection of meticulously cataloged old books in the shop's backroom that caught her eye.

She left Sharon ogling the estate jewelry in the glass-topped case up front and wandered toward the back of the store. Perusing the poetry section, she found herself drawn to the brownish-red cloth spine of a book crammed onto an upper shelf. Without really knowing why, she found a stool and stepped up.

Taking the book down from the shelving, she saw it was a volume of poetry by Elizabeth Barrett Browning, *Sonnets from the Portuguese*. Maggie already owned a copy though not a first edition like this one. Holding the book, she felt her fingers tingling with a strange, prickling heat and her heart rate suddenly picked up. *Wow, I must have really overdone it on the caffeine and sugar.*

The pocket-size edition was marked for sale at fifty dollars, a bargain though as Richard would say, she needed it like a hole in the head. Nonetheless, she found herself opening the book, her eye going directly to the inscription, the penmanship neat, elegant—and by now hauntingly familiar.

> To my dearest, darling Ethan, whom I love "to the depth and breadth and height my soul can reach." Love Always, Isabel.

Oh, my God. Seized by a strange urgency, she started turning pages, not sure of what she was searching for, yet searching all the same. Marking the page for sonnet number forty-three, from which Isabel had paraphrased her inscription, was a small metal-plated photograph known as a tintype. Maggie picked up the picture with a shaking hand. Bringing it closer, she suddenly felt as if the shop, indeed her whole world, were spinning like a carousel. The woman in the picture wore an 1860s-era dress complete with lace-edged round collar and leg-o'-mutton sleeves, but what caught and captured her attention was the face. It was her, Maggie, right down to the mole at the corner of her left eye. She recognized the dress as the same one she'd seen Isabel, herself, wearing in her *dream.*

Talk about getting hit with a double whammy. Unless she'd had a body double who had lived back in 1862, Ethan must be right. Not only was he a ghost—not a hallucination, but a ghost—but she was the embodiment, make that reembodiment, of Isabel Earnshaw.

"What do you think of these earrings?" Startled, Maggie looked up to see Sharon standing in front of her holding one of a pair of antique earrings up to her lobe.

"They're...great." Oh, my God, they were the very earrings Isabel—she—wore in the picture.

Ethan's voice came to her as if haunting her from a distant place and time. *"I don't have a ring to plight our troth but these ear bobs belonged to my grandmother. I want you to have them, Belle, and know when you wear them you have my very heart, as well."*

Feeling perspiration break out on her forehead, Maggie said, "They're great, Shar, but to be honest they're just not you."

Sharon's smile dipped downward. Dangling, unique jewelry was kind of her thing and the amber inlays cinched it. "They're not? Are you sure? You know how I love amber."

Mouth dry, Maggie gave a hard shake of her head. "Positive. They just don't work. You know, they really look more like Lucia's style to me."

"Lucia?" Sharon greeted that pronouncement with a puzzled look. "But she only ever wears those little diamond studs she got on her eighteenth birthday. Other than to clean the posts, I've never seen her take them out. These are way bigger and they dangle, see." She tapped the curved edge of the earring, setting it to swinging.

Reaching out, Maggie snatched the earrings from Sharon's hand. "The last time we talked, she mentioned she was looking to make a style change—wear bigger jewelry, branch out from diamonds to earth colors. And she has a birthday coming up, remember?"

"Not until November." Sharon looked a little put out.

"Perfect. I'll get these for her and tuck them away until then." Hooking an arm around Sharon's shoulders, she led her back toward the counter. "In the meantime, let's go pick out something that's more you."

SHOPPING BAG IN HAND, Maggie opened her front door. Now that the initial shock was fading, she could hardly wait to see Ethan to tell him she believed him. Oh, several fairly weighty questions remained to be answered, such as what had happened to Isabel—to her—but those would keep for a while at least. Hopefully he'd come to her again that night, though of course, with him being a ghost, there was no way to know if she would see him then—or again at all.

"Welcome home."

Ethan sat in her window seat, his long, booted legs stretched out in front of him and Willie purring in his lap. Wow, he even liked cats. Talk about her dream man. If he weren't dead, he'd almost be too perfect to be real.

Dropping her bag inside the door, she asked, "What are you doing here?"

He set Willie on the cushion next to him and stood. "Not quite the greeting I'd imagined, but I suppose it'll do."

"Sorry, I didn't mean it like that. It's just that it's…well, it's still daylight. I just assumed ghosts had to wait until after sundown to materialize. Don't tell me you got a heavenly hall pass?"

Other than worrying over how much of his energy they were consuming with this unscheduled visit, she was glad, so very glad, to see him. Determined not to waste one precious nanosecond of their time together however long—or short—she closed the short distance between them.

She slid her arms about his waist and hugged him tightly against her. He felt so warm, so solid and so altogether alive that even after the afternoon's revelations, she still had trouble believing he wasn't all of those things.

He tucked a strand of her hair behind her ear. "A hall pass?"

Tingling at his touch, Maggie explained, "You know in high school when you get a signed slip of paper from your teacher… Oh, never mind, it's not important. Just kiss me.'"

"With pleasure."

He bent his head to hers, his tongue sliding along the seam of her lips, teasing them apart. Kissing him back, she felt the very last of her doubts melt away. A part of her had been wondering if the incredible chemistry between them wasn't because of the clandestine nature of their previous sexual encounters, but it turned out that kissing Ethan in full daylight was every bit as thrilling as doing so in shadow.

Pulling back, he asked, "Did you have a nice day?"

In the past six months of dating, Richard had asked about her day maybe twice. She smiled up at him, loving that he cared. "I did. I met my friend Sharon for coffee and then we did some shopping."

He glanced beyond her to the shopping bag she'd left by the door. "I'm glad to know that at least some things about ladies haven't changed in one hundred forty-five years." He took a step back from her, broad palms resting lightly on her shoulders in that special way of his that made her feel cherished yet lusted after, protected yet free. "What did you purchase?"

Feeling shy suddenly, she admitted, "I got you a present."

"A present for me?"

"Sure, why not?" The afterlife probably didn't have a lot of storage space for earthly items—death was a fabulous opportunity for downsizing—but her senses told her it was fundamentally important that she give the sonnets to Ethan…again.

Turning away, she retrieved the book from the bag. "I was going to wrap it, but that was when I thought I wouldn't see you until tonight." Watching his face, she held the book out.

He didn't need to look down to know what it was. She could see from the somber look on his face he recognized it immediately. "*Sonnets from the Portuguese.*" He swallowed hard. "Where did you get this?" Taking it from her, he smoothed a palm over the tattered cover.

"I bought it at a shop on Caroline Street. There must have been hundreds of books there, maybe thousands, but for whatever reason, I was drawn to take it down from the shelf. I, uh…read the inscription. I gave you this, didn't I?"

He nodded, a faraway look in his eyes. "It was the September before we were ordered to cede our position holding the town and instead march on Richmond. I swore I'd be back to bear you home to Boston as my bride after the war, but you weren't so sure. I gave you a pair of amber ear bobs as a keepsake. I'd thought to sell them once I made Richmond and use the money to buy your wedding band, but you were so distraught at my leaving, I decided to give them to you instead so you might know just how very much you meant to me."

"You mean these?" She reached into the bag and took out the small, tissue-wrapped bundle. Unfurling it, she dropped the earrings into her palm and held them out for him to see.

He lifted his incredulous gaze to hers. "The very ones. My God, Isabel—I mean, Maggie—where did you find these? I'd always thought they must have been buried with you."

For the first time it hit her that being the reembodiment of Isabel Earnshaw meant she'd died a human death once already. Maggie shivered, suddenly feeling as if someone had walked on her grave.

She shook her head. "I guess you could call it a miracle or at least one hell of a coincidence. I'd just opened the book and found the tintype of Isabel, me, tucked inside when my friend came to show me the really cool earrings she'd picked out of the case. I don't know. Seeing the picture just made it all real somehow."

"Maggie, are you saying what I think you are?"

Now that she'd overcome the barrier of her self-imposed resistance, Maggie found it as easy to read his thoughts as he had hers. "Yes, Ethan, I think I'm finally ready to believe."

BELIEVING HAD A POWERFUL impact on Maggie. She didn't just know she was Isabel—she felt it. Looking up into Ethan's dear, handsome face, she said, "Come upstairs to the attic with me. Make love to me as you and Isabel—as we—made love that very first time."

She'd anticipated them walking up the main stairs arm in arm and then the narrow attic stairs single file but the next thing she knew Ethan blinked and they were standing facing each other, not in the foyer but the attic, her head doing a crazy spin.

"You stood just there." His eyes wearing a faraway look, he pointed to the eave from which the dried lavender still hung. "You pulled a ribbon from your hair and tied up the lavender sprigs you'd gathered from the herb garden your maid kept out back."

"Like this?" Maggie wasn't wearing a hair ribbon but a scrunchie. Pulling it out, she shook out her hair and pantomimed the action. Taking his silence for assent, she turned to face him. "What did I say afterward?"

She thought she knew, or rather remembered from reading

the diary. Even so, she didn't want to revisit the memory alone. She wanted them to go back together.

Ethan swallowed hard. "You said, 'Now it's our bridal bower as if we were man and wife in truth.'"

Throat thick with emotion, she turned to him and smiled though she was so close to crying, she could feel it. "Now it's our bridal bower as if we were—are—man and wife in truth."

He advanced a step toward her. "Then I came up behind you and put my one hand upon your hip and with the other I brushed your hair to the side and laid my lips along the nape of your neck. I whispered that you shouldn't be frightened, that I'd take every care with you, and then I pulled you back against me and let you feel how hard I was for you, how much I loved and wanted you in every way a man can want a woman."

Slowly, very slowly, Maggie turned back around. *Come to me, Ethan. Make me your wife and yourself my husband as you did all those many years ago.*

A warm hand settled on her hip. He swept her hair to the side and laid his lips along the line of her neck, drawing her shiver. "God, Belle, the Lord alone knows how I've wanted you. How I've waited." He pulled her back into the cradle of his thighs, and she felt his erection brushing her buttocks.

"No more waiting." Looking down, she saw she no longer wore her T-shirt and jeans but the brown dress with the lace collar and cuffs from the tintype. Feeling a weight pulling at her ears, she reached up to the amber earrings swinging from her lobes.

He undressed her slowly, thoroughly. Never once rushing, he stripped her bare layer by layer, piece by piece, stopping to trail soft kisses over her clavicle, to exclaim over the beauty of her breasts and draw her swelling nipples ever so gently into his mouth.

Maggie stepped out of the ankle-deep pool of petticoats,

chemise and corseting, stark naked save for her garters and stockings, and opened her arms to him. "Come to me, Ethan."

He went down on his knees before her, mouth pressed to her belly, to the sensitive inside of her thighs. Looking up at her through those thickly lashed blue eyes, he said, "Spread your legs for me, sweetheart. I need to see you, touch you and suckle the sweet fruit of your womanhood lest I die."

Throat dry and eyes damp, Maggie widened her stance and braced her hands upon his broad shoulders. Ethan dipped his head and found her with his mouth, suckling and tasting and savoring her like a starving man given his first bite of bread. Just when Maggie felt herself being brought to the brink, just when she felt as though one more swipe of his tongue would have her coming in his mouth, he stood and lifted her into his arms.

She thought he meant to carry her over to the desk as he had that first magical night when she'd thought he was an intruder but instead he lowered her to the floor, or rather to the wool cloak he'd spread there.

Making a pillow of his arm beneath her head, he held her gaze with his and swore, "I'll make it good for you, sweetheart. I'll be as gentle as I can."

Maggie licked her parched lips, a contrast to the wetness jetting between her thighs. "You're always gentle with me and you always make it good, so very good."

Excitement coursed through Maggie. Her lips tingled, her breasts tingled, and between her legs she was wetter and warmer than she'd ever been before. At the same time, she felt strangely shy, more like a nineteenth-century virgin than a twenty-first-century thirtysomething.

Jaw tense, Ethan reached down between them to unbutton the flap of his fly. His erection sprang free. She felt the exquisite weight and pressure of it as he ran it along the inside of her thigh. "Feel how hard I am for you, Belle. How much I want you."

Reaching down, she tested the moist tip with her thumb, already knowing how amazing he would taste, how fragrant he would smell—like lavender only better, his own unique musk. "I feel you, Ethan, and I want you, too, not just for now but for always."

His roughened fingers traced the outline of her cheek. There was so much love in his eyes she thought she might drown in it. "You have me always, forever more. Down whatever path life—or death—may take us, know always that our souls are joined, two halves of the same whole."

There was a second's pause and then he was inside her in one long, beautiful thrust that filled her body and soul. She arched to meet him, her hands sliding beneath his shirt, fingers playing on the sweat sheathed muscles of his back and then sliding downward beneath the waist of his trousers, all at once remembering how afterward when she was braver, Isabel—she—had dared undress him and nudge him over onto his belly to sprinkle kisses from his broad shoulders down the line of his spine to the firm lobes of his buttocks. Straddling his bare back, she'd leaned in and whispered into his ear, "From here on, I must be with you always, your wife in every way. Something that feels this right, this perfect, must surely be God given and…right."

Reading her memory, Ethan said, "You are my wife and I am your husband in every way that could possibly matter. I shall love and cherish and keep myself true to you not only until death does part us but beyond death. Whom God has joined together, let no man put asunder."

She opened her mouth to answer him but he thrust into her

again, stealing her breath, her will, her soul. The orgasm hit her like a streaking comet, a starburst of pulsing heat radiating from the drenched place between her thighs to the warm glow enveloping her heart. She wrapped her arms about him and buried her head against the mat of his chest and let his blood-warmed flesh and bone mute her satisfied cries.

Only when the last contraction ebbed did she trust herself to open her eyes and look up at him. *My husband.*

A single tear sliding down his lean cheek, Ethan smiled down at her. *My wife.*

A WHILE LATER, MAGGIE lifted her head from Ethan's shoulder and steeled herself to ask one of those weighty questions she'd hoped to save until later. "Who was Damian Grey?"

They were still lying on his cloak on the attic floor, too languid to bother with moving downstairs to her bed. Leaning over her, he traced slow, sensual circles around the areola of her breast. "Do you know that in my day this very color was known as Ashes of Roses?"

"What was?"

"The color of your breast just there. It's the very shade of dusty pale pink known as Ashes of Roses." He bent his head and drew her nipple into his mouth, a diversionary tactic—and a very effective one.

Determined not to succumb, not just yet, anyway, Maggie said, "Why is it I have this feeling you're avoiding my question?"

Venting a sigh, Ethan stilled his hand. "Very well, Damian was a sutler who made camp with my regiment and peddled his wares. Mostly he made a tidy profit from selling whiskey to desperate, homesick men and stirring up trouble when the spirit moved him."

"I gathered that much from reading Isabel's—my—diary.

I also found out from doing some research at the library that after Isabel's family died, he bought this house at auction. What I don't understand is why he went to the trouble and then only lived here a month before boarding it up and running off to Richmond."

Ethan lifted a dark brow and looked down at her. "He didn't run off to Richmond. I chased him off."

"Why?"

He let out a heavy sigh. "If ever a man deserved haunting, it was Damian. He bore false witness against me, forged a document of our general's plans for the assault, which I supposedly wrote and then had passed on to Lee, trumped up treasonous charges that caused me to be hanged as a Confederate spy. He murdered me as sure as he placed the noose about my neck himself. Purchasing the house where we'd loved was the final insult. Still, my haunting him was piddling punishment compared to what he deserves. To put the past to rest once and for all, he must repent his crimes not only to me but to the world and the powers that be beyond it."

She reached out a hand to the cloth he still wore wrapped about his neck, trailing light fingers down the side, pulling away when he flinched. Having only just accepted him as a ghost, she hadn't thought before to ask how he'd died. "Oh, Ethan, no wonder you want to find him. But what was his motive in doing you such harm?"

His gaze shuttered. "He coveted…something I had, something rare and precious and very dear." Angling his head to look down at her, he asked, "I take it you haven't gotten around to finishing the diary?"

Sensing he already knew the answer, she shook her head. Accepting Ethan as a ghost and herself as the reembodiment of Isabel Earnshaw had amounted to quite a drain on *her* reserve of physical energy. She hadn't been feeling all that well lately, and the headaches were getting worse, not better.

"I'm about three-quarters of the way through. Have…have *you* read the diary?"

He pressed a kiss to the top of her head. "I don't have to, sweetheart. I lived it."

12

September 1, 1862

The Federal forces have decamped for Richmond, Ethan among them, blowing up our bridges in their wake. To distract myself from my misery, I took myself into Pa's office at the lumber mill to help out with the books as the regular bookkeeper fled with his family to Lynchburg last spring.

Feeling eyes upon me, I looked up from the column of figures I was reckoning to find a tall, thin man staring down at me. It was the sutler I'd caught staring at me in church, the one who'd been traveling with the Federals. Apparently he'd elected to stay behind.

Eager to get back to my ledger, I asked, "May I help you, sir?"

He stared at me a long moment and then as if suddenly remembering his manners doffed his derby, revealing a crown of thick, straight blond hair. "Damian Grey at your service, miss. Pardon my ill manners, Miss Earnshaw, but for the moment your beauty rendered me speechless."

Not so very long ago, such blandishments would have seen me flirting in return, but that was before Ethan. Enemy officer though he might be, he was still my heart's desire, my soul's mate. Though the sutler was a young and attractive man, neither his golden looks nor his overly gallant manner moved me. If anything, I found myself repelled by his pale, fixed stare.

"I was passing through town on my way back to Stafford Hills, and I thought to stop by and show you my wares."

Looking down to the black carpetbag he carried, I shook my head. "I've no funds for fripperies, sir, and you're sure to find yourself greeted by the same answer as you travel about town. Most folks who've stayed on have precious little money as it is for firewood and food."

It wasn't only the Union blockades causing our misery but the greed of war profiteers such as he who drove up the cost of just about everything. Quinine fetched sixty dollars per ounce, a cake of store-bought soap cost a dollar twenty-five, and the going rate for a pair of plain boots was thirty dollars. If the war went on much longer, we'd soon be giving up bathing and going about barefoot. Whereas we were reduced to darning socks, wearing homespun and turning old clothes inside out to keep ourselves decent, the sutler's clothing looked store-bought and shiny new.

"Pretty girls should have pretty things. I like pretty things myself," he added, looking at me in a way that made me uneasy. "Were you to let me call on you, I fancy a great many fine things would find their way into your possession."

I lifted my chin and looked him square in the eye. "I have a beau already and even if I didn't, no quantity of ribbon or lace would induce me to stoop to step out with a carpetbagger such as you."

A cold look came into his eye, and at once I regretted my hard words if only for fear of what mischief he might make for me or those I loved. "Is that so, Miss Earnshaw? We'll just have to see about that."

Saturday aka Day of Reckoning.

MAGGIE CLOSED THE DIARY, a chill crawling up her spine. Isabel's diary entry had confirmed what she'd known already in her heart. The precious, rare and very dear possession of Ethan's the sutler had coveted had been her. Though Damian had lived more than a hundred years ago, the predatory behavior Isabel described in her diary could have easily fit a modern-day date rapist or stalker, only in 1862 there wouldn't have been any sexual harassment laws or any laws against stalking, either. With the wartime occupation relaxing the customary social rules, Isabel must have felt vulnerable indeed.

Maggie would have liked to read on, but it was already eleven-thirty. Richard would be here by noon, and she hadn't showered yet. As much as she was dreading the face-to-face breakup talk, in her heart she knew it was the right thing to do. The next few hours wouldn't be the most pleasant she'd ever spent but anticipating the relief she'd feel afterward, she felt ready to get on with it, not only the afternoon but the rest of her life.

Richard must have pushed his Porsche Boxster to its limit because she was just stepping out of the shower when she heard his impatient knocking below. *Shit.* She quickly finished toweling off and then pulled on her sundress before hurrying downstairs to let him in.

"You're early." Admittedly not the warmest of greetings but

then again she was about to break up with him. No point in sending a mixed message.

Luggage in hand, he stepped inside. "Traffic was light." Glancing down at the black bag in his hand, he said, "I'll put this in the bedroom." He started toward the stairs.

At his mention of going into her bedroom, panic set in. "No. I mean, you can't. I put the cat in there."

Richard purported to be highly allergic though she'd never so much as seen him sneeze. He swung around to her, a scowl on his face. "That's a hell of a place for him. What am I supposed to do?"

"I shut him in so he wouldn't bother you." Actually it was the other way around. She didn't really trust Richard with her cat, a pretty sorry statement about their so-called relationship. "Just set your bag by the door for now. I'll…figure something out. Have a seat in the living room. I'll be down in ten minutes."

"No rush." He dropped the luggage inside the door and moved to take her in his arms. "You smell nice. Shower-fresh." He leaned in to kiss her.

She jumped back. "I still need to dry my hair."

He lifted a damp strand from her shoulder and wound it around his index finger. "I like you with wet hair. In fact, I really like you wet." He wiggled his eyebrows and the gesture along with the erection tenting the front of his jeans confirmed he wasn't talking about her hair.

She took a moment to study him. Richard was slightly built compared to Ethan but his workout sessions definitely were showing results. Wearing a fitted long-sleeved black shirt and ass-tight designer jeans, a day's growth of golden stubble offsetting his chiseled jaw, he could have stepped off the page of a Calvin Klein ad. Most women her age would find his designer-brand good looks highly appealing—most women, but not her and especially not now. Since being with Ethan, her definition of sexy came in the form of dark hair and blue eyes, a broad chest dusted with dark hair and big, capable hands that knew exactly how and where to touch you. That he was always so gentle, so unfailingly kind was the biggest turn-on of all.

"I really need to finish getting ready." Stomach knotting, she turned to go upstairs.

He gripped her by the shoulders and spun her around to face him. "Hey, what's the rush? Aren't you happy to see me?"

Nerves set in, causing her carefully rehearsed breakup speech to stick in her throat. She was being ridiculous. All she really had to say was "I don't want to see you anymore." How hard could that be? Why was she so afraid to speak up to him? It wasn't as though he was an authority figure, at least not anymore.

Losing her courage, she said, "I thought you wanted to see the downtown before dinner? Our reservation is for six o'clock."

"The downtown, right." He let out a snort, hands sliding down her upper arms. "Get real, Mags. We're in the equivalent of Mayberry, U.S.A. I'm sure there'll still be plenty of tables open whenever we get there." He backed them into the living room and through the open pocket doors to the dining room.

She jerked back, feeling his fingers digging into her flesh. "I know this is hard for you to get but the people who staff the downtown restaurants are members of my community. It's not like D.C. where people leave work and go home to somewhere else. I don't want to start out being branded as a no-show."

"What about me? I drive all this way to spend the weekend with you, and you act like you don't want to come within fifty feet of me. What gives?"

A golden opportunity to have that breakup; she'd never get a better one. "Well, Richard, to be honest—"

His mouth closed over hers, cutting off the rest of her sentence as well as her breath. The kiss was hard, bruising, more brutal than passionate.

He wrenched his mouth away. "Since that fucking cat of yours probably has his ass parked on the bed, let's get the party going here in the dining room, a little appetizer before dinner—it's about time you served up something hot on that antique table of yours." His hands squeezed her buttocks, and he crushed her against his thighs.

"Richard, stop it. I'm trying to have a conversation with you."

He lightened his hold but only marginally. "We can do all the talking you want later at dinner or you can talk dirty to me in bed. Right now, I am so hot for you, so *fucking* hot."

With his hard-on digging into her abdomen, she felt suffocated and disgusted and something more—an inexplicable certainty that this scene or one very much like it had played out between them in the past. But that was crazy. Until now, Richard had never exhibited any signs of being a physical abuser. And yet wasn't his persistent putting her and others down a form of assault? Was physical violence really so very different from verbal abuse or were they part of the same spectrum of aggressive behavior?

"Maybe this is what you've needed all along—a little walk on the wild side to get the juices flowing." He slid a hand to the space between her thighs and gave her mound a hard squeeze.

"What I want is for you to let go of me—now!"

Pushing against him, she caught a flash of movement out of the corner of her eye. Willie? But no, she'd left him closed in upstairs.

"On second thought, we can start out by testing out just how solid those precious plaster walls of yours really are."

Bypassing the table, he backed her across the room until she bumped up against the wall. She shoved at his hands, which had started on the buttons fronting her cotton sundress.

Richard was small compared to Ethan, but he was still a lot bigger and stronger than she was. She couldn't budge him, and it wasn't looking like she could reason with him, either. She was seriously considering smashing her knee into his groin when she saw Ethan in the far corner. Raw fury washing over his face and ham-size fists at the ready, he looked like someone with murder on his mind. Gladness to see him battled with fear of what he might do to Richard. One ghost per house was more than enough.

She mouthed the words, *No, don't do it,* but it was too late.

Following the direction of Ethan's stare, she looked up to see her solid Baker breakfront cabinet shaking as though they were in the midst of an earthquake, the blue pottery vase atop it dancing as if on legs.

"Richard! Heads up."

"Yes, baby, yes! Give me head." He stepped back and smacked a hand to either of her temples, pulling her downward. "That's right, suck me, baby, suck me hard!"

Even though she'd known what was going to happen, the thud followed by the splintering crash had her letting out a small scream. Richard's hold on her slackened and then dropped off. He staggered, pale eyes rolling back in his head and blood matting his hair. "Mags?"

Before she could answer, he folded to the floor.

13

Later that evening, Maggie stepped inside her front door after putting in a three-hour stint waiting in the local hospital emergency room for Richard's head to be X-rayed and then stitched. Because he'd lost consciousness, though only briefly, the doctor had wanted to keep him overnight. Tomorrow she could look forward to picking him up and driving his car back to D.C. Unless Sharon agreed to help her out by following them in Maggie's car, she'd be taking the train back to Fredericksburg.

But in the big scheme of things, getting Richard back to D.C. and herself back to Fredericksburg was only a logistical inconvenience. It would ruin her Sunday but certainly not her life. What really ate at her was the niggling fear that once she broke up with him, Richard might decide to sue. The so-called accident had occurred on her property, and he was always running on about structural damage and unsafe conditions. If she'd gained her dream house—the dream house purchased with her family's blood money—only to lose it to a dick like her soon-to-be ex-boyfriend, she'd never forgive herself—or Ethan, for that matter.

Throwing her keys down on her marble-topped foyer table, she scanned the downstairs for Ethan. Like a hit-and-run driver, he'd vanished the moment she'd looked up from

Richard's prone form. She hadn't seen him since, which either meant that the assault had seriously depleted his energy and he'd gone off to recharge or he was hiding from her—maybe a bit of both.

"Ethan, I know you're here somewhere. There's no use in pretending you're sleeping because I'm guessing ghosts don't nap. And don't give me any more crap about your needing to make another withdrawal from your earth energy reserve. You obviously had enough juice in your batteries to split Richard's head open like a melon."

Now that she knew Richard would be okay, her biggest gripe with the way the day had turned out was that she hadn't gotten to break up with him. You didn't tell your boyfriend the two of you were over while the E.R. doctor was stitching up his scalp—especially when you were afraid he might come back and sue you for damages. Afterward, he'd been too groggy from the painkillers to focus on anything beyond getting some sleep. Watching him ease back into his hospital bed, she'd almost envied him. Broken skin would heal in time but what about a one-hundred-forty-five-year-old broken heart? Just how did you handle being in love with a ghost?

"Ethan, come out. We need to talk."

She was about to take her search upstairs to the attic when Ethan's deep baritone answered her from the stair landing. "Personally, I hold to the adage that actions speak louder than words."

Stalking over to the bottom of the stairs, she looked up at him and demanded, "What's that supposed to mean?"

He shrugged. "That I saw you being manhandled, and I acted to protect you."

Would Richard really have taken rough handling to the point of raping her? She didn't want to think so and yet the bruises on her upper arms didn't lie. "I could have handled it myself. I was handling it."

Ethan shook his head, looking as weary as Maggie felt. "Sweetheart, I know what I saw, and the only one handling anything was Richard."

As she had no immediate rebuttal to that, she sallied forth with what she did know. "He had to have stitches—twelve to be exact. You could have injured him badly, killed him even."

He shrugged. "He strikes me as a thick-skulled sort."

"We sat in the emergency room for three solid hours. On a lesser note, that vase you broke was my favorite piece of Phil Chapman pottery from his final raku firing. It can never be replaced."

She'd been too focused on getting Richard to the hospital to stop and sweep up the mess. Unless Ethan had saved enough energy to wield a broom, it would be there waiting for her. She stomped into the dining room to find her suspicion confirmed. The shards of broken pottery were still scattered across the floor. Ethan might be a one-hundred-forty-five-year-old ghost, but he was still a guy—a guy who didn't think about cleaning up after himself.

"Why do you let Richard treat you in such a miserable fashion?"

She swung about to see him standing in the center of the pulled back pocket doors leading in from the living room, one hand braced against the wall. "Well, Ms. Steinem, what I'm asking myself right now is why I'm putting up with having to clean up a mess I didn't make." She cast a significant glance out onto the floor.

"Very well."

Venting a sigh, he lifted his hand and waved it in the vicinity of the breakage. Maggie was just about to tell him to cut the theatrics when she noticed the dust cloud swirling around the broken pot. Not dust but pixel points of golden light. Awed, she watched the cloud increase until it covered the vicinity of the vase, bathing the breakage in brilliant light. The whirling gradually slowed to a standstill, leaving the vase once more intact.

Ethan folded his arms over his chest. "Satisfied?"

She walked over to inspect the pottery's seemingly smooth surface. Bending down, she ran her hands over it, unable to find a single chip or crack. Looking back at him, she said, "That's amazing. You can't even see any cracks beyond the raku."

Ethan came up behind her. Even while she was furious with him, she was keenly aware of how close he stood, how amazing he smelled. His scent, his presence, his heat were more real to her than those of any flesh and blood man she might meet in a bar or pass on the street. It was impossible to forget all the things they'd done together, all the things she wanted to do with him still if only they might be granted the time.

His breath was a balmy breeze striking the back of her neck, his voice a soft whisper. "That's because there aren't any. It has been restored to a state of perfect wholeness."

Distracted by his closeness, she started toward the kitchen to get the footstool.

"There's no need," he assured her, reading her thoughts yet again. He blinked and the vase levitated, traveling above the china cabinet and then resuming its former place of honor as though set there by invisible hands.

Looking back at him over her shoulder, she asked, "I don't suppose you'd consider doing the same for Richard's head?"

He frowned. "There's a lot more broken in Richard than a patched crown. In my day, a gentleman showed a lady the utmost courtesy and respect."

Hands fisted on her hips, she whirled around, ready to do battle. Richard wasn't there to break up with, but Ethan was. "Give me a break. In your day, women weren't even allowed to vote."

"Is it really so much better now, in *your* day?" He speared her with one of his penetrating stares, a silent reminder he was privy to everything about her, her hopes, her fears and her not-so-secret fantasies.

"Of course it's better."

He lifted a dark brow, his expression openly skeptical. "If you'll pardon my asking, how old are you—in this life, that is?"

She hesitated, thinking how old she would seem to him coming as he did from an era where it was commonplace for a woman to die in childbirth before ever seeing the age of forty. "Thirty, but thirty is the new twenty in case you haven't heard."

He shook his head. "You're a thirty-year-old spinster who lives alone with her cat. Other than to visit the library, you scarcely stir from this house. When you do, it's to step out with a man who courts you yet makes no mention of marriage. Is that really better?"

Anger flared within Maggie, as sudden and unpredictable as thunder slashing through a placid summer sky. "I am not a spinster. I am a single woman, single by choice and in the prime of my life." She felt tears welling and turned her head. Age was a tender topic ever since she'd crossed the line to thirty, but it was that his words were an echo of every unspoken self-doubt she'd ever had that upset her most. "I just earned my doctorate, something a woman never could have done back in your time. In a few more months, I'm starting a great job, a tenure-track position that will let me teach and do research, as well. I have a great house I just purchased all on my own—or at least I thought it was going to be great until…"

His gaze narrowed. "Until I came along and spoiled things, you mean?"

She'd gone too far to turn back now. Lifting her chin, she met his gaze head-on. "Yes. Yes, as a matter of fact, that is exactly what I mean. I didn't ask for this. I was doing fine on my own, fine without you popping in and out whenever you please, breaking things and moving things around and making me wonder just how close to crazy I've really come."

"I can see my presence offends you, ma'am, and so I shall remove myself forthwith and trouble you no more." He took a step toward the stairs and then another. Coming up to the wall, he melted into the plaster and disappeared.

SITTING IN FRONT OF HER computer later that evening confronted by a blinking cursor and blank screen, Maggie reminded herself that peace and quiet were what she'd moved to Fredericksburg for in the first place. It seemed she'd finally gotten her wish. Other than Willie occasionally rubbing against her ankles for a snack, not a creature stirred within her four walls, not a mouse and apparently not a certain sexy—if sulky—ghost.

Making the final edits to her dissertation wasn't brain surgery, but the work required concentration—a commodity in short supply these days. Since firing up her computer, she'd tried to focus, but the material in front of her seemed if not irrelevant, certainly far removed from any immediate concern. With not one but two souls hanging in the balance, it was hard to invest her energy into a thesis that only a handful of people would ever read. It was the not knowing whether or not she would see Ethan ever again that really hurt. It was like sleeping with a man and waiting for him to call you, knowing that if he didn't, sooner or later you'd run into him in a bar or on the street, one of those awkward accidental meetings that were an inevitable part of single life. Only in the present case, it wasn't the fear of running into Ethan at some future point, but rather the fear their paths would never again cross, that had her reaching for the Ben & Jerry's. Unfortunately not even Chunky Monkey—her favorite flavor—could cure a soul hurt that ran this deep.

She shoved the ice cream back in the freezer and traded it in for a glass of wine. Sitting down to sip it, she replayed the quarrel with Ethan in her mind. Now that her anger had cooled, she admitted he'd made some worthwhile points. Why did she choose manipulative yet emotionally remote men like Richard for her lovers? Why did she put walls up to keep the people she cared about at arm's length? Was she just shallow or was it that she was afraid of losing anyone else she loved? Had she lashed out at Ethan purely because his words had stung or had anger been an easy excuse for pushing him away, too, before he got any closer?

Around midnight, she gave up on working, shut down her computer and went upstairs to bed. Staring up at the shadows crawling across the ceiling, the bed had never seemed so empty to her, sleep so far away—or the silence so dead. Who would have guessed that one day she'd lie in bed awake hoping for a ghostly bump in the night?

Switching on the lamp, she reached for her glasses—and the diary, its musty lavender aroma greeting her like an old friend.

November 16, 1862

Now that the Federals are back in possession of us, the situation in town has worsened progressively. Though the woman in me embraces their occupation as a means to keep Ethan close by, the part of me that is still a daughter of the South cannot help but mourn for our poor bleeding Dixie. The Yankees have taken possession of every vacated house in the neighborhood with much ransacking thereof. We are entirely shut in by their line of pickets and just this morning word came from their provost marshal there would commence a house-to-house search for fugitive rebels.

It is with these grim tidings swirling about my brain that I received Ethan's handwritten message delivered by way of the drummer boy in his company, Jem Sparks. Meet me at noon was all it said but of course I knew the place. Our attic hideaway.

Ethan was waiting for me when I stepped inside. Instead of rushing into his arms, I held back by the door. "You must be pleased."

"Belle?" Wearing a puzzled look, he rose from the chest upon which he'd seated himself. Even with my anger mounting, I took note of how gaunt and hollow-cheeked he looked. The Federal army must not be eating all that much better than we were.

I folded my arms over my breast. "Only this morning I heard that poor Mr. Potter was carried off to jail for harboring his fugitive son in the stockroom of his store. After they dragged him out, they torched the store, burned it fair near to the foundation. You must find that highly satisfying."

"I never wanted this war. It was the South that started the whole damned thing by pulling out from the Union, a union our forefathers bled and died to form."

Next to curiosity, my temper is my mortal failing. I lifted my voice from our usual whisper, for the time being not caring who might hear me below. "Only because you Yanks tried to seize our liberty and make us subject to you as surely as our ancestors were subject to England."

Expression more weary than angry, he shook his head. "It wasn't your liberty we mean for you to surrender, Belle, but your slaves."

"We don't own slaves. Our housemaid, Clarice, is a freed woman and has been for more than a decade. She stays with us of her own free will."

"But that's not the way of many Southern households, is it? I've witnessed firsthand the state of slaves laboring in the cotton fields of Georgia, and I wouldn't stand by and see a dog or a mule treated so foully, let alone a fellow human being."

As I'd never traveled farther south than Richmond, I had no answer to that. Instead I satisfied myself with sending him a fuming stare.

At length, he said, "I can see my presence offends you, ma'am, and so I shall remove myself forthwith and trouble you no more." He walked over to the window as if to leave in earnest.

In these uncertain times, none of us ever knows if the present day might not be our last. The prospect that I might be sending him off in harm's way, perhaps even to his death, with only bitter words between us overrode my anger.

I rushed to him and cast myself in his arms. "Oh, Ethan, forgive me. I don't know what came over me just then."

His arms went about me. He rubbed soothing circles over my back and let me weep into his neck as though

I were a child. "Lord, Belle, I'd sooner face the whole of Lee's army single-handed than see you cry and know I'm the cause."

Pulling away to look up into his dear, handsome face, I shook my head. "It's not you, it's this damned war." For someone who'd grown up without ever saying a swear word, I'd cottoned on to the habit mighty well of late. "I never know when or if I'll see you again and every time I do I worry it will be our last."

"I know, sweetheart, I know, but it won't always be this way. No war lasts forever, not even this one."

An hour or so later, Ethan departed amidst many sweet kisses and soft words. It was as though we'd never quarreled, and yet as the day wore on I couldn't put the episode from my mind. Pleading a headache, I excused myself from the dinner table and spent the remainder of the afternoon in my room, not lying in bed but kneeling beside it. Hands clasped in that age-old posture of supplication, I begged for the willpower to guard my foolish tongue in the future. Were I to give us away, I'd never forgive myself. Without the promise of our future together after the war, there would be no reason to go on living, no purpose in life at all. As for marrying anyone other than Ethan, I'd sooner go to my grave a spinster than let the likes of Damian Grey lay so much as a finger on me.

I'd sooner be dead.

TEARS IN HER EYES, MAGGIE closed the diary. The passage struck a chord deep within her and not only because of the earlier argument. How she wished she could go back and erase the past few hours and, this time, find the wisdom to put aside her pride as her earlier, twentysomething self, Isabel, had done. Instead, she'd stood by and watched him disappear. So much for age and wisdom going hand in hand.

Recalling their earlier argument, she remembered how exhausted Ethan had looked, how drawn. Toppling that vase onto Richard must have taken more of an energetic toll on him than he'd let on. What if he'd used up so much that he couldn't come back to her even if he wanted to? God, what if she'd blown her second chance at love after all?

Switching off the light, she squeezed her eyes shut and let the tears fall. As much as she tried, she couldn't put the latest diary passage from her mind, particularly the final cryptic note—*I'd sooner be dead.* Hadn't she said the same to herself when grief over losing her family had led her over to the bathroom medicine cabinet where a razor or a bottle of pills had promised release from all that earthly pain?

Had Isabel known a similar sort of despair and only been unable to find the willpower to resist it? Was that why there was no record of her death or burial? Maggie lay back in the cool darkness contemplating that sad thought when the proverbial elephant in the room hit her like a pie in the face. Whatever had happened to Damian Grey, specifically his soul? If she and Ethan had both been sent back to earth to work through the past—albeit in different forms—wouldn't Damian have had to come back, too?

14

WHEN MAGGIE PICKED RICHARD up from the hospital Sunday morning, he was feeling better than anyone had predicted, including him. She hadn't realized how worried she'd been that he might not be able to take care of his wound by himself until the discharging doctor assured them he was fine to go home. If that had been the case, she could have found herself stuck with him as a houseguest for the whole of the coming week. Talk about a lucky escape.

Carrying his antibiotics prescription and suitcase out to his Porsche parked in front of her house, she felt a twinge of guilt. Prick though he undoubtedly was, he'd been through a lot in the past twenty-four hours.

"If you have any problems along the way, if you start feeling woozy or anything, call me on my cell and I'll come and pick you up, okay?" She slid his suitcase onto the backseat and turned back to hand him the white paper pharmacy bag.

"Okay, thanks." He went to get in the car, and then hesitated. Turning back around to her, he said, "Hey, Mags, about the other day, I'm sorry."

Richard apologizing—this was a first. "All that talk about doing me in the dining room did freak me out a little," she admitted, thinking maybe, just maybe, someday he might morph into a decent human being after all.

He blinked as though trying to make sense of what she'd just said. "What, oh that." His dismissive tone suggested mauling her was a matter of course. "I was talking about dinner. I was supposed to take you to that train station restaurant, remember?"

"Claiborne's, right." Leave it to Richard. He finally found it in him to apologize, and he did so over the wrong thing. So much for thinking that bump on the brow might have helped him grow a conscience—or a soul, for that matter. "That's okay. I called the restaurant after I got home last night and explained we'd had an emergency."

"How about a rematch?"

She hesitated. After the previous day's fiasco, she was beginning to think breaking up over the phone might not be such a bad idea after all. "That's not necessary."

"No, really, I want to. How about this Friday night? I'll drive down after work, and we can have a late dinner."

Once she broke up with him, he'd either be driving back that night or booking a hotel room, but she could hardly say so at the moment, not when his surgical bandage was showing signs of seepage. Instead, she said, "Won't you miss working out at your gym Saturday morning if you stay over?" She belonged to a downtown gym that allowed members to bring a guest for a small fee, but when they'd glanced inside the other day, Richard had made it clear the facility wasn't up to his standards.

He shrugged. "I may have to lay off the rest of the week anyway until my head heals."

Feeling slightly sorry for him—even if he had been a jerk to her, he was a human being, after all—she stepped back while he slid behind the wheel. "Okay, I'll see you on Friday."

She waited at the curb to make sure he got off okay before

turning to go back inside. Her head pounding with another of her stress headaches, she was thinking maybe a nap might be in order when her cell went off. Her first thought was to let whoever was calling leave a voice message but very much like her previous incarnation as Isabel, curiosity remained one of her chief strengths—and chief failings.

She clicked on the cell. "Is this Maggie Holliday?" The middle-aged female voice had a slight Southern twang.

"Yes, how can I help you?"

"It's Carol from the library. I work in the Virginiana Room. You came in about a week ago to do some research on your house."

It took Maggie a handful of seconds to jog her memory. "Oh, right. Hi, Carol. What's up?"

"I don't usually like to bother people on the weekends, but since the library is usually quiet on Sunday afternoons, I thought why not use the time to tackle that research query of yours?"

Talk about dedication. Holding the cell to her ear, Maggie took a seat on her porch swing. "That was awfully nice of you."

"It was my pleasure. In fact, I'm calling because I've found something I think you might find of interest."

Excited, Maggie waited for her to say more. When she didn't, she prompted, "You've got me on the edge of my seat. What is it, Carol? What did you find?"

Building the anticipation, Carol blew out a breath. "What would you say if I told you I'm holding a copy of the last will and testament of Damian Grey?"

Maggie was already on her feet. "Hold tight, Carol. I'm only a block away. I'll be right there."

> *I, Damian Wilson Grey, being of sound mind and body, do in the year of Our Lord 1892 hereby make my last will and testament…"*

THE VERBIAGE FOR WILLS hadn't changed all that much in the past century and a half. There was a laundry list of assets to be disposed starting with Maggie's house, which had gone to a male relative who lived in New Hampshire. Maggie recalled from her previous research that the cousin, Fairchild Ellis, had sold the house and land at auction, setting into motion a chain of one-generation owners leading up to her own recent purchase. It was all interesting stuff but nothing that couldn't have waited until Monday morning.

Tamping down her impatience, she continued to wade through the list of dispositions, including those related to not one but several businesses. Despite his relatively humble beginnings as the nineteenth-century equivalent of a traveling salesman, Damian had done well for himself after the war. Feeling as though her eyes were crossing, she came to the final paragraph.

> I do hereby repent of all mine offenses, notably the wrongs I committed in this life against one Ethan O'Malley, a captain in the Union Army of the Potomac against whom I bore false witness, producing forged evidence that he had tipped Burnside's hand to one of Lee's lieutenants, prompting the Rebels to position their sharpshooters on the high hill known as Marye's Heights and thereby win the battle. In so doing, I caused an innocent man to be court-martialed and hanged as a traitor, all because I did covet his sweetheart, Isabel Earnshaw, for my own.
>
> May God have mercy on my soul.

Maggie thought for a moment. The will was dated December 16, 1892, exactly thirty years to the day of Ethan's hanging. Damian would have been in his late fifties or early sixties, old for his time. By that time he'd been living in Richmond for almost thirty years. Why come back to Fredericksburg to write his will when he could have easily stayed in Richmond and done the same?

Looking up from the photocopied document to Carol, seated across from her at the worktable, she said, "This is great stuff. The one thing I don't get is why Damian Grey would come back here to make out his will. Richmond must have had plenty of lawyers."

Carol's plain face lit up like a Christmas tree. "That's the part I've been saving until you read the will." Carol opened her manila folder and took out a photocopy of a microfilmed newspaper article. She slid it across the table. It was an obituary.

"Carol?"

The librarian nodded and explained, "Damian Grey took the train here from Richmond on the sixteenth of December. Instead of checking into a hotel, he returned to the Caroline Street house that had been boarded up for almost thirty years. With the furniture buried beneath sheets and everything shrouded in thirty years of cobwebs and dust, it must have looked like a haunted house indeed. Can you imagine?"

Maggie certainly could. "Go on, Carol."

"He went out once to have the will notarized, and then came back to the house and hanged himself—in the attic, to be specific."

Maggie ran a hand through her hair. "Damian Grey committed suicide?" Talk about fact being stranger than fiction—a lot stranger. "But why would he want to kill himself when he'd apparently gotten away with murder, so to speak?"

Carol shrugged. "Who knows? Maybe his conscience caught up with him and he couldn't live any longer with what he'd done. Too bad he confessed thirty years too late to help that poor young army captain who was hanged—and his sweetheart. On the bright side, it kind of makes you feel better about your own life, doesn't it?"

Maggie hesitated, weighing just how very much she still had at stake. "Well, Carol, I'd have to say yes—and no. One thing's for sure, you've got to hand it to history. Real life has stories to top anything the most talented of fiction writers could make up."

MAGGIE WALKED HOME MULLING the latest information over in her head. It was clear now as it never had been before that she, Ethan and Damian were each one corner of a classic love triangle. If Ethan's coming back to present-day Fredericksburg had been scheduled to coincide with her moving there, then wasn't it possible, even likely, that Damian was here, as well? He might be any number of people. She hadn't exaggerated when she'd told Richard the city was home to roughly twenty-one thousand people, though of course not all of them lived within the forty-block historic district. The latter narrowed the field to the occupants of seven hundred households give or take—still a staggering number to sift through assuming she was even on the right track.

She would have liked to talk over her discovery with Ethan, but she hadn't seen hide nor hair or him since their argument the previous day. Even before, he'd been highly tight-lipped on the topic of Damian Grey. Was that because he was on some level embarrassed at having been bested by such a slimy soul or was this yet another attempt to protect her? Since he wasn't around, or at least not visibly so, that left her to draw her own conclusions—and plan her own next steps. She still hadn't discovered what had happened to Isabel but with all the suicides and confessions swirling about, she couldn't believe it had been good.

Lost in thought, she was back at her house before she knew it. She headed straight for her bedroom and the diary. She knew from glancing ahead that the final entry was dated December 16, the day after the battle. For whatever reason—a sense of foreboding perhaps—she'd been putting off reading it, but she knew she was meant to, that the universe had guided her to discover the diary for a reason. Ethan had once told her to look for the answers she sought in her own soul. She figured finishing Isabel's diary, her diary, was about as close to taking his advice as she could come.

December 16, 1862

> Ethan is to be tried for treason, court-martialed by a makeshift military tribunal of his peers as a spy for the Confederacy when nothing could be further from the truth. One of the charges against him is giving aid and comfort to the enemy—me! Even without being privy to all the particulars, I know in my heart this must be Damian's doing. Ever since that day in Pa's office, he has set his cap for me if only out of spite.
>
> My parents have me locked in the attic, for my own good, Pa says. What bitter irony to have my home spared only so that I may be made a prisoner in it. I hear raised voices coming from below, my father's and, yes, that of Damian, though even with my ear pressed to the locked door, I can't rightly make out the words.
>
> There is a knock outside the attic door. "Isabel?" It

is my little sister's voice. For the first time this dark day, a beacon of hope finds its way to my breast.

"Lettie, you must find a way to get the key from Clarice and let me out."

"I can't. If I do, they'll come and drag you away. Mr. Grey says so."

"Lettie, what did you hear? Tell me everything, and don't spare a word."

"It's the sutler, Mr. Grey. He says if Pa doesn't give you to him as his wife, he'll see you hauled off to the Old Capitol Prison and hanged for spying, too."

If Damian's word held sufficient sway to have a Federal Army captain court-martialed and sentenced to hang, surely a Southern woman, a rebel, couldn't hope for better justice.

Lettie went away, promising to return and I sat down and tried in vain to pray and quiet my mind. I can't be certain how long I sat thus, but some time later footfalls sounded up the attic stairs.

The door opened and I ran to it, thinking it was Lettie, but instead Damian stepped inside. "How fares my bride?"

Blinking at the sudden rush of light, I answered with a violent shake of my head. "Ethan will come for me and bear me away. If I'm anyone's wife, it's his."

"Such earthly actions are beyond him now. You see, he's been hanged as all traitors must be. I just came from him, in fact, sitting astride his horse with the noose about his neck."

At that moment, a boom sounded from across the river, not the salvo discharged to announce the commencement of battle but the single cannonade to mark a death by execution.

Speechless, I sank down to the floor, feeling all my will to live draining out of me. "You'll not get away with this, Damian."

Hands in his pockets, he walked over to me. The smile he wore as he stared down on me, I can only describe as demonic. "It appears, my dear Isabel, I already have."

It wasn't until he left that I found the strength to rise. To think that but a year ago my biggest worry was to fret over wearing spectacles. I feel as though I've journeyed a lifetime since then. Looking back, I can't help thinking what a simpleton I was back then. But then how could I know that dying unmarried was hardly the worst that fate might have in store for me?

You, Dear Diary, are blessed to possess no life, only wood-pulped pages and unfeeling ink. You will never suffer the pangs of remorse or of a perfect, soul-true love won only to be lost. Such suffering belongs to we flesh-bound mortals. You will never know that terrible, soul-sick longing that comes when you miss someone so much that your heart twists and your stomach drops and a sick hollowness creeps in, filling you back up but with the absence of things—loneliness, despair, yearning. It's the feeling that comes over you when you own the terrible truth that the person you love best in the world is the one you can never be with, at least not beyond the realm of your dreaming.

My own sweet dream is dead to me for surely by now Ethan is living amongst the angels. As for my future husband—and to call him such makes a mockery of the very institution of marriage—how can I share my bed with a man year upon year knowing that every time he reaches for me, it is with hands covered in my beloved's blood?

I cannot, I will not, submit to live in such a hellish state. Judas's wife I never shall be. I must take my fate into my own hands and pray that my heavenly Father will have mercy on my soul.

Wait for me, Ethan. Wait…

MAGGIE CLOSED THE DIARY before one of the tears might splash onto the page and blur the ink. Isabel must have hidden her diary behind the wall and then found a way to take her life, sowing the seeds of her present life's triumphs and tragedies. Unlike in the past, though, she knew she was strong enough not to make that particular mistake. Her life might not be picture-perfect—soon she would have to say goodbye to Ethan all over again—and yet this short time on earth was precious all the same—too precious to waste arguing. Determined not to let pride get in the way of her happiness, not Ethan's and not hers, either, she set the diary on her nightstand and got up to find him. The strains of what sounded like a harmonica stalled her in her steps.

Backtracking to her wardrobe, Maggie opened the double doors—and screamed.

15

HAP HAD BEEN WATCHING Ethan and Isabel—Maggie—engage in a standoff, each too proud to seek out the other. Being obliged to carry your dismembered head about with you like a jack-o'-lantern made it mighty hard to play matchmaker, but Hap was determined to do what he could. He'd seen how miserable Ethan was and had watched Maggie moping around the house. Someone had to do something to bring those two lovebirds together once and for all, and the way he reckoned it, headless or not, there was nobody else but him.

"Howdy, ma'am. You come for this?" Holding his head by the hair, he handed over the hanger with her little black dress. "Women's dresses have sure as shoot changed. You modern ladies get away with a lot less material than a dance hall girl in my day."

Dragging a hand through her hair, she shook her head. "Let me guess, you're a friend of Ethan's?"

He nodded, or rather the head he held did, and hopped out of the wardrobe. "The captain and I, we go back a long ways. He saved my life more than once, I don't mind telling you. That boy means the world to me. I'd do just about anything for him."

"I see," she said, looking uncomfortable.

"Name's Hap Longacre, and I'm pleased to make your acquaintance, ma'am." Though manners dictated a lady offer her hand first, Hap wasn't about to let a silly old rule get in the way of salvaging a one-hundred-forty-five-year-old true love. Determined to be friendly, he stuck out his free hand.

"Maggie Holliday." Reaching around his head to shake hands, she jumped back when her fingers passed through his energy field as though it were empty air. Cheeks flushing, she said, "Sorry, I suppose I should be used to that by now."

"It takes some getting used to even for us." Seeing she wasn't yet sure what to make of him, he glanced over to the bed. "Mind if I sit a spell? I promise I won't take more than a minute of your time."

"Okay, I...I guess." She followed him over to the bed.

Settling on the edge, he dropped his head in his lap and turned it to face her. "Look, here's what I come to say and I might as well just come out with it and then get outta your hair. Ethan loves you. He loved you when you were Isabel and, if it's purely possible, he loves you even more now that you're Maggie."

She sank down beside him. "I love him, too. But why won't he show himself to me?"

Hap grinned. This was going even better than he'd hoped. "It's called pride and pride always goeth before a fall. In Cap's case, his pride is one of the challenges his soul is supposed to work on conquering but even if it weren't, just because he's dead don't mean he ain't still human. It's hard on a man having to sit back and watch his woman gad about with another fella under his very nose. It hurts him, it hurts him plenty."

That got her attention. He could tell by the way her pupils grew to fill out her eyes all of a sudden, turning them from chocolate brown to coal black. "I'm not *gadding* about with

Richard, I'm dating him, or at least I was. If you must know, I'm going to break up with him."

"Break up with him?" True, he didn't have a chance to converse with all that many folks among the living, but from what he could tell their newfangled phrases seemed to have a lot in common with pig latin.

"I'm going to tell him I don't want to…step out with him anymore."

"Well, why didn't you just say so in the first place?" He dug an elbow into her ribs though of course she didn't feel it, least-ways not beyond a slight stirring of air. "Does Cap know?"

She frowned. "I assumed he did. I mean, he reads all my other thoughts like I'm an open book—make that an open diary."

Hap shrugged. "It all depends on the signals you're sending out. If a mortal's thoughts are tangled in any way—say for instance you're feeling guilty about this Richard fella, maybe even telling yourself you owe him, which you most definitely do not—then the signals can get crossed."

"They can?"

"Yep, same as one of those newfangled telegraph machines you modern folks are always holding up to your ears and jawing into—telephones, I believe you call 'em—only instead of hearing the person you're talking to answering you back, it's some stranger cutting in." Eying her, he added, "You want my advice?"

She arched a dark brow. "Do I have a choice?"

"Humans always have free will. You might say that's part of the problem. But the fact that you can see and hear me tells me the powers that be mean for you to hear what I've got to say."

"And that is?"

"Go find Ethan and tell him what you just told me."

She shook her head. "I don't even know if he's still in the building, so to speak."

Reaching over, he patted her shoulder. "Oh, he's here all right, upstairs in the attic pretending to study the city map he got from something called a Visitors' Center. Go to him, girl, while there's still time. Life's too short—and the afterlife's too damned long—to fritter either away being alone when you don't have to be. Trust me, I should know."

TRUE TO HAP'S WORD, MAGGIE found Ethan in the attic. Seated at the desk, the latest tourist map spread out before him, he didn't look any happier than she was. Catching sight of her, he rose from the chair. "Maggie, what are you doing here?"

"I was hoping to talk to you and a…friend of yours told me I might find you up here."

"Damn it. Hap always was the camp busybody. You'd think after all this time he'd learn to mind his own business." He hesitated. "He didn't scare you, did he?"

"A little at first." She hesitated and then confessed, "Okay, a lot, but after I got past the whole headless thing, he was really sweet." She glanced over to the chair he'd vacated. "Would it be okay if I joined you?"

"Of course. It's your house, after all. I'm just a guest, an unwanted guest, I might add."

"Ethan, that's not true."

"The other day you made it clear you're content with your life as it is. I've done a great deal of thinking since then, and I've come to agree with you on one point at least. I've no right to interfere with your plans." He turned away to stare out the one window, the one with the loose shutter that was responsible for bringing them together again. Sharon's words from the other day came back to her. *Second chances are like catching a falling star or finding a four-leaf clover. When a miracle like that comes your way, it's always for a reason.*

She walked over to stand beside him. Stretching out a hand, she laid it on his shoulder. Instead of passing through his energy field as it had when she'd tried to shake hands with Hap, her palm met with blood-warmed flesh and solid bone. As much as she'd hurt him, he was still expending his precious energy to put on his human body for her.

"Ethan, look at me…please. I don't love Richard. The fact is I don't even like him very much. He's cold and petty and self-absorbed and controlling—the exact opposite of the warm, giving and very sexy man I'm in love with—the very opposite of you."

He turned to face her, and the stark misery in his eyes caught at her heart. "Whatever faults Richard has, at least he's alive."

"Then explain to me why I feel so dead whenever I'm with him—and so very alive whenever I'm with you?"

"Maggie?"

She reached out and took his face between her hands, loving the sandpaper roughness of his jaw against her palms, the way his eyes lit up when she touched him. "Whether I'm Isabel Earnshaw or Maggie Holliday or some crazy combination of the two, I'm the woman who loves you. I see now why none of my past relationships with men ever really worked out. All this time I've been holding back, waiting for you to come for me."

"What about Richard?"

"I'm going to tell him I don't want to see him anymore. No more procrastinating, no more waiting for that perfect time that will never come. Come hell or high water, I'm telling him when we have dinner on Friday."

He took her hand from his cheek and carried it palm up to his lips. Pressing a kiss to the sensitive flesh, he looked up. "I don't suppose you'd consider sending him a telegram?"

"I don't suppose I can—or a Dear John e-mail, either."

"You've finished the diary, haven't you?"

She nodded, wondering if it was telepathy talking or if he'd been watching over her. "Why didn't you tell me Isabel committed suicide? That is what happened, isn't it?" Silly perhaps to mourn a woman who'd been dead one hundred forty-five years and yet when that woman was you, or rather had been you, it was hard not to care. "Answer me, Ethan. Please, I have the right to know."

He hesitated as if weighing his words. "You took your life on the eve of the day I was hanged. It was a fatal dose of laudanum administered by your own hand."

An overdose—the similarity to her close call with the medicine cabinet sent a chill sweeping through her. She shook her head, amazed at how life, or rather lives, had a way of repeating themselves. "I always assumed Isabel died of a broken heart or in childbirth or in some other…I don't know, *natural* way."

"Unfortunately you took matters into your own hands and hurried things along. You went to sleep and never woke up."

With a lump in her throat, she asked, "Why weren't you waiting for me on…you know, the other side?" Instead of death parting them, it would have been a case of death bringing them together again, a happy ending of sorts—only for whatever reason, it hadn't worked out that way.

He shook his head. "The universe operates according to a strict set of rules. Each earthly embodiment a soul undertakes provides a set of experiences designed specifically for learning particular lessons that present the optimal challenge for that unique being. Just as we can't escape our earthly problems by running away, we can't escape them by hastening our deaths, either. You took your life to escape your future as Damian Grey's wife. In your grief, you imagined killing yourself would be a means of reaching me. But the opposite was true."

Oh, my God. She dragged a hand through her hair. It was so much to take in, so much to believe. "Are you saying I'm the reason we can't be together, that our souls have been separated for one hundred forty-five years!"

He graced her with a gentle smile. "Don't be so hard on yourself. Purgatory isn't an entirely bad place. Besides, Damian's black soul bears the brunt of the blame. He took my life and then drove you to end yours."

"I found his will, by the way. Actually Carol at the library found it for me. At the end he confessed that he'd framed you for treason and caused you to be hanged."

He nodded. "I know he did. I haunted him for that very purpose, hoping to at least clear my name. But by that time, there was no one left living to care."

She shook her head. "I've cost you not only your physical life but your afterlife, as well. I wouldn't blame you if you hated me."

His arm went around her, hugging her close. "I could never hate you. Even though your actions were misguided, your motive was love and your heart was and is as pure as the mountain stream I fished as a boy. No, Belle, I could never hate you. I'd gladly wander in limbo as you call it until the end of time for the chance to be with you like this once every fifty-year earth cycle."

"Oh, Ethan." She lifted her head and shifted to face him. "I don't know what I ever did to deserve you, not one hundred forty-five years ago and not today, but I'm glad, so very glad, to have you in my life for however long that turns out to be. Whatever happens to us, I'll still be thankful every day for our having this time together."

16

SEATED ACROSS FROM RICHARD at the white cloth-covered table in Claiborne's main dining room on Friday night, Maggie was beginning to feel frustrated. Every time she opened her mouth to get the breakup rolling, a server came by to refill their water glasses, check on their wine or offer them more bread.

Dapper in a dark Italian suit and silk tie with his blond hair combed low over his forehead to cover most of his bandage, Richard looked as though he was on the mend from his previous week's ordeal. "Are those new?"

Lost in thought, Maggie looked up from the filet she'd been pushing around her plate. From the single bite she'd taken, she knew it was excellent but no matter how fancy the food or fine the wine, when you were sharing them with the wrong person, grade A steak might as well be cut-rate hamburger. "Pardon me?"

Spearing a scallop on the end of his fork, he gestured toward her ears. "Those earrings. I've never seen you wear them before."

"Oh." Maggie reached up and touched one of the amber ear bobs. "They were a gift from a friend." Her *friend* had given her another, more recent gift over the past week—a tintype portrait of himself similar to the one taken of Isabel.

As much as she loved her earrings, the photograph of Ethan was her most precious possession.

Scowling, Richard looked about the room. "Where is that damned waiter?" He picked up the cloth-wrapped bottle of chardonnay and started to pour more wine into her glass.

"No, thank you." Maggie glanced at her half-full glass. Though she'd ordered a beef entrée, he'd chosen a white wine to complement his mixed seafood grill.

"As George Washington said, 'Waste not, want not.'" He splashed wine into her glass anyway.

"It was Benjamin Franklin, actually." Feeling more defiant than tense, she pushed the wineglass away.

"What did you say?"

She thought about letting the subject drop—it was such a small thing considering all the crap she'd taken from him over the past six months—and yet suddenly it seemed symbolic and so very important to win.

"'Waste not, want not' isn't a quote from Washington. It's from Franklin, his *Poor Richard's Almanac,* actually."

"Really? Are you sure about that?" His cold tone confirmed he didn't care to be challenged. "I'm certain it was Washington."

She opened her mouth to remind him that American History was her field, after all, when Leslie Fallon, a British faculty member from the history department at Mary Washington sidled up to their table, her peaches and cream complexion offset by a pale pink chiffon dress that unfortunately clashed with her shoulder-length carrot-red curls.

Addressing Maggie though her slanted green gaze fell on Richard, she said, "I was having a drink in the bar with some mates when I spotted you. I didn't want to leave without saying hello. Oh, but you're in the middle of dinner," she added as though only just noticing their entrée plates and half-full bottle of wine. "Carry on, then." She turned as if to go.

"Why not sit down and join us for dessert?" Richard interrupted, shifting over in his chair.

Maggie didn't particularly care for Leslie. In their brief interaction at her faculty interview and then at the welcome-aboard lunch, she'd thought the woman shallow, even a bit sly. But looking at the way Richard's face had lit up, it occurred to her that Leslie might be the answer to her prayer, or at least her immediate problem.

Leslie didn't require much arm-twisting. She had her bar bill transferred to their tab, hailed their waiter for a third chair and happily squeezed into their table for two. At Richard's insistence, coffee and dessert—Southern fruit cobbler and coconut custard pie—turned into more coffee accompanied by a round of brandies. Watching them interact from the sidelines, chatting in apparent oblivion to the waitstaff sweeping floors and putting up chairs around their table, Maggie decided that Richard and Leslie just might be perfect for one another. Two attractive, self-absorbed people oblivious to anyone's needs but their own—talk about a match made in heaven. If it wouldn't come off as pimping, she'd ask for Leslie's home phone number—to give to Richard.

They ended up closing the place down, the entrance door bolting behind them and the outside lights switching off. Richard insisted they walk Leslie to her car. Watching the redhead slide behind the wheel of her candy-apple-red Volkswagen Bug, Maggie realized the only thing her backpedaling had accomplished was to delay the inevitable. Instead of blowing the whistle on their relationship, all she'd blown was her chance to break up in a public place where he wouldn't be inclined to make a scene. Now she'd have to deal with him back at her house or on the short drive there; otherwise, he'd be spending the night.

As much as she hated confrontation, especially the no-holds-barred variety with no one else around to serve as a buffer, bringing Richard back to her bed was simply not an option. The ghostly presence with whom she'd been spending her nights was the only man with whom she could imagine being intimate.

Predictably Richard lit up before they got in the car. Slipping into the passenger-side seat, she rolled down her window and looked out to avoid the smoke. As much as she wanted to get the weight of those yet-to-be-spoken words off her chest, gut instinct had her holding back until they got to her place—to Ethan. Thinking back to the previous week's episode in her dining room, she decided having a sexy supernatural on her side couldn't hurt.

"Earth to Maggie." Richard's voice snapped her out of her reverie.

"Sorry?" She turned to see him pull the keys from the car's ignition. They were back at her house already. Time to face the music—and inside her head, it was playing taps.

Gaze dropping to her breasts, he reached across the seat for her hand. "You looked like you were a million miles away just then."

Pulling out of his reach, she turned to unbuckle her seat belt. Not a million miles—but perhaps one hundred forty-five years. "I guess I've got a lot on my mind." Boy, was that an understatement.

Stomach tightening, she led the way up her front steps. Willie Whiskers was waiting inside the front door. Grateful for the support, she scooped him up in her arms. "How's Mommie's precious boy this evening. Hungry, hmm?"

Pulling the door closed, Richard scowled. "Really, Maggie, you treat that cat like it's a person. It's an animal for Christ's sake." He slung his keys onto her marble-topped hallway table.

"Willie's not an *it*, he's a he. And yes, I realize he's an animal—the extra two legs and the tail are a huge tip-off. He also happens to be a living being who loves me unconditionally."

"Whatever. Just keep him away from me."

"Not a problem." And it wouldn't be because in a few short minutes Richard, not Willie, would be out of the picture—permanently.

She carried Willie out into the kitchen where she fed him. When she came out again, she found Richard making himself at home in her living room, loosened tie dangling around his neck and a snifter of Baileys cradled in one hand.

Plopping down on the couch, he leaned over to the coffee table papered with copies from her library expedition. "What's all this?" He picked up a photocopied survey plot and frowned. "It doesn't look like your dissertation data to me." His voice held an edge of disapproval that used to cow her but now had her clenching her jaw.

Coming up beside him, she snatched the paper from his hand. "That's because it isn't. I'm doing some research on the house…for fun," she added out of habit, and then reminded herself she didn't have to explain herself to him anymore. Indeed, she never really had.

But Richard wasn't so easily put off. "I didn't realize you had that much time on your hands." He leaned over, liquor dribbling off the side of his glass.

Looking down, she saw several fat drops of Baileys atop the tintype of Ethan. Heart lurching, she grabbed for the picture. "Richard, watch what you're doing. That tintype is almost one hundred fifty years old." She snatched up a handful of tissues to blot the photograph dry, not sure if that was the right thing to do.

"Relax. If you want, I'll bet you can walk into any antique store here and get a handful of old photographs of dead people."

Once Ethan crossed back over to the other side, the tintype would be all she had of him. It was her most precious possession, and Richard had ruined it like he ruined everything else good in her life. He couldn't have hurt her worse if he'd taken a baseball bat and gone room to room smashing things. She snatched the photograph out of his hand. The alcohol in the cordial had acted like acid eating away at the surface image. Fortunately Ethan's face had survived unscathed but the impression of his broad shoulders and big, beautiful hands folded in repose had been eaten away.

Richard jumped up. "Jesus, Maggie, I don't see why you're getting so upset. Whoever he is, make that was, the guy lived and died more than a hundred years ago."

"His name is—was—Ethan O'Malley. He was a captain in the Union Army of the Potomac who was court-martialed and executed the day after the First Battle of Fredericksburg. But beyond any of that, he was once a living, breathing human being, a human being with hopes and dreams and feelings just like you and I have."

Richard certainly had preferences but as to actual feelings, she had her doubts. Feelings required having some sort of depth of soul, and she didn't think she'd ever met a more shallow man.

He backed up to stare at her. "Okay, okay, I get it. There's no need to be hostile."

"I'm not being hostile. I'm being honest. After all those therapy sessions where you kept pushing me to get in touch with my true feelings, I'd think you'd appreciate that."

The brazenness of her tone shocked both of them. In the past, her usual response was to button her lip and quietly seethe. But this felt better—pretty damned good in fact. Speaking up for herself wasn't nearly as hard as she'd imagined it would be.

He stared at her as though she'd grown a second head. "What's gotten into you? You're talking like you're fixated on the guy, maybe even hot for him. Really, Margaret, necrophilia doesn't become you."

He was back to calling her Margaret again, which meant he was pissed off. But like Rhett Butler in the final scene of the film version of *Gone with the Wind,* Maggie frankly didn't give a damn.

"Don't be disgusting, Richard. Ethan O'Malley's is a fascinating story ending in the Federal court-martial of an innocent man. I'm not sure yet, but I think it might have potential for a book." It was the first time she'd voiced that hope even to herself but now that she had, why not? Exonerating Ethan once and for all—if they couldn't be together in life, then at least she could give him that timeless token of her love.

"A book? You've got to be kidding me." Richard threw back his head and laughed, the cutting sound slicing through her like an electric carving knife. "At best, you'd be lucky to squeeze a journal article out of it. Even then it sounds pretty sketchy."

"Ethan's story deserves to be told—and heard. He deserves a broader audience than a handful of academics subscribing to some boring journal."

Richard's mouth twisted into an ugly leer. "Ethan does, does he?" When she didn't answer, he said, "Is this what it takes to get that dry pussy of yours wet? Costumes, props? Am I supposed to dress up like some crackpot reenactor to turn you on?"

The anger pouring out of him stunned her more than his vulgarity. She looked him in the eye and instead of feeling guilty or unsure as she might have in the past, she was one hundred percent certain of what she had to do. "I tried to tell you earlier but the fact is, I don't want to see you anymore."

He must have sensed she was serious because he backed down. "Maggie, calm down. What I just said, I was out of line, but there's no reason to blow it out of proportion."

Fisting her hands on her hips, she faced him down. "Out of line, is that what you call it?" Thank God she'd never gotten around to giving him a house key; otherwise, she'd have to worry about getting the locks changed.

"All right, you win. It was completely inappropriate. But, baby, we've been through so much together. When you were ill, I was the one there for you, picking up the pieces."

It was the old guilt trick only this time, it didn't have a prayer of working. "Oh, you were there all right, there right on top of me. I trusted you, and you took advantage of me. For the past six months, you've taken every opportunity to psych me out whenever it looked like I might be getting strong enough to step out on my own. Ever since I first told you I'd signed a contract on this house, you've been nothing but negative—make that vicious—even though you knew moving to Fredericksburg has been my dream for a long time. Well, guess what? The abuse stops here and now. I don't need your kind of *help* anymore, *doctor*. I'm beginning to see I never did."

He slammed his drink glass down, setting ice cubes flying. "You ungrateful little bitch. You'd be in some hospital psych ward wearing four point restraints if it weren't for me."

She'd confided her close call with swallowing the pills when she was still seeing him for therapy. So much for doctor-patient confidentiality—another of the many trust factors he'd breached. "You can insult me all you want, throw out every put-down in the book, but it's not going to work this time. We're over." She pointed to the door. "If you've drunk too much to drive safely, you can leave your car here for the night and get a room at the Kenmore Inn. It's just a block up on Princess Anne, and I know for a fact they have some vacancies."

Ignoring her offer, he said, "It's not over until I say so."

She swung around, not because of what he'd just said but because she didn't want to miss his expression when she told him to fuck off. "I don't need your permission, Richard. You can't bully me into staying with you anymore."

"I'm warning you, Maggie, I don't give you permission to break up with me." He took a step toward her, menacingly close. He was a small man compared to Ethan but as she'd learned the previous week, his lean body held a wiry strength.

Steeling herself not to back down, Maggie pulled out the trump card she'd hoped she wouldn't have to play. "Is that so? I seriously doubt the district's medical review board would agree with you. I would imagine having sex with a client would be grounds for a malpractice suit. And I also suspect I may not be the first female client you've tackled on that therapy couch of yours." She'd been fishing, but his dropping jaw confirmed the hook had hit home. "You never know, the state medical review board might rule to revoke your license to practice."

Looking as though she'd punched him in the gut, he backed away. "But, Maggie —"

"No buts. Get out, Richard, and don't ever try to contact me again."

17

"BRAVA." THE CLAPPING brought Maggie swinging around to see Ethan standing in the center of the open pocket doors leading into the dining room. This evening's ensemble was rolled-up shirtsleeves and buckskin breeches. "You were splendid." His breath was a warm caress on her nape, his scent and warmth closing around her like an embrace.

Her breath caught in her throat not because he'd startled her, but because she was so very glad to see him. Smiling, she walked toward him. "You were watching me again."

It wasn't a question or a problem. His dropping in and out didn't bother her as it once would have, a sure sign she was getting used to having him around. What she would do when their time together came to a close she couldn't say, but for now she wanted him, just wanted him.

He didn't bother to deny it. "I've never had anyone defend me so fiercely before." A smile, or at least the ghost of one, hovered on the corners of his sexy mouth. "I wish you'd been at my court-martial. You just might have talked them out of hanging me."

I wish I, or rather Isabel, had been there, too.

I wish I could go back with you now before you fade away for good. Dead or alive, resting in peace or walking the line between life and death, either way, I'll love you any way, every way, I can.

His smile dimmed along with his eyes. "Don't wish your life away, Maggie. It goes by faster than you think."

"You're reading my thoughts again." His clairvoyance used to drive her crazy but it didn't anymore. Instead she found it comforting, almost as if the universe had gifted her with a kindred spirit. Or maybe that was what soul mates really were.

"Guilty as charged."

He smiled again though the sentiment didn't reach his eyes, and she wondered if he was thinking back to his trial. Given her increasing attunement where he was concerned, she was almost certain he must be.

"You look beautiful, by the way." His gaze skimmed the length of her, and she realized she'd worn the little black dress not for Richard but for afterward when she'd come back home, home to Ethan. "How do you feel?"

She paused to think about that. How *did* she feel? "Relieved, lighter than I've felt in some time, maybe ever—and hungry. I'm starving, actually."

He smiled at that. "I can have Hap rustle you up something. He was the best camp cook we ever had but, being dead, he doesn't have much call to put his cooking skills to work. What would you like? Pheasant under glass, squab roasted with chestnuts—"

"Actually, I was thinking I'd just nuke—I mean, heat up—my dinner leftovers."

As much as she liked Ethan's friend—and the whole headless thing was beginning to grow on her—she didn't want to share Ethan, not tonight. Breaking up with Richard counted as a major milestone for them both. Whatever the future might bring or not bring, this night, this moment, belonged to the two of them.

"I'd be glad to share, but I don't suppose you can join me?"

Ethan shook his head. "My temporary embodiment doesn't

extend to eating or imbibing, but it would give me great pleasure to bear you company."

Thinking of the very great pleasure he'd given her on more than one occasion, Maggie felt her knees go weak. Grateful for the dining room chair he held out, she sank into the seat.

From the head of the table, he said, "I've been saving a case of some of the best French Bordeaux ever seized in a Federal blockade. Unless dining customs have changed dramatically, a full-bodied red wine should serve as a suitable accompaniment to beef."

"That sounds lovely." It did but then as long as he looked at her like he was doing, his gaze warm with equal parts love and lust, he could have offered her unfiltered river sludge from the Rappahannock and she would have sipped it as though it were nectar.

A blink of his eye brought a wine bottle and a crystal goblet materializing onto the end of the polished mahogany table. Watching him pour, Maggie slipped off her high heels, the shoes knocking against the uncovered floor.

Looking up from massaging her aching arches, she said, "I hope you don't mind. I know ladies in 1862 didn't kick off their shoes, but the truth is, my feet are killing me." His gaze dropped to her feet, and she was suddenly reminded that a woman's ankles were considered highly erotic and forbidden territory in his day. Feeling herself blushing, she reached for the wineglass he handed her. "It's a good thing I didn't stick to my original plan and break up with Richard at the restaurant. I'm not sure I could have walked all the way back in these heels."

He lifted his gaze to her face. "I'm glad, too. This way I could be here to watch over you." Though he couldn't drink, he'd filled a glass for himself, which he raised to her.

The crystal met with a soft clink. Warmed by his admission, Maggie took a sip of the excellent wine, savoring the subtle flavors and the warm glow of his presence before asking, "You were watching over me the whole time?"

Setting his untouched wine on the table's edge, he nodded. "I was, indeed I have been since the day you were born, or rather reborn. Watching and waiting and praying to the powers that be for the chance to come to you in a way that you could see and feel me, too."

"There have been times over the years when I thought I sensed a…presence. When I was little, my mother used to say it was my guardian angel watching over me. Are you saying that all along, it was you?"

He nodded, his expression solemn. "I don't have a halo or wings, and I certainly can't lay claim to being any angel, even less so a saint, but I love you, Maggie, with all my being, all my soul. I always have and, come what may, I always shall."

Looking up at him, Maggie felt the power of her feelings washing over her like a cleansing wave. "I love you, too, so very much. Please forgive me for not believing you. I promise I'll never doubt you or us again." She pushed back her chair and stood.

"Maggie?"

"It's my turn to show you, Ethan. To make you believe."

Praying there was time yet to show him just how heartfelt every word was, she walked toward him. Standing before him, wearing her heart on her sleeve and her love in her eyes, she reached behind her, caught the tab of her dress's zipper and brought it very slowly down.

UNGRATEFUL BITCH.

With boxwood branches digging into his crotch and his gaze riveted to Maggie's dining room window, Richard felt his alcohol-fueled temper bubbling to the boiling point. The sexy scene playing out inside the house was straight out of a porn movie. And though from where he crouched he couldn't see the man with her, he also knew Maggie wasn't the sort of woman who stripped down to her bra and panties in the middle of her formal dining room by herself. No, those slow, salacious movements meant she had an audience of one there with her, an audience that didn't include him—at least not by invitation.

Cursing the fucking foliage that blocked him from having a clearer view, he replayed the past ten minutes' roller-coaster ride in his mind. After she'd broken up with him and thrown him out, he'd gotten into his car and headed out to the interstate. He'd just turned onto Route 3 when it struck him—he wasn't going to let her get away with it. Slamming on the brakes, he swung a hard left onto William Street and circled back into town. Even on a Saturday night, the historic district was as dead as a cemetery. He parked the Porsche on a side street and snuck around to the back of Maggie's house. The inside lights were still on, including those on the downstairs level. She hadn't gotten around to pulling the blinds on her back windows, and coming up on the house, he could see straight through. Hunkering down behind the boxwood, he saw Maggie standing by the dining room table, face animated and glass of wine in hand. He couldn't be sure but he thought her mouth was moving and she was gesturing with her free hand to one of the empty chairs. A second wineglass was set out on the table. The situation was even more disgusting than he'd thought. Not only was she fucking someone else, but apparently she'd had the guy hidden in the house the whole time! Her lover must have heard every word of their breakup, including her threatening to report him to the medical review board. Judging from the satisfied smile breaking over her face, the radiance in her eyes, the two of them must be sharing not only a celebratory bottle of wine but also a good laugh at his expense. Bitch!

In breaking up with him, she'd struck not only a nerve but the heart of his ego, not just as a psychiatrist but more fundamentally as a man. No matter how well-developed his muscles got from those pounding workouts at the gym, the fact was his love muscle was modest…okay, small. That someone as gorgeous and brilliant as him was saddled with such an embarrassment just wasn't fair.

Buying that vibrator had been a huge sacrifice on his part, an act of selfless love. Of course, he'd also gotten off more than once envisioning how she'd look with a bubble-gum-pink dildo sticking out of her pussy, her long legs spread wide, her back arched, her tight ass lifting off the bed. Even now when he wanted nothing more than to wring her slender neck and pound the smile off her pretty face, he felt the hard-on tenting his trousers.

If only she'd cooperated, the dildo could also have been put to practical use. He'd planned on taking a picture of her playing with herself, maybe more than one. Similar to the mirror exercise he'd recommended, the premise for the photo shoot would have been to free her libido from her overzealous superego—blah, blah, blah—but in reality he would have held on to the photos as insurance against her ever trying to walk out or fuck him over. It might be 2007 but American society hadn't entirely purged itself of its Puritan roots. No parents were going to pay big bucks college tuition to have a nymphomaniac teach history to their kid.

Squinting, he made out what looked like a man's jacket hanging over the back of one of her dining room chairs. He was no expert—history bored him—but it looked a lot like the old style military uniform the dead guy in the photograph had been wearing. So it was a reenactor she was fucking. For whatever reason, that struck him as especially sick. If he wasn't afraid she might slap him with an assault charge, he'd go back inside and show her just what all his working out had made of him.

Of course, if he confronted her now, he'd have to deal with her lover, too, and judging by the breadth of that jacket, he must be a pretty big guy. Wondering if he was large everywhere, Richard swallowed hard. A moment later the blind came down, blocking his view.

That was okay, though. He could be patient when he had to be, and he'd get back at Maggie in his own sweet time. She wasn't going anywhere, certainly not tonight. In the interim, he would watch and wait. Sooner or later, his chance would come and then he'd seize it to hit her where it would hurt her the most. By the time he was finished, Maggie wouldn't be able to show her pretty face in her precious Fredericksburg—or anywhere else. She'd be lucky to get a job teaching a survey history course at a community college. For the first time since he'd stormed out her front door, Richard found his smile.

"Better cover that tight ass of yours, Mags. Paybacks can be hell."

MAGGIE STEPPED OUT OF the puddle of black dress at her feet. Wearing a black lace bustier, thong, hose and garters, she opened her arms.

Ethan swallowed hard, his throat tight with emotion. She was so bright and beautiful, so truehearted and good. That he'd found her again was nothing less than a miracle. He couldn't see how he could possibly let her go a second time.

As much as he'd loved her as Isabel, as his thoroughly modern Maggie, she was doubly dear.

She slipped her hands about his neck and looked up at him with shining eyes. "Stepping into your arms always feels like coming home. If this is what it means to be haunted, then I hope you'll haunt me for the rest of my days."

If only it might be so. Though he'd yet to find Damian, he could feel his energy ebbing by the hour. Ere long, he'd be called to go back, he could feel it.

He cocked his head to the side and smiled. "How is it I'm the one who's the ghost when it's you who's haunted me all this long while?" He planted his hands on her supple waist and pulled her to him.

"You certainly don't feel like a ghost." Her smile turning wicked, she slid a hand down between them. "This is your real body, isn't it? What I'm touching is real flesh and bone. And this?" She settled her palm over his erection.

Her kneading fingers were a slice of heaven on earth. He bit back a groan. "Yes, that's real, too."

"This time I want to see you, Ethan, every beautiful inch of you." She reached up and trailed gentle fingers down the side of his wrapped neck. "Please."

The ligature scars on his neck were embedded on his soul's energy imprint as well as his mortal body, his cross to bear until he found a way to make peace with his past. As much as he hated having his soul branded with the constant reminder of his violent, unjust death, the aftermath could have been so much worse. The hangman had been a fair hand at his trade and his actual dying had been accomplished with a quick, clean snapping of the vertebrae. Had he endured the agony of swinging for an hour or more, his neck would have stretched like a game goose hung out to dry. Still, the abraded flesh wasn't a pretty sight. He'd had almost a century and a half to get used to looking at it, but to Maggie it would seem startling. He didn't want to frighten her or, worse yet, suffer her pity or disgust.

"Be careful what you wish. You might regret asking once you have it."

She shook her head. "I already know you were court-martialed for treason and that the penalty was death by hanging."

Fixing his gaze on hers, he said, "I didn't care what they did to me. I just wanted to see you one last time."

Tears filled her eyes, spilling over onto her cheeks. "I wanted to come. I tried to come. Oh, God, Ethan, I tried. I did." She stopped in midsentence, realizing as did he that she'd spoken of Isabel in the first person.

Holding her gaze, he reached up and began to slowly untie the elaborate knot. "Did you know this particular style of neck cloth fold is called a waterfall? The Englishman Beau Brummel made it the fashion during the Prince Regent's day, and it held for decades after his death."

She answered with a watery smile. "Some things are timeless, the good things at least."

He unwound the cloth and then pulled it free, laying bare not only his neck for her but his soul, as well. "Very well, then, only remember I warned you."

"Oh, Ethan." She leaned in and brushed her lips over the ruined flesh.

Despite his promise to himself to be stoic, he jerked back. Until that moment, the last physical sensation he'd felt on his throat had been the horrors of strangulation. "I don't want your pity."

Solemn-eyed, she looked up at him and shook her head. "Pity, is that what you think I'm feeling right now?" When he didn't answer, she reached for his hand, drawing it down to the juncture of her thighs. "Touch me, Ethan. Touch me and tell me if this feels like pity to you?"

The thong she wore had a slit at the crotch. To his delight, the edges of the lacey opening were already drenched with her dew. She was warm and wet, supple and ready, and when he stroked her, his exploring digit slid straight in.

Clenching her inner muscles around him, she leaned forward and whispered in his ear, "Do you feel how hot for you I am, how wet?"

"Yes." Drowning in her heat and musk, he caught her mouth with his and slid a second finger inside.

Like the fairy-tale maiden induced to kiss the frog prince, the curse—this facet of it at least—was broken. Forgetting about his throat, forgetting everything but her, he braced his hands on her waist and lifted her onto the edge of the mahogany table.

She opened her legs wide for him, her firm thighs creamy white as milk, her pretty pink sex framed in black lace, looking as succulent as a summertime peach. Stepping inside her open legs, Ethan knew there would be no need for words between them that night and perhaps not ever again. Theirs was a perfect understanding, a perfect love, a union strong enough to transcend the physicality of time and space.

Maggie braced her hands on his shoulders, her eyes never leaving his face. *Come inside me, my love. Make me yours in every way.*

Holding her gaze, he released his trouser flap and entered her in a single slow, sweet thrust. *You're already mine, sweetheart, as I am yours. Until we can find a way to be together, I'll haunt you every chance I get—until the end of time.*

18

ETHAN VANISHED AFTER their lovemaking in the dining room. Maggie went into the kitchen for a glass of water and when she came out he was gone. Panic hit her when he didn't answer her call—had he gone back for good, *crossed over,* as he called it, or had he simply needed to disappear long enough to gather more energy? Her gaze fell on the sprig of fresh lavender he'd left on the table for her, and she relaxed fractionally. Picking up the herb, she held the vibrant purple flower up to her face and breathed in its calming scent. Surely leaving the sprig behind was Ethan's way of telling her their earth cycle together wasn't yet over. He would find a way to come to her again, but for how much longer?

Maggie couldn't say for certain what possessed her but the next afternoon she found herself walking down Caroline Street toward the Visitors' Center. She knew it wasn't only the opportunity to play tourist in her own town that led her there. She'd been coming to Fredericksburg for almost a decade and had seen most, if not all, of the attractions at least once if not several times. Still, in spite of feeling drained, she was way too wired to focus on finishing her dissertation or getting any home projects out of the way. Instead, she'd found herself walking the house's big, empty rooms wondering when or if she would see Ethan again, which was making her crazy—

literally. Maybe a little hometown R & R was just what she needed?

The Visitors' Center was housed in a neat, Federal-style brick building at the far end of Caroline Street. According to the bronze plaque marking the entrance, it was originally a confectioner's shop. Though Maggie had passed it many times, she'd never gone inside, but for some reason, she felt compelled to do so now.

The moment she crossed the threshold, the headache hit her like a hammer to the back of her head. Tension, it had to be; either that or she was coming down with one hell of a case of the flu. Until recently she'd never had a problem with headaches, but the past week must be making up for lost time. This episode was the worst yet. If it didn't pass, she'd have to stop into Goolrick's Pharmacy on her way home and pick up some more Motrin.

The brief orientation film playing in the minitheater at the building's back was pleasant and informative, but as American history was her discipline, it offered nothing new. Wondering why she was even there, she walked back out to the front. She was scanning the pamphlet section for some attraction she may have missed seeing when she glanced through the window and spotted a woman in Civil War–era dress standing on the sidewalk outside.

Maggie started, wondering if she were seeing a ghost—another ghost—and then smiled at her own foolishness. The woman's full striped skirt and straw hat looked authentic enough but she was also wearing lipstick and modern-day high-heeled shoes. She must work as a tour guide or docent in one of the many downtown historical attractions. *Yes, Maggie, there are indeed such persons as real, live reenactors. Not everyone in period dress is dead, after all.*

Ever curious, Maggie walked up to the counter. Catching the eye of the blue-haired lady working behind it, she asked, "Who is that costumed lady standing outside?"

"That's Mavis Trumble, or Judith Beaton, as she prefers to be called."

"Judith Beaton? I'm sorry, but I don't know who that is."

The woman smiled. "*Was,* actually. Judith Beaton was a schoolteacher who lived in Fredericksburg during the Civil War. You can purchase copies of her diary in the Fredericksburg Area Museum gift shop and some of the local antique shops carry them, as well. Mavis has really gotten into her character. She gives a wonderful walking tour of the city. Nobody knows Civil War history better than Mavis—at least nobody still alive," she added with a wink.

"Thanks. It sounds great. I'll have to check it out."

Leaving the center, Maggie walked up to Mavis, who was chatting with the carriage tour hostler. Turning to Maggie, she said, "Hi there. May I help you?"

Still wondering what she was doing, Maggie admitted, "I'm a history professor up at the college, or at least I will be once the fall semester starts. I'm also playing with the idea of writing a nonfiction book about a Union officer who was killed here during the Civil War, court-martialed actually. The lady inside recommended I take one of your walking tours."

"You must mean Captain Ethan O'Malley?"

Startled, Maggie said, "Why, yes, how did you know?"

Mavis seemed to find the question amusing. Breaking into a smile, she said, "Oh, honey, it's one of Fredericksburg's oldest ghost stories, a classic tragic love triangle. Captain O'Malley was hanged by his fellow Federals for passing on information to Lee that helped the Confederates win the 1862 battle. I can't say I've looked much into that—it's the human angle on the legend that always interests me."

A cold draft trickled down Maggie's back. Having a feeling she knew the answer already, she asked, "What might that be?"

"He was seeing a town girl in secret, which didn't look too good for him once the charges were brought. Legend has it that they met by chance in this very store." Mavis gestured her gloved hand toward the Visitors' Center.

Feeling another chill run through her, though the thermometer was already pushing toward the high seventies, Maggie said, "But this was a confectioner's shop, wasn't it? I read the historical marker before I went in."

The slight frown creasing Mavis's forehead suggested she didn't take kindly to being second-guessed. "Originally, yes, but remember, Fredericksburg was chartered in 1728. During the Civil War, Caroline was Main Street and this shop housed a dry goods store."

Maggie's heart slammed into her chest. "Mr. Potter's mercantile. You mean, the rumor was false? The Yankees didn't burn it after all!"

Mavis stared at her for a moment. "Why, you've got me there. I can't say I recall the store owner's name, but you could certainly check the deed and find out."

Blushing at her outburst, Maggie suddenly understood. Ethan was always telling her there was no such thing as random chance, that all actions and reactions on earth, both good and evil, served a higher purpose, and she sensed her casual stroll was no exception, that for some reason, she'd been *guided* here.

Mavis picked up the thread of her ghost story. "Captain O'Malley's sweetheart killed herself that very day after hearing the single shot from across the river in Stafford Hills announcing his death. Some say she was driven to swallow an overdose of laudanum—that's a tincture of opium and perfectly legal back in the 1860s—because she was brokenhearted over losing her lover. Others say it was to keep from marrying another Yank, a civilian who traveled with the Union troops and had his eye on her. I've always thought it was probably a bit of both."

Maggie didn't mention having found Isabel's diary. She still meant to donate it to a historical archive collection, but until she figured out the best home for it, she wanted to keep it to herself. Holding on to it was like holding on to Ethan—neither really belonged to her and yet she wasn't ready to let go, at least not yet.

Mavis's voice pulled her back to the present. "It's said she still haunts the attic of a Caroline Street house where she killed herself—one of the private homes, not a house museum. Who's to say whether or not that's the case, but it's always struck me as odd that nobody ever lived in that house for more than a generation. Nowadays with folks moving so much, it makes some sense, but back in the old days, houses tended to stay in the same family year after year."

Maggie had it on the tip of her tongue to tell Mavis that she'd bought that very house, but again she held back. The last thing she needed in the middle of figuring out her future was to have walking tour groups peeking inside her windows. Being head over heels in love with a ghost felt like enough of a challenge.

Instead she said, "I'd like to take your tour. Where do I sign up?"

"Right here with me. We have two versions of the daytime walk and then there's a special ghost walk I give once a week—more often as we get closer to Halloween. In fact, I'm giving it tonight. Which would you like? I can give you a brochure with the descriptions of the sites included in each." She indicated the straw basket of brochures looped over her wrist.

"That won't be necessary. The ghost tour, definitely."

Mavis smiled. "Good enough. We leave from the front of the Visitors' Center at seven o'clock sharp and end up in the old Federal cemetery. The full moon tonight should make it perfect."

HARMONICA MUSIC ANNOUNCED Hap was nearby. This time it was the soft strains of "Home, Sweet Home" filtering into the attic chamber, the gentle, plaintive melody matching Ethan's wistful mood. These precious days with Maggie, of getting to know her present-day incarnation and falling in love with her all over again, had been a homecoming in so many ways, not just a reunion of physical bodies but a reunion of souls.

"Whatcha got there, Cap?"

Ethan looked up from the faded hair ribbon he held to Hap sitting on the rafter beside him. "I guess you could call it a memento."

The ribbon was Isábel's from 1862, the very one she'd used to tie together the lavender for their bridal bower. When he'd returned from making love to Maggie last night, he'd found it lying on the floor along with a small pile of dust and pollen. The century-old-plus nosegay had finally succumbed to the pull of time. Given his situation, that struck him as sadly symbolic.

"Thinking about going back, are you?"

Ethan nodded. It wasn't as though he had a choice. Lately each subsequent embodiment was taking more and more of a toll on him. He could feel his energy field weakening by the hour. Not even his lovemaking sessions with Maggie, magically fulfilling as they were, sufficed to bolster him for long. Last night after they'd made love on her dining room table, he'd barely had enough strength left to get himself back to the attic before he collapsed.

But what really worried him more so than his own weakening was the toll he was taking on Maggie. She might not know it yet but the physical fatigue and headaches she was starting to experience weren't due to what modern-day people called *stress*. Being with him was beginning to siphon her energy, her life force. So far her symptoms were mild but if he stayed on, it was only going to get worse.

"I'm going to have to go back soon, and when I do Maggie will be heartbroken—again."

He held back from adding that the knife cut both ways. He'd endured one hundred forty-five earth years' worth of heartache since losing her the first time. Now that he was about to be called away from her again, he sincerely hoped all that heartache hadn't been wasted.

If he'd accomplished only one thing this earth cycle, he'd made sure it was that no matter what life dished out to her, Isabel—Maggie—wasn't going to make the same mistake again. She wasn't going to try and take her own life. Maybe he hadn't succeeded in coming to terms with Damian, but at least he was leaving the woman he loved in a stronger, better place.

Some days being dead could be a hell of a lot of work.

Hap turned the head in his lap to the side and looked up at him. "You're not just sweet on her, are you? You love her, don't you, boy?"

Looking down into his friend's keen-eyed gaze, Ethan sensed it wasn't really a question, but he answered it as such anyway. "Whether she's called Isabel or Maggie, she's the answer to my heart's prayer, the missing half of my soul. Without her, I'm incomplete, empty…lost."

Hap shrugged his headless shoulders. "So what's the

problem? When your time's up, just toss her over your shoulder and take her back with you."

Ethan shook his head. "I can't do that. I can't decide for her. That would be selfish, just plain wrong. Maggie has to choose for herself."

Hap gave the head in his lap a good shake. "You have some mighty confounded modern notions, Cap, I'll give you that."

Even a week before, Ethan might have considered Hap's suggestion but now doing anything to impose on Maggie's free will was simply out of the question. His love might be the reembodiment of Isabel, but she was also very much a modern-day woman. Thinking of how adventurous she'd shown herself in bed, brazen by the standards of his day, Ethan couldn't help but smile. Of all the earthly pleasures he was going to miss after relinquishing his human body, making love to Maggie by far topped the list.

Turning to Hap, he asked, "If you could have your head back—on your shoulders, I mean—what would be the first thing you'd rush out to do?"

Hap didn't hesitate. "Play my harmonica again."

"That's it?"

Hap's rheumy eyes took on a faraway look. "The way I see it, sometimes that's everything."

IT WAS DUSK WHEN THE SMALL tour group came upon the Federal cemetery. Led by Mavis, each of the five walkers, including Maggie, held a lantern. The lanterns helped to set the mood of being in a previous era but they also had a practical purpose—once you ventured off the main streets, it was friggin' dark.

Coming up on the cemetery gate, Mavis pulled the park service key from her pocket and they filed inside. After giving a brief orientation on some of the more famous soldiers buried there, she turned them loose to walk around on their own.

"Watch your footing in the dark. We'll meet up at the gate in ten minutes, all right?"

Maggie found herself wondering about the markers, saddened at how many unknowns were buried so far away from their loved ones. She was about to head for the gate when a sagging marble tombstone caught her eye.

Ethan O'Malley. Beyond the name and date of birth and death—December 16, 1862—the rest of the inscription was too faded to make out.

Looking down at the marker, reality hit her like a sucker punch to the gut. She thought she'd accepted the fact that Ethan was a ghost and yet staring down at the irrefutable proof, she felt tears filling her eyes.

"I'm not there, you know." She jerked her head up to see Ethan standing just behind the gravestone. "All that grave holds is my physical body or what little's left of it. A heap of dry bones isn't me, Belle."

She could tell he was in spirit form because his energy field was so thin she could see through him to Mavis waiting by the gate. Knowing that at any moment he might fade away forever prompted a painful pull in the vicinity of her heart.

She shook her head, willing this not to be goodbye. "I knew you were dead, *are* dead, but seeing your grave makes it all so…*real*."

"It is real, Belle, but it's also going to be all right. That's why the powers that be guided you here, to help you understand that—and to help you let me go."

"But I don't want to let go. I love you."

"I love you, too, sweetheart, but as you can see, a love as deep and strong as ours takes many forms."

"What about Damian? If you don't find him this earth cycle, doesn't that mean you'll have to keep coming back?"

He nodded. "All of life is a cycle and earth cycles for spirits run every fifty years. If we don't prevail this time, I'll come back every fifty years until we do. It's only time, after all. You may have trouble understanding this now, but in the vastness of the universe, fifty years is but the blink of the eye."

Glancing around to make sure no one was looking, she dropped her voice and said, "In fifty years, I'll be an old woman. Assuming I'm still alive, you'll have to come haunt me in the assisted living village." At his blank look, she clarified, "An old folks home, the modern-day equivalent of old people being put out to pasture."

He cocked his head and smiled at her though his eyes were sad. "I would, you know. Young or old, you'll still be my Isabel, the mate to my soul, the love of my life—and beyond."

"Easy for you to say. You've already passed on. Days, weeks, years—time's all the same to you. You can just float around or whatever it is you do…up there, but I'll be left behind to slog through every empty hour, waiting for only God knows what."

"What are you saying?"

"That I don't have a fantasy that doesn't have you in it, and I don't know what I'm supposed to do with that because—and please don't take this the wrong way—you're dead and I'm not. And yet…"

"Yes?"

"I've never felt as alive as I do when I'm with you, and well, I don't know what to do with that, either. I don't know much of anything anymore. Oh, Ethan, it's all such a mess, and the worst part is you're the only one I can talk to about it unless I want to risk trading in this outfit for a hospital nightgown and four point restraints."

He took a step toward her. “We’ve been together before. We’ll figure out a way to be together again. We’ve already had one miracle.”

“What do you mean?”

“Can’t you see it was no coincidence, you buying the house? It was the answer to my prayer—and yes, Isabel, the dead can pray as well as the living. Your coming to Fredericksburg was the direct consequence of my soul calling out to your soul. And I’m telling you, Belle, when it comes to loving I’m just as alive as you are.”

19

One Week Later

BREAKING UP WITH RICHARD, and staying broken up, had been easier than Maggie had anticipated. It had been a week since that ugly episode in her living room, and so far there hadn't been so much as one phone call or e-mail from him. She must have really shaken him up with her threat to file a complaint with the medical review board—or maybe he and Leslie had hooked up after all. Either way, she was glad to be rid of him. Having him out of her life had freed up her time and energy to accomplish other things. She'd finished the edits to her dissertation and delivered it to the dean's office just the other day. With that off her plate and school still weeks away, she'd begun jotting down some notes for that book. You just never knew.

Sadly, Ethan's energy field was growing weaker by the day. He had to take longer and longer periods to recharge between embodiments and even then, the results were mixed. The other day his lower torso had disappeared, only to flicker back in; the day before that it had been his arm. He still came to her at night but instead of making love, he slipped into bed beside her and they held each other tight. She felt like he was dying, which was crazy because he was already dead. Dead or alive, it couldn't be much longer now before he was called back to cross over. Instead of having weeks left, she suspected they were looking at only a few more days.

Under the circumstances, Maggie hated to leave him, but she didn't have a choice. While the fall semester started after Labor Day for the students, faculty ended their summer break and began preparing for the new term much earlier. In her case, the new faculty orientation was already starting up. Having classes on how to have classes—go figure.

She packed her portfolio case with articles and items she thought she might need. If there was any downtime in the program, perhaps she'd find a spot outside and work on her book. Standing at the front door, brass knob in hand, she couldn't resist turning back to the stairs just in case. Even though there was no sign of a presence, she called up, "Goodbye, Ethan, goodbye, Hap. I'll be home around four."

It was a habit she'd gotten into over the past week. She wasn't even sure if Ethan could hear her but she hoped he did. She was even less sure he'd still be there when she got back.

PARKED FARTHER DOWN THE street, Richard watched Maggie pull out of her gravel driveway and head down Caroline Street. Checking the university Web site had been the easy part. The faculty information portion of the site was password protected but fortunately for him, one of his female patients, a high school girl, happened to be an ace hacker. Manipulating the crush the little geek had on him, it hadn't taken much persuading to get her to agree to hack into the university's system. The new faculty orientation would keep Maggie away from the house for several hours. Perfect.

She didn't know it but he'd slipped one of the spare house keys into his pocket the day he'd helped her move in. He darted around back and let himself in through the side kitchen door. He wasn't sure what he was looking for, but he'd know it when he found it.

Willie was right there at the door when he entered. He kicked the cat away, smiling when the animal cried out in pain. If he had time later, he'd take the mangy feline for a nice little roadside ride. Maggie had spoiled the animal until he was more like a child than a cat. Richard wouldn't give him much above an hour in the wild, and the big benefit was Maggie would be heartbroken. To get Willie back, he'd bet she'd be willing to humiliate herself in all sorts of delicious, delightful ways.

The sound of a car pulling up at the front door caused him to jump. Looking out the bedroom window, he saw Maggie pull her Ford Escort up to the curb. Knowing her as he did, he surmised she'd forgotten something. She was always laying down keys, parking tickets, you name it. The bitch would lose her head if it weren't strapped to her shoulders.

But that was okay—he was more than ready for her.

MAGGIE KNEW FORGETTING HER faculty ID badge was a sign of how distracted she was but fortunately the university was only a five-minute drive from her house. She'd given herself plenty of time to get there and park, so it wasn't any big deal to circle back to the house. She only hoped that once she got there she'd remember where she'd left the badge.

As she entered, the house seemed to throb with an eerie silence. Her time with Ethan hadn't just opened her mind and heart but sharpened her intuition considerably, and though she couldn't yet say what, something just didn't feel right. For one thing, Willie wasn't at his usual greeting post by the door.

Pulling the door closed behind her, she went from room to room calling his name. "Willie?"

She finally found him upstairs inside her bedroom wardrobe

cabinet. When she went to pick him up, he let out a little cry. Gently running her hand along his lean body, she took in his panting breaths and dilated pupils. "What is it, sweetie? Did something hurt you? Did somebody scare you?"

"Boo!"

Maggie let out a scream, sending Willie leaping from her arms. She whirled around as Richard stepped out of the shadows, a lit cigarette in one slender hand. Holding her racing heart, she said, "Richard, what are you doing here? How did you even get in?"

Grinning, he patted the pocket of his khakis, scattering ashes onto her new Paymon Persian carpet. "Keys are amazing things. The day I helped you move I borrowed one of your spares."

"In that case, you can leave it on the hallway table on your way out."

"I won't be leaving, not just yet."

Too tired to be having this conversation with him, she took a backward step to the bedroom door. "Richard, in case you didn't get it last week, we're not together anymore."

"I think you're the one who doesn't get it, Maggie. I don't want to date you—you've shown you don't deserve that kind of consideration from me."

Maggie blew out a breath. "Then what do you want?"

He couldn't hurt her with words, not anymore. But that he'd been prowling her home while she was gone seriously creeped her out. If she hadn't forgotten her ID, she wouldn't have been back for hours.

"For starters, I want to watch you use the vibrator I gave you—and don't tell me you don't have it because it's in your night table drawer."

She must have been in a dark hole of depression indeed to

have spent six months, even six minutes, with such a sicko. "You have no right to go through my things. Get out."

Acting like he hadn't heard her—some things never changed—he said, "I want to see you put it in your pussy and fuck yourself. If that's not enough to get you off, if you need more, I have five fingers on each hand and, baby, they're all yours." He lifted his empty hand, digits wiggling.

Oh my God, was he actually suggesting fisting her? Backing up to the door, she wasn't only disgusted but beginning to feel more than a little afraid. And to think only last week she'd argued with Ethan over the vase incident. What she wouldn't give for the intervention of her sexy ghost right about now.

"You're sick, Richard, and apparently more delusional than any of your patients if you think for a minute I'd even consider…performing for you."

She'd expected him to be furious but instead he only smiled. "I guess you don't want this anymore, then?"

He picked up her diary from the nightstand where she'd left it out in plain view. Once Ethan was gone, the book and the tintype tucked inside it would be all she had left to remember him by.

She pushed away from the door and took a step toward him. "Give that back."

He smiled. "Fuck yourself first, and I'll consider it."

"No."

He shrugged and slid the cigarette into the side of his mouth. "Suit yourself." He took out his cigarette lighter. "How did that old slogan go—Flick my Bic?" He snapped the lighter on, the flame dancing close to the edge of the page.

"No!" She rushed him and made a grab for the diary but he only held it above her head. "Beg for it. Go down on your knees and suck my cock and beg for it." He grabbed hold of her elbows and threw her down on the bed.

But Maggie wasn't going anywhere—at least not without a fight. She raised her hand and raked her nails down the side of Richard's face.

"Bitch!" His backhanded blow landed squarely across her jaw, as the diary skittered across the bare space of uncovered floor. She fell back on the bed, the breath knocked from her lungs.

Richard stripped off his leather belt and walked toward her. "It's payback time, Mags."

Blue eyes blazing, Ethan materialized by the door. "Leave her be."

Richard dropped the belt and jerked his head up. "I take it you're the reenactor Maggie's been fucking?" He glanced down to where Maggie was pulling herself up on her elbows and smirked. "Well, I don't mind a ménage à trois as long as you don't mind waiting your turn."

Pulling his gaze away from the red mark marring Maggie's cheek, Ethan started toward Richard, murder on his mind when suddenly it struck him. "You can see me, can't you?"

Richard shrugged. "Of course I can. Why wouldn't I? Maggie here is the one who needs glasses, don't you, Mags?" He took a drag of his cigarette and exhaled a perfect smoke ring into Ethan's face.

Staring at the curl of smoke as he had on that long ago December day, Ethan felt something buried deep inside him surface—and then snap free.

"Damian!"

Drawing on every ounce of earth energy he still possessed, he launched himself forward, smashing his fist into Richard's startled face. His human knuckles met the cartilage of

Richard's nose with a soul-satisfying crunch, the impact sending the slighter man crashing into the far wall, cigarette shooting from his slackened mouth.

Ethan turned back to Maggie. "Are you all right?" He reached down to pull her up.

Grabbing hold, Maggie rose to her feet. "I think so." Standing side by side, they looked across the room to Richard slumped over, apparently out like a light, the cigarette burning a hole in the leg of his Lands' End khakis.

Ethan turned to her. "Aren't you going to chastise me for hitting him—again? It is the second time in as many weeks."

Tasting blood from where Richard's blow had caused her to bite the inside of her cheek, Maggie shook her head. "Whatever number life he's on, I hear he has a pretty thick skull."

"UP AND AT 'EM, BOY, TIME'S a wastin.'"

Richard cracked open an eye to see fingers snapping in his face. Pain pounded through his swollen nose, making it hard to inhale. Breathing through his mouth, he cast his gaze about the room's four corners. He was in the attic, Maggie's attic, and seated on a very hard, very uncomfortable chair. He tried to shift to a more comfortable spot but he was pinned in place. Beyond his head, his body felt as limp and nerveless as a jellyfish.

Panic rising, he scoured his brain to piece together the chain of recent events. The last he remembered, he'd been in Maggie's bedroom holding the diary and threatening to set it afire. He didn't remember much beyond that, at least not after the large fist had connected with his face.

"Helpless—not such a good feeling, is it?"

A squat old man who couldn't have been much more than five feet tall sidled up to him. With his collar-length matted gray hair, bulbous nose and lazy eye, he could have been the prospector character from any old Western B movie except that he wore not a miner's slouched hat but a blue uniform jacket and a checkered-cloth apron over that. Richard relaxed fractionally. If this was the best Maggie could come up with for someone to work him over, he might be okay after all.

"Who the hell are you?"

"The name's Hap. I'm a friend of Maggie's. She has a lot of friends watching over her, and we ain't too pleased with how you've treated her."

Eyeing Maggie's friend's stubby, bowed legs and stiff stride, Richard was beginning to feel better by the moment. "Fuck off."

"Why, I oughtta wash your mouth out with soap. In fact, I reckon I will."

A bar of brownish soap appeared in Hap's hand and the next thing Richard knew, half of it was being shoved into his mouth. Gagging, he tried to get up but he still couldn't move. Lye burned his throat, threatening to make him bring his breakfast up.

"Oh, God. Stop…please."

"Well, seein' as you said please, all right then." The soap bar disappeared from the old man's hand. Whatever else he was, he must be an amateur magician. The sleight o' hand was a classic parlor trick, but Richard had bigger problems on his mind then figuring it out. Starting with getting himself out of this situation—and this fucking chair.

Hap leaned in, bringing his weathered face within inches of Richard's. "Tell me, boy, you ever lose track of things?"

Eyes watering, Richard was starting to wonder if they'd drugged him with some kind of hallucinogen. "Huh?"

"You know, keys, umbrellas, pocket change—that kind of thing?"

Richard wasn't sure where this was leading, but until he

recovered enough to get out of the chair, he thought he'd better play along. "Uh, sure, sometimes. Once in a while."

Hap backed away from him, and the glint in his eye made Richard nervous indeed. "Why, wouldn't you know a feller said just this morning about my good friend Maggie that she'd lose her head if it weren't strapped to her shoulders? Funny thing, that's my problem, too."

Jesus, did they have the house bugged? But no, he'd only thought that about Maggie, he hadn't said it aloud—had he? He opened his mouth to ask what the hell he had to do for them to let him free when the old guy reached up and lifted his head off his shoulders like a box lid.

Sweat stinging his eyes, Richard felt his limp body start to shake. "Okay, I am not seeing that or, if I am, it's got to be another trick."

"If you like that trick, you'll love this one." Holding the dismembered head by the hair, Hap brought his arm back and then swung it forward. "One, two, *three!*" Like a bowling ball released down the lane, the head rolled toward Richard, crashing into his feet.

"Ahhhhhhhhhh."

"How'd you like that trick, boy?" the head asked him.

Richard squeezed his eyes closed. *I am not seeing any of this. When I open my eyes, they'll be gone.*

"I wouldn't count on that if I were you."

Unless the old man was a ventriloquist, too, someone else had joined them in the room. Feeling something tickling the top of his head, Richard opened his eyes and looked up to the noose dangling over his head.

"Bearing false witness against a man is not a sin the Lord will let go unpunished, Damian."

The tall, broad-shouldered man wielding the rope was the

reenactor guy who'd decked him downstairs. Flinching at his approach, Richard realized he really did look a hell of a lot like the dead guy in the old Civil War photograph. His blue wool uniform coat was unbuttoned and hanging open and he wore a pair of like-colored trousers and knee-high riding boots. How had such a big man managed to creep up on him so softly? And why was he calling him Damian?

The latter was an odd coincidence because *The Omen* had been his favorite movie growing up, though perhaps not the most appropriate material for an impressionable young mind. A latchkey kid, he'd been able to watch what he wanted. He must have seen it fifty times. He'd really identified with the main character, Damian. Being the son of Satan had seemed like a sweet deal.

Determined not to let them break him, he forced himself to meet the man's hard-eyed stare. "If you don't let me go, I'll call the police and file a report."

If the big man was cowed, he didn't show it. "Threats, Damian, even now? You'll have to find a way out of here first, won't you? Out of here alive, I should say."

Oh, shit, would Maggie really go so far as to have him killed? "You must have me mixed up with someone else. My name's Richard. Dr. Richard Crenshaw."

"Oh, I know who—and what—you are, *doctor.* The question of the hour is, do you know me?"

"Of course not. I've never seen you before in my life."

"In this life, perhaps."

The chair beneath Richard began to shake and belatedly he realized that his shuddering body had set it to rocking. "What…what other life is there?"

The big man seemed to find the question amusing. "What indeed?"

He reached up with his free hand and pulled at the white cloth wrapping his throat. The neckwear fell away revealing a broad neck collared in a cross-hatching of scars, the flesh whittled away in places down to raw muscle. Staring in morbid fascination, Richard didn't see how someone who'd sustained such an injury could have survived.

"Not a pretty sight, is it? But the very worst part of dying was the knowing that I was leaving the woman I loved more than earthly life behind for the likes of you."

Richard started to say he must have him confused with another man when the noose dropped around his throat. Holding the rope firm, the reenactor slowly cinched it until the knot rested on the soft spot just below Richard's right ear.

"How does it feel, Damian, to be the one on the receiving end of the rope?"

Richard felt as though the attic were spinning around him, his feet melting into the floor, the reenactor's voice reaching him as an echo. The part of his brain that still functioned rationally told him he was having an anxiety attack combined with a dissociative reaction—both thoroughly normal under the current circumstances—but with a noose around his neck, who the fuck cared?

"Oh, my God, please don't kill me." Voice hoarse, Richard shook his head back and forth, urine streaming down the inside of his pants leg. "Please, please, I didn't mean to hurt Isabel. I just wanted her, wanted her so badly, but no matter what I did, I couldn't make her want me back. I thought once you were out of the way, that maybe..."

Richard stopped in the middle of his sputtering. He'd meant to say Maggie—hadn't he? And he'd never met this reenactor guy before today—had he?

The noose fell away. The reenactor looked down on him,

shaking his dark head. "You're not worth killing. You'll have to live out your embodiment like everyone else and, given the twisted existence you've created for yourself, that should be punishment enough. But I tell you this, if you ever come near Maggie again, in this life or any other, there'll be the very devil to pay. Speaking of which…" Stepping back, he turned to the old man. "Hap, are you thinking what I'm thinking?"

Head sitting on his shoulders once more, the old guy broke into a broad grin. "I don't rightly know, Cap, but I reckon I may just be."

Turning back to Richard, the reenactor smiled in a way that had every muscle in Richard's suddenly enervated body twitching with fear. "Now that he won't be seeing Maggie anymore, I think Dr. Crenshaw here may be in need of some female companionship."

"Why, Cap, I think you may be right."

The geezer tented his hands like a bullhorn. "Oh, Yvette, *vite vite?*"

Mouth trembling, Richard looked between the two grinning men. "Who's…who's Yvette?"

The sharp tap on his cheek had Richard whipping his head around—and freezing with fear. The old African woman leaned in, foul breath blowing across his face, yellow teeth bared and snapping. Even seeing the evidence up close and personal, Richard couldn't believe someone could be that ugly and still live. The whites of her eyes were cloudy as cottage cheese, her nose and chin were covered in warts and hairy moles and her grizzled gray hair hung midway to her thick waist along with a necklace of assorted bones and animal teeth. He blinked and a sleek black cat hopped onto her crooked shoulder.

Arms crossed, the old-timer regarded him with a grin. "Being a New Orleans voodoo queen and all, Yvette here is real partial to cats, and she didn't much care for your plans for Maggie's Willie. Besides that, she says you never did pay her for the last load of shirts she done washed and pressed for you."

Turning back to the voodoo queen, Richard prepared to plead his case. "Look, I don't know about any shirts, but I was just venting about the cat. Honestly, I didn't really mean…" She dropped her gaze to the space between his thighs, and Richard decided he'd better pick up the pace on his apology. "I wasn't really going to…" Licking her lips, she reached out and clamped her claw over his cock. "Oh, God, please not there, not that…"

The old man let out a chuckle. "Don't worry, boy. I'm sure you two can work something out. Yvette's horny as hell. Last time that gal had sex Custer was headed to Little Big Horn."

Feeling Yvette's talons raking over his nuts, Richard couldn't take it any longer. Head knocking against the chair back, he opened his mouth and screamed.

"Maaaaaaaaaaaaaaagggggggiiiiiiiiiiiiiiieeeeeeeeeeeeee."

THE CRONE STEPPED ASIDE AND Maggie took her place. "Why Richard, that scream of yours was loud enough to wake the dead." For whatever reason, she and her three *friends* seemed to find that funny. "Can I assume you're ready to discuss a deal?"

With sweat pouring into his eyes and urine running down his leg, Richard had never been so happy to see someone in his life. "Sure, whatever you want, just please no more. Make them stop. Better yet, make them go away. I'll do anything, anything you want."

"Anything?" Arms folded, she stared down at him. "In that case, Richard, I'd say you have some writing to do."

MAGGIE STOOD OVER RICHARD, whom they'd moved to the secretary desk. Knowing Ethan needed to conserve what energy he had left, she said, "Why don't you and Hap wait outside the door. I'll be fine."

Ethan hesitated. "Are you sure?"

Maggie looked over at him, feeling her heart lurch. He had a supporting hand braced against the wall and his big shoulders drooped. It was obvious he was fighting hard to hold on to his physical body and yet at the same time, all his concern was for her.

"I'll be fine—won't I, Richard?"

Elbows on the table, Richard managed a nod. Cheek bloodied, snot running from his swollen nose and his pants soaked with urine, her former boyfriend was definitely looking the worse for wear.

Hap stepped up to her side. "If you need anything, darlin', you just give a holler."

"Okay, I will. Thanks."

Watching Hap brace an arm around Ethan and lead him away, Maggie felt her heart lurch. Knocking Richard out and then using his energy field to pin him to the chair had drained Ethan in a major way. He was almost down to the dregs of his earth energy and rapidly losing what little he had left.

Alone with Richard, Maggie laid Damian's will on the desktop in front of him along with clean white paper and pen: the supplies she'd picked up from a local stationery shop specializing in nineteenth-century reproductions.

Looking back over his shoulder at her, he said, "What's all this?"

Rather than answer—she was more than done explaining herself to him—she said, "I want you to recopy the last paragraph of this document word for word with one exception. Instead of December 16, 1892 at the top, I want you to date it December 16, *1862*. Got it?"

"Why would I copy by hand a document that already exists? Can't you doctor the date and photocopy it, for God's sake?"

"Just do it. Unless you'd rather I call my friends back. I think Yvette has the hots for you. Once you get over your cat phobia, you two might just have a future."

Face contorting, he picked up the pen. "Okay, okay, I'm writing."

RICHARD HANDED THE HANDWRITTEN page over. "Satisfied?"

Adjusting her glasses, Maggie bent to inspect the new document. Wow! Talk about a match made in heaven. Looking between it and the will, it was amazing how closely, make that identically, the penmanship matched. She wondered that Richard didn't see it himself—or maybe he did. Given his earlier outburst, she suspected that on some level he knew who he was and what he'd done.

"It'll do. You can go now, but if you ever—"

"I got it, okay. I'll leave you alone." He got up and started for the attic door. Pausing, he turned around. "Was I really that bad, Maggie? I mean, we had some good times, didn't we?"

She shook her head. "You're a sexual predator, Richard. You're not really all that different from the perverts who hang out at playgrounds or men who rape their dates. Like them, you prey on people who've put their trust in you, only you charge their insurance for the privilege. Speaking of which, my threat to file a conduct complaint with the district's medical review board is still on the table. If I were you, I'd think twice before taking any more female clients for a ride on your office couch."

He shook his head at her, a familiar gesture only now all she could think was how pathetic he looked. "Jesus, you used to be so sweet. When did you become such a bitch?"

Maggie thought for a moment, and then she smiled. "The way I see it, I've been through a hell of a lot in the last one hundred forty-five years. I guess I decided it was time to toughen up."

MAGGIE OPENED HER FRONT DOOR, and Richard barreled out—but not before she made him hand over the stolen house key. Even with it in her pocket, she promised herself she'd have the locks changed tomorrow just in case. It wasn't looking as if she'd have her sexy resident ghost around all that much longer to watch over her.

Heart heavy, she climbed the stairs back to the attic. Ethan was slumped in the desk chair Richard had just vacated, a sad-faced Hap at his side, harmonica music playing the plaintive score to "My Old Kentucky Home."

It was clear Ethan was being called home. The bottom half of his body had disappeared entirely, his breathing was labored and his eyes were rimmed in dark circles.

She and Hap exchanged glances. "Cap's not doing so good."

Ethan raised his head at her approach. "Afraid it's…my…time."

She'd promised herself she'd be strong, but until now, she hadn't realized just how hard saying goodbye would be when the love—and the hurt—ran this deep. She rushed forward and dropped to her knees at Ethan's side.

Stepping away, Hap reached down to his head and swiped at the tear tracking down his leathery cheek. Holding a checkered hankie down, he blew his bulbous nose. "I'd best let you two say your goodbyes in private. Cap, I reckon I'll see you knockin' around the ole astral realm?"

Ethan managed a nod. "Take care of yourself, Hap—and thanks."

Maggie leaned over and planted a kiss on Hap's head. "Thank you for being such a good friend. I'll miss you."

"Aw, shucks, I hate goodbyes. You take care of yourself, missy." Pocketing his harmonica, he turned to go. Music ebbing, he melted into the wall.

Ethan looked down into Maggie's upturned face. "I'm sorry you have to see me like this."

In answer, she wrapped her arms about his waist, willing her life force to pour into him. She'd gladly shave off twenty years or more from her current embodiment for another few days with him.

Weak though he was, he wound his arms around her. "It's no use, Maggie. I'm fading and you don't have enough energy to keep me here any longer. If anything, my being here is draining you." She lifted her head from his chest to protest but he shook his head. "The headaches and fatigue you've been suffering lately aren't from stress. They're from you giving your energy to me. It worked for a while, but you don't have enough life force to sustain two bodies. If you keep trying, you'll make yourself ill."

She shook her head. "I don't care. I'd do anything and give up anything if it meant you could stay with me even a little while longer. If it weren't for Richard, you wouldn't have had to expend all that energy at one time. We might have had a few more days together."

Resting her cheek back against the hard plane of his chest, she still had trouble believing he was dead, let alone leaving her for good. She could feel the scratchiness of wool beneath her cheek, smell the musky scent of his skin, feel his breath brushing over her as he tucked her head beneath his chin and held her close, so wonderfully close that she imagined herself melting into him at any time, much as Hap had melted into the wall. But it was Ethan who would shortly be melting—away.

He shook his head. "Everything happens for a reason, Maggie. Richard was meant to come here today just as I'm meant to go back now. There's no point in trying to fight the current of life. The universe has a plan for every one of us, even Richard. It is wiser than us all."

She tried to cling tighter, but her hands went right through him. His energy field wasn't solid mass anymore but instead free-flowing. Crying, she pulled her head from his chest. "I can't feel you. I can't feel you anymore. You're fading, aren't you?"

"I am. I can hear the powers that be calling me back home. It's time, Maggie." He started up.

Maggie bolted to her feet. "I don't want you to go. I thought I could stand it but I can't."

He gripped her shoulders though she couldn't feel anything beyond a vague sensation of warmth. "Listen to me, Maggie, you can and you must. If it helps, remember that this isn't farewell but goodbye. If need be, I'll be come back in fifty years to haunt you again."

"Fifty years might as well be an eternity."

He managed a weak smile. "Trust me when I say eternity is a good sight longer. As for your life, it goes by quicker than you might think or want. Live it well, Belle. Don't waste so much as one precious drop on regrets." He let her go and backed away. "Remember, I'll always be with you, and I'll always love you. When your time comes to cross over, I'll be waiting for you on the other side with open arms."

"Ethan, wait. Come back!"

"Goodbye, Belle. Goodbye, my love." He lifted his hand in a wave, his energy field flickering in and out of view and then fading to ash until nothing was left to mark his place beyond the dust motes dancing in the air.

Sinking to the floor, Maggie was sure she'd never felt so very cold or so very alone in any life.

20

One Year Later

IT WAS GOOD TO BE HOME. The book tour had been a huge success, better than even Maggie or her publisher had hoped. With so many cases of power-hungry politicians, corrupt corporations and profit-motivated wars making the headlines, the American public was hungry for a hero. Ethan's story, *Betrayed: The Hanging of a Civil War Hero* had made it onto the bestseller lists the first week out of the gate. Maggie might not be regarded as a historian on par with Doris Kearns Goodwin, but she took tremendous satisfaction in having set the historical record straight once and for all.

After Ethan's departure, she'd thrown herself into not only her teaching but also researching the book. Additional delving had turned up documented acts of heroism Ethan had been far too modest to ever admit. During the Battle of Marye's Heights, he'd risked his life not once but several times, running into open fire to carry his wounded comrades beyond the Sunken Road to safety. By rights, he should have been decorated by the U.S. government. Instead he'd been hanged.

Suitcase in hand, she walked in the front door half expecting to find Ethan there but, of course, that wasn't going to happen, not for another fifty years at least. The prospect of waiting that long for their next reunion still made her sad, but now she'd come to see that being alone and being lonely didn't have to be the same thing. Ethan had taught her so many things in their short time together, namely that no one was really ever alone. Whether you thought of them as guardian angels, ghosts or best buddies who'd crossed over to the other side, everyone had at least one benevolent being watching over them at all times. It had taken an almost two-hundred-year-old dead man to teach her the art of living—how ironic was that?

As for Richard, though she'd never made good on her threat to have him brought before the medical review board, she was happy to simply have him out of her life. The parents of a former client, a female high school student, had been less forgiving. Apparently he'd manipulated the girl's crush on him to have her hack into some university's computer network. The board's revoking his license apparently pushed him over the edge. She'd heard through her friend Becky, who lived in D.C., that he'd been hauled in as homeless by a police officer who'd found him wandering Dupont Circle hallucinating about voodoo queens and headless men.

Prancing in circles around her feet, Willie Whiskers meowed and looked up at her with wide, welcoming eyes, pulling her back to more positive thoughts. As happy to see him as he was her, she set down her suitcase and scooped him up. "Was Mommie's darling a good boy for Auntie Sharon?" She planted a kiss on his little wet nose.

Anyone who heard her baby talking her cat would think she was some kind of nut but Willie was the closest to a child she'd ever have now. Knowing she and Ethan were soul mates connected across time and space, knowing he was looking down on her from the astral realm and waiting for the day when she could cross over to the other side and be with him made it impossible to consider being with anyone else.

She put Willie down and walked out into the kitchen to pour herself a glass of wine. The note from Sharon was taped to the refrigerator door.

> Willie Whiskers was an absolute angel. I'd catnap him in a heartbeat except the demon dog would eat him. Give me a call when you're back in town. If I don't hear from you, I'll come over in the morning and check on him just in case…"

Sipping her wine, she thought back over the last whirlwind month. Hanging out with film and media celebrities in the greenrooms of national talk shows, doing book signings in stores across the country, addressing the symposium of a prominent national historical society had all been heady stuff, but the downside was that the nonstop pace had wiped her out. The headaches, which had stopped after Ethan's leaving, had returned with a vengeance, as had the fatigue. Maybe this time she really was fighting the flu or jet lag or…well, who knew? Whatever the cause, she couldn't fight her body's needs any longer. Unpacking would have to wait.

"Hey, Willie, what do you say we take a catnap? We can call Auntie Sharon when we wake up. She'll still be at work, anyway."

Good boy that he was, he trotted up the stairs before her. Lagging behind, Maggie had to stop midway to catch her breath. *Wow, I am really wiped.* Making it to her bedroom, she set her wineglass down on her night table, pulled down the bedcovers and crawled beneath. Beyond kicking off her shoes, she was too tired to bother undressing.

"Belle."

She snapped upright to see Ethan standing at the foot of her bed. "I must be dreaming."

He shook his head, sending her one of his signature sexy smiles. "Not dreaming, Belle. I said I'd come back for you when it was time, and I have."

She hesitated, confused. "But I thought we had to wait another fifty years?"

"Indeed, so did I, but your actions accelerated the plan."

"What actions?"

"The book you wrote cleared my name, Belle, and in doing so, expunged the remaining darkness from my energy imprint and set my soul free." He gestured to his uncovered neck, the taut flesh smooth and free of scars. "That was your life's work, and you've completed it fifty years ahead of schedule."

She'd always known it paid not to procrastinate but this was something else. "Are you saying—"

"The powers that be have granted you a choice. You can wait another fifty years to cross over or you can come with me now."

To think you had to wait fifty years and then suddenly have the choice to leave immediately land in your lap was a shock. Go now or wait another fifty years—talk about going from one extreme to the other. Her mind racing, Maggie took a quick inventory of all she'd be leaving behind. This house was still her dream house but without her very special resident ghost it also felt hollow, empty. Her immediate family had already passed over but Sharon and Becky and Lucia were like surrogate sisters. Leaving them behind would be really hard, but they had their own lives to lead, and hopefully she'd see them all again someday.

A plaintive meow drew her attention back to the bed—and

the very special furry, four-legged friend she'd be leaving behind, as well. Willie Whiskers stood at the foot of the mattress, pupils huge and fur standing on end, staring straight at the spot Ethan occupied. She remembered she'd only put down enough food and water to last a day, but fortunately Sharon would be over in the morning to check on him. Who knew, maybe her friend would adopt Willie and the demon dog would just have to deal with it? If not Sharon, then maybe Becky or Lucia would take him in once they figured out she was…gone.

Looking sad, Ethan backed away.

"Ethan, wait. Don't go. Not yet."

"I must, Belle, but don't fret. I've waited all these many years. Another fifty or so won't kill me." He tried for a smile but he was fading fast, his form flickering in and out.

Seeing his energy imprint growing steadily smaller and frailer, she felt a painful stabbing in the area of her heart. Fifty years might seem like a drop in time to him, but to her it would be an eternity—an eternity spent without him. If her life's work was accomplished, if the love of her life along with her family had passed over to the other side already, what in the world was she waiting for?

"Ethan, wait, I'm coming with you." Turning back, she picked up Willie. Instantly, he started purring. Tears welling, she brushed a kiss on his silky head. "Be a good boy for Sharon, okay?"

She tried setting him down, but he dug in, claws clinging to her like Velcro, and suddenly she understood. He didn't want to be left behind without his special person any more than she did.

The cat in her arms, she whirled around. Ethan was barely visible now, the cone of white light encasing him grower ever fainter and smaller—the size of a football bobbing in midair. "Ethan, wait for me. I'm coming, Ethan. I'm coming!"

Clutching Willie, Maggie ran toward the light.

"SOMETHING JUST DOESN'T smell right." A healthy, young woman turning up dead for no apparent cause. It still doesn't make any sense to me."

Standing in the funeral home's private viewing room, Mac McMillan, a junior detective with the Fredericksburg City Police Department, looked down at Maggie Holliday's flower-decked coffin and shook his head. Wakes weren't really his thing and he'd only met the guest of honor once in passing. Even so, after the past two days of looking into her sudden and, to him, mysterious death, he felt almost as though she was a friend.

The senior detective on the case, Charlie Jones, shook his head. Mac was a decent guy and a pretty good detective, but still, he was from the D.C. area. Yankee Locusts, the local newspaper called them, newbie Northerners like Mac who'd descended on Fredericksburg in the past decade, driving up house prices and clogging roadways and generally mucking with the character of what used to be a nice, friendly little Southern town.

Reaching for his patience, Charlie said, "Look, we've been over this all before. The coroner tested her for toxins. There were no traces of drugs in her system and her blood-alcohol level was well below the legal limit. That half-finished glass of wine set out on her night table was probably all she'd had to drink."

Mac glanced over to a trio of attractive early thirty-something women huddled in a nearby corner. "The friend, Sharon Walker, said Maggie hadn't seemed like herself since making the move here."

Sharon Walker was the one with the artfully mussed ash-blond hair, catlike green eyes and slinky black wrap dress that hugged her petite shape just so. Even with tears streaking her pretty heart-shaped face, she was certifiably hot.

Pulling his gaze back to Charlie, he added, "She'd been staying inside her house a lot, making excuses not to go out. Apparently there was a guy she'd been seeing but she wouldn't say who."

Charlie shrugged. It was an old story. The guy was probably married and playing around on the side. He glanced again at the wall clock. He had two gorgeous rib eyes from Ukrop's marinating in the fridge at home and the season finale of his favorite detective drama recording on TiVo. Unless he left in the next five minutes, the odds of him beating traffic on Route 3 were looking pretty slim.

"So the woman was maybe turning into a couch potato or an Internet geek or getting a little somethin' on the side, so what? Maybe she was working on her next book. Hell, it's not like folks move here for the nightlife."

Frowning, Mac started to cut in. "Still—"

Almost tasting the cold beer on his tongue, Charlie was having none of it. "Look, there's not one shred of evidence to point to foul play or suicide. She'd had rheumatic fever as a kid and lately she'd pushed herself with the book tour and, well, it looks like the stress caught up with her. She had a heart attack, pure and simple. It may not happen often but it happens. Case closed."

"What about the cat?"

"The cat?" Jesus, the kid was like a rottie with a bone—he just didn't know when to drop it.

"Her cat was found dead in bed beside her, remember?"

Charlie shrugged, failing to see the problem. One less cat in a city infested with ferals wasn't exactly a tragedy in his book. "What about it?"

"Don't you find it kind of odd that the cat's heart gave out at the same time? What are the odds of that happening?"

Eager to fire up the grill while the light held, Charlie was fast approaching the end of his patience. "How should I know? Do I look like a fucking vet?"

Mac dragged a hand through his closely cropped blond hair. "I just think it's odd. I mean, what are the chances of two concurrent natural deaths in—"

Patience at an end, Charlie waved a hand, cutting him off. "Listen, kid, this is Fredericksburg, America's Most Historic City, or so the slogan goes. Maybe that's just some bullshit line we put out there to reel in the tourists or maybe it's the God's truth but either way we're definitely one of America's more haunted cities. Crazy shit happens here all the time. I should know. My family's been in these parts for one hundred sixty years give or take. We've seen and heard it all or just about all. You come-heres really need to dial it down and mind your own business."

Mac didn't bother to hide his annoyance. He hadn't been in Fredericksburg long and while most people he'd met had been welcoming, the cliquishness of the old-guard set was starting to sour his view of city life. "Maggie Holliday was a come-here, as you call it."

Charlie transferred his gaze from Mac to the coffin. "Yeah, she was, wasn't she? And look what happened to her."

Epilogue

A Federal Military Encampment
Stafford Hills, Fredericksburg, Virginia
December 16, 1862

ETHAN GLANCED AT THE EGG YOKE dripping down his shoulder. To waste precious rations, his former comrades-in-arms must hate him indeed. No matter; it was time. Determined to meet his maker head-on, he turned to look out onto the assembly of onlookers, some curious, others, like the egg-hurling heckler, openly hostile, but all impatient to get on with the retreating march.

"Hold, I say. Hold! Go no further for that noose binds the neck of an innocent man."

Heads turned to look back at the tall young woman who'd spoken out. Hair streaming and cheeks flushed, Isabel pushed a path through, her cloak catching the wind like a ship's sail and one hand wrapped about the handle of a wicker basket. Heart lifting, Ethan thanked the powers that be for granting him his final and dearest wish after all.

Breathless, she came up beside him. "Oh, Ethan, thank God. I feared I'd be too late."

Wishing he might touch her yet knowing that would be greedy indeed, he settled for running his gaze over her, a silent caress. "Indeed, a moment more and you would have been. Jem said he saw you locked in the attic of your father's house."

"And so I was. I coaxed Lettie to lift the key from Clarice and let me out."

"Ah, my brave girl, you've made me happier than you can ever know, but you should go now." As much as he wanted her with him, he wasn't so selfish that he'd condemn her to watch him die. "After I'm gone, seek out Jem. I've left my money purse with him. It's not much but it's enough to purchase your safe passage away from Fredericksburg—and Damian. You can go to my family in Boston or anywhere you wish—only hurry. You must get away."

She started to answer him when a burly soldier, the sergeant at arms, came up beside her and took hold of her arm. "Ma'am, I'm afraid you're going to have to step aside."

Pitching her voice to be heard by the crowd, she reached beneath her cloak and shoved a folded paper toward him. "Take me to your ranking officer at once. This paper is the signed confession of one Damian Grey. In it, he admits to forging documents and bringing false charges of treason against Captain O'Malley."

"I'll fetch him straightaway, miss." Eyes bright, Jem sped off.

A few minutes later, the officer came forward, pulling a cloth napkin from his collar as though he'd been in the middle of a meal. Isabel handed the paper to him, and they waited in tense silence as he read the few lines.

Looking up, he demanded of his sergeant at arms, "Where is the sutler?"

From the onlookers, the laundress, Yvette, called out, "He done cleared out his tent and run off in the wee hours this morning, mumbling some foolishness about headless men.

Damned fool never did pay me for them shirts I washed and pressed for him."

The battalion commander turned to Jem. "Cut the prisoner down."

"With pleasure, sir." Beaming, Jem leaped onto the platform steps and set to work sawing away at the rope with his knife while Isabel held the horse steady.

Ethan felt the rope fall away from first his neck and then his hands. He was off his horse in an instant, the blessed ground firm at his feet and Isabel soft in his arms.

A cheer went up. Several soldiers who'd cursed him earlier came by to shake his hand and slap him on the back.

Smiling, the commander divided his gaze between Ethan and Isabel. "It looks as though you are a free man once more, Captain, and a damned lucky one at that. To have won the heart of so brave and bold a woman is rare good fortune indeed."

Smiling into Isabel's tired but shining eyes, Ethan answered, "Why thank you, sir, I'd have to agree." He hesitated. "If you don't mind, sir, I'd like to impose upon you for one final favor."

"Under the circumstances, Captain, I will hear it."

Ethan looked from Isabel to the chaplain standing by the makeshift scaffold steps, the closed Bible tucked beneath his arm. "That preacher fellow, do you reckon he can read marriage lines as well as last rites?"

Beneath his handlebar mustache, the commander's mouth broke into a grin. "I believe that can be arranged."

It wasn't until later when Ethan and Isabel were alone in his tent, him seated in a borrowed chair while his bride of less than an hour bent over him tending to his neck that he had the presence of mind to ask, "How did you come by it, Belle? Damian's confession, I mean?"

She tied off the bandage into a neat little knot and stepped back to survey her handiwork. "Why, Ethan, that's the most peculiar part. Someone pushed it beneath the attic door this morning along with this." She reached into her skirt's pocket and brought out a harmonica.

Taking the instrument from her, he recognized it at once. "This belonged to Hap Longacre, our company's cook and a great friend of mine. He was killed at Marye's Heights the other day." Poor Hap's head had been cut clean from his body by a cavalryman's saber or so he'd heard. But knowing Hap, he'd find a way to get it back in heaven if not on earth.

Isabel bent and brushed a kiss over his mouth, one of several they'd shared since the company chaplain had pronounced them husband and wife. By this time tomorrow, they'd be on a train bound for Boston. Ethan had been granted leave so that they might make their honeymoon trip, a small concession for having very nearly wrung his neck.

He glanced over to her cat stretched out dead center of his camp cot. "Once we get that feline of yours north of the Mason-Dixon Line, we're going to have to rename him, you know. Jefferson Davis or even Mr. Davis won't do."

Isabel's beautiful brow was marred with the slightest hint of a frown. "Well, headed north or not, no cat of mine will be saddled with Abraham Lincoln for a name. I know. We'll call him William after the Norman brute who invaded and conquered a neighboring land—Willie for short."

"Willie it is, then." Smiling at her small display of stubborn mischief, one of the many qualities he loved about her, Ethan anchored his hands to her slender hips. "As usual, my love, you are the perfect diplomat. Were you president of these United States, sure there'd be no war at all."

At his mention of the current conflict, Isabel's smile

dimmed, and she looked down at him with wide, searching eyes. "Oh, Ethan, but there is a war and I can't help but feel bad about leaving my family behind to face it without me."

"Don't fret, sweetheart. I've already made arrangements for them to meet us in Boston. In fact, they're en route even now. Your parents might not be overjoyed to have a Yankee in the family, but at least they'll be clear of the fighting. They and your sister are welcome to stay with us for as long as need be."

"Oh, Ethan!" She threw her arms about his neck. "I'm so very happy and yet I'm halfway to believing none of this can be true, that it's all a beautiful dream I'll wake up from and find myself in that attic and you lost to me still."

He laid his lips low on her flat belly, inhaling the fragrance of lavender and her own womanly musk. Thinking about the great pleasure he would take in slowly undressing her in just a little while, he looked up and said, "Ah, Belle, I'm no philosopher but only a simple man. Still, there are those who'll swear that all of earthly life is but one big dream. I don't rightly know about that, but I'll tell you what I do know, down in the depths of my very soul. Loving as we do, sweet Isabel, we've not only the whole of our earthly lives to look forward to sharing but the whole of eternity, too."

* * * * *

Dante Raintree stood with his arms crossed as he watched the woman on the monitor. The image was in black and white to better show details; color distracted the brain. He focused on her hands, watching every move she made, but what struck him most was how uncommonly *still* she was. She didn't fidget or play with her chips, or look around at the other players. She peeked once at her down card, then didn't touch it again, signaling for another hit by tapping a fingernail on the table. Just because she didn't seem to be paying attention to the other players, though, didn't mean she was as unaware as she seemed.

"What's her name?" Dante asked.

"Lorna Clay," replied his chief of security, Al Rayburn. "At first I thought she was counting, but she doesn't pay enough attention."

"She's paying attention, all right," Dante murmured. "You just don't see her doing it." A card counter had to remember every card played. Supposedly counting cards was impossible with the number of decks used by the casinos, but there were those rare individuals who could calculate the odds even with multiple decks.

"I thought that, too," said Al. "But look at this piece of tape coming up. Someone she knows comes up to her and speaks, she looks around and starts chatting, completely misses the play of the people to her left—and doesn't look around even when the deal comes back to her, just taps that finger. And damn if she didn't win. Again."

Dante watched the tape, rewound it, watched it again. Then he watched it a third time. There had to be something he was missing, because he couldn't pick out a single giveaway.

"If she's cheating," Al said with something like respect, "she's the best I've ever seen."

"What does your gut say?"

Al scratched the side of his jaw, considering. Finally, he said, "If she isn't cheating, she's the luckiest person walking. She wins. Week in, week out, she wins. Never a huge amount, but I ran the numbers and she's into us for about five grand a week. Hell, boss, on her way out of the casino she'll stop by a slot machine, feed a dollar in and walk away with at least fifty. It's never the same machine, either. I've had her watched, I've had her followed, I've even looked for the same faces in the casino every time she's in here, and I can't find a common denominator."

"Is she here now?"

"She came in about half an hour ago. She's playing blackjack, as usual.

"Bring her to my office," Dante said, making a swift decision. "Don't make a scene."

"Got it," said Al, turning on his heel and leaving the security center.

Dante left, too, going up to his office. His face was calm. Normally he would leave it to Al to deal with a cheater, but he was curious. How was she doing it? There were a lot of bad cheaters, a few good ones, and every so often one would come along who was the stuff of which legends were made:

the cheater who didn't get caught, even when people were alert and the camera was on him—or, in this case, her.

It was possible to simply be lucky, as most people understood luck. Chance could turn a habitual loser into a big-time winner. Casinos, in fact, thrived on that hope. But luck itself wasn't habitual, and he knew that what passed for luck was often something else: cheating. And there was the other kind of luck, the kind he himself possessed, but it depended not on chance but on who and what he was. He knew it was an innate power and not Dame Fortune's erratic smile. Since power like his was rare, the odds made it likely the woman he'd been watching was merely a very clever cheat.

Her skill could provide her with a very good living, he thought, doing some swift calculations in his head. Five grand a week equaled $260,000 a year, and that was just from his casino. She probably hit them all, careful to keep the numbers relatively low so she stayed under the radar.

He wondered how long she'd been taking him, how long she'd been winning a little here, a little there, before Al noticed.

The curtains were open on the wall-to-wall window in his office, giving the impression, when one first opened the door, of stepping out onto a covered balcony. The glazed window faced west, so he could catch the sunsets. The sun was low now, the sky painted in purple and gold. At his home in the mountains, most of the windows faced east, affording him views of the sunrise. Something in him needed both the greeting and the goodbye of the sun. He'd always been drawn to sunlight, maybe because fire was his element to call, to control.

He checked his internal time: four minutes until sundown. Without checking the sunrise tables every day, he knew exactly when the sun would slide behind the mountains. He didn't own an alarm clock. He didn't need one.

He was so acutely attuned to the sun's position that he had only to check within himself to know the time. As for waking at a particular time, he was one of those people who could tell himself to wake at a certain time, and he did. That talent had nothing to do with being Raintree, so he didn't have to hide it; a lot of perfectly ordinary people had the same ability.

He had other talents and abilities, however, that did require careful shielding. The long days of summer instilled in him an almost sexual high, when he could feel contained power buzzing just beneath his skin. He had to be doubly careful not to cause candles to leap into flame just by his presence, or to start wildfires with a glance in the dry-as-tinder brush. He loved Reno; he didn't want to burn it down. He just felt so damn *alive* with all the sunshine pouring down that he wanted to let the energy pour through him instead of holding it inside.

This must be how his brother Gideon felt while pulling lightning, all that hot power searing through his muscles, his veins. They had this in common, the connection with raw power. All the members of the far-flung Raintree clan had some power, some heightened ability, but only members of the royal family could channel and control the earth's natural energies.

Dante wasn't just of the royal family, he was the Dranir, the leader of the entire clan. "Dranir" was synonymous with king, but the position he held wasn't ceremonial, it was one of sheer power. He was the oldest son of the previous Dranir, but he would have been passed over for the position if he hadn't also inherited the power to hold it.

Behind him came Al's distinctive knock on the door. The outer office was empty, Dante's secretary having gone home hours before. "Come in," he called, not turning from his view of the sunset.

The door opened, and Al said, “Mr. Raintree, this is Lorna Clay.”

Dante turned and looked at the woman, all his senses on alert. The first thing he noticed was the vibrant color of her hair, a rich, dark red that encompassed a multitude of shades from copper to burgundy. The warm amber light danced along the iridescent strands, and he felt a hard tug of sheer lust in his gut. Looking at her hair was almost like looking at fire, and he had the same reaction.

The second thing he noticed was that she was spitting mad.

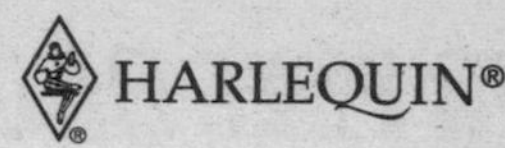

COMING NEXT MONTH

#321 BEYOND SEDUCTION Kathleen O'Reilly
The Red Choo Diaries, Bk. 3
The last thing respected talk-show host Sam Porter wants is to be the subject of a sex blog—but that's exactly what happens when up-and-coming writer Mercedes Brooks gets hold of him…and never wants to let him go!

#322 THE EX-GIRLFRIENDS' CLUB Rhonda Nelson
Ben Wilder is stunned when he discovers a Web site dedicated to bashing him. Sure, he's a little wild. So what? Then he learns Eden Rutherford, his first love, is behind the site, and decides some payback is in order. And he's going to start by showing Eden *exactly* what she's been missing….

#323 THE MAN TAMER Cindi Myers
It's All About Attitude…
Can't get your man to behave? Columnist Rachel Westover has the answer: man taming, aka behavior modification. Too bad she can't get Garret Kelly to obey. Sure, he's hers to command between the sheets, but outside…well, there might be something to be said for going wild!

#324 DOUBLE DARE Tawny Weber
Audra Walker is the ultimate bad girl. And to prove it, she takes a friend's dare—to hit on the next guy who comes through the door of the bar. Lucky for her, the guy's a definite hottie. Too bad he's also a cop….

#325 KISS AND DWELL Kelley St. John
The Sexth Sense, Bk. 1
Monique Vicknair has a secret—she and her family are mediums, charged with the job of helping lost souls cross over. But when Monique discovers her next assignment is sexy Ryan Chappelle, the last thing she wants to do is send him away. Because Ryan is way too much man to be a ghost….

#326 HOT FOR HIM Sarah Mayberry
Secret Lives of Daytime Divas, Bk. 3
Beating her rival for a coveted award has put Claudia Dostis on top. But when Leandro Mandalor challenges her to address the sizzle between them, her pride won't let her back down. In this battle for supremacy the gloves—and a lot of other clothes—are coming off!

www.eHarlequin.com

HBCNM0407